PRAISE FOR
DANIEL KALLA

THE DARKNESS IN THE LIGHT

"Trust Daniel Kalla to come up with the perfect post-COVID thriller. "

The Globe and Mail

"Emergency room physician Daniel Kalla is one of Canada's best-selling and most impressive writers, and his latest novel, *The Darkness in the Light*, demonstrates why."

Zoomer

"Kalla's Alaskan whodunit delights. . . . Just remember that Vancouver E.R. doctor Daniel Kalla not only writes superb medical thrillers with a pronounced social edge—his books are also terrific murder mysteries."

Winnipeg Free Press

"A very good read, and very timely."

CBC's The Next Chapter

"*The Darkness in the Light* is a gripping, heartbreaking, and enthralling suspense so vividly immersive that I was hooked from the first page. With crisp, powerful writing and two extremely compelling voices, Kalla draws you in to the remote, intriguing world of the Arctic and the tragic, inexplicable suicide clusters that have ravaged a small, tight-knit town. Kalla is a clever master of surprise, dropping subtle clues and expertly changing course, so you can't possibly look away until the mystery is solved. It's an absolute must-read from a remarkable talent."

SAMANTHA M. BAILEY,
USA Today and #1 nationally bestselling author of
Woman on the Edge

"Kalla is unparalleled in his ability to create compelling characters that embody societal trauma and medical complexities. *The Darkness in the Light* explores rural northern health care, the unrelenting pressure of depression and pharmaceutical treatments with great care. Both heartbreaking and brave, this is a boldly written story that fans will love and new readers will devour."

AMBER COWIE,
author of Last One Alive

LOST IMMUNITY

"Kalla ratchets up the suspense as a cover-up is exposed . . . a truly scary scenario from a writer who knows his medical thriller lingo down to the final line."

The Globe and Mail

"Kalla . . . has a knack for writing eerily prescient thrillers."

CBC Books

"Always there to hold up a mirror to society—his last book, *The Last High*, took on the opioid crisis—Kalla's new *Lost Immunity* book sits smack dab in the middle of what the world has been going through for the last year."

Vancouver Sun

THE LAST HIGH

"Kalla has long had his stethoscope on the heartbeat of his times. . . . In his latest, the focus is on Vancouver's opioid crisis. . . . A lively story."

Toronto Star

"Kalla is terrific at building suspense as the case progresses, uncovering a web of dealers, sellers, and users."

The Globe and Mail

"If you want an engrossing, edge-of-your-seat thriller that combines good detective work, corruption, savage criminal practices, a dark, seamy portrait of a large Canadian city, and a hard-hitting lesson on the medical and emotional effects of opioid drugs, then *The Last High* certainly fills that prescription."

Montreal Times

"A thrilling, front-line drama about the opioid crisis."

KATHY REICHS

"A riveting thriller . . . This important, must-read book is not only well-researched and entirely realistic, it gives a human face to a devastating epidemic."

ROBYN HARDING,
internationally bestselling author of
The Arrangement and The Party

ALSO BY DANIEL KALLA

FIT
TO
DIE

A THRILLER

DANIEL KALLA

PUBLISHED BY SIMON & SCHUSTER CANADA

New York   London   Toronto   Sydney   New Delhi

SIMON &
SCHUSTER
CANADA

Simon & Schuster Canada
A Division of Simon & Schuster, Inc.
166 King Street East, Suite 300
Toronto, Ontario M5A 1J3

This Simon & Schuster Canada edition May 2023

SIMON & SCHUSTER CANADA and colophon are trademarks of Simon & Schuster, Inc.

For information about special discounts for bulk purchases, please contact Simon & Schuster Special Sales at 1-800-268-3216 or CustomerService@simonandschuster.ca.

Manufactured in the United States of America
10 9 8 7 6 5 4 3 2 1

Library and Archives Canada Cataloguing in Publication
Title: Fit to die / Daniel Kalla.
Names: Kalla, Daniel, author.
Description: Simon & Schuster Canada edition.
Identifiers: Canadiana (print) 20220285594 | Canadiana (ebook) 20220285608 | ISBN 9781982191429 (softcover) | ISBN 9781982191436 (ebook)
Classification: LCC PS8621.A47 F58 2023 | DDC C813/.6—dc23

ISBN 978-1-9821-9142-9
ISBN 978-1-9821-9143-6 (ebook)

In memory of my mom and
her special soul

CHAPTER 1

"**S**omeone killed him," the woman murmurs.

Her cheeks are splotched. Her pupils huge. And her outstretched finger trembles, pointing to the corpse near her feet.

How else is a mother supposed to respond? Detective Cari Garcia wonders with a sympathetic nod as she glances around the tidy bedroom, its walls lined by framed black-and-white posters of marathon runners and races. A pair of crime technicians in white bunny suits survey the scene, acting as usual as if they're the only living souls present. The victim lies on his back with his right leg flopped out to the side, bent at the knee, and a pool of vomit puddled under his chin, which accounts for the faint sour odor drifting to Cari's nostrils.

Cari had been on her way to dinner when the captain phoned with his urgent request. It was almost a relief to be called out to a case. She had only agreed to go on the date to appease her best friend, Benny, who insisted Cari had been "on the bench" too long since Mattias.

Cari looks back over to the mother, whose whole body is now shaking.

"I see how it looks." Her finger has turned on Cari. "Just another teen suicide. Or maybe an accidental OD. Another addict who fooled his parents. No fucking way! I know my Owen." Her voice cracks and her chin drops, fractionally. "Never, never, never . . ."

"We don't make any assumptions from the outset," Cari says.

"Somebody must have killed my son!"

Cari has witnessed the same response too many times in her career. The outrage. The shock. The denial. But not in this setting. Not with the victim still splayed on the floor of his own bedroom. The uniforms would never have allowed the mother to stay in the room while two crime scene techs scoured the scene, were she not one of California's most influential state senators—a fixture on the local news—and, according to some pundits, the front-runner to succeed the current governor.

"We're going to find out what happened to Owen. I promise you, Senator Galloway." Cari has to stop herself. It's not the time or place to pose the usual questions: Did her son have mental health issues? Were there substance use concerns? Had his mood changed of late? Was there a recent breakup or any other crisis in his life?

Without any visible signs of trauma, murder is already near the bottom of Cari's list. Statistically speaking, fentanyl or some other opioid would be at the top. Suicide, a close second. Granted, there are a few anomalies, like the lack of any visible drug paraphernalia or pill bottles. Perhaps even natural causes? The boy is rail-thin. Regardless, the LAPD's Robbery and Homicide Division would not normally have been called to a scene as tragically familiar as this one.

The finger stills and the senator's hand drops to her side. The voice is calmer. The visage of the seasoned politician re-emerges. "What's next, Detective Garcia?"

"We'll start with the forensic evidence we find here." Cari waves toward the nearest crime scene tech, who is examining the pinkish rug where Owen lies.

Cari can tell by the way the tech avoids direct contact with the body that he's uncomfortable with the mother's presence. She steps out into the hallway and, without looking back, senses the senator's hesitance to leave her son's side. Cari cannot begin to imagine her torrent of emotions. And, as usual, she refuses to try. "Don't catch feelings. Feelings are the investigator's kryptonite," her old Detective Training Unit instructor used to drill into them. "They will blind you."

The senator finally joins Cari in the hallway, which is mercifully out of the sight line of her son's body.

"It could be homicide." Cari spreads her hands. "No question. Owen might've been drugged or poisoned. But the autopsy—and especially the toxicology screen—will be essential in establishing what happened to him. And how."

The senator eyes her steadily. Her voice is eerily calm now, almost affable. "I get it, Detective Garcia. Anything to appease the grieving mother. You'll go through the motions. The toxicology will find fentanyl or something even worse. And you'll file your report. It will all be very professional and respectful. Maybe you'll call it an accidental overdose to protect the family's reputation." She goes quiet and the thrum of the air conditioner fills the void. "But someone did this to my Owen. And I expect you to find out who."

CHAPTER 2

Storage. Julie Rees knows it's ridiculous, but she can't stop focusing on it. Standing in front of the spacious walk-in closet, she's reminded how it was the one feature that tipped her into buying the two-bedroom condo. Even more so than the sleek new concrete-and-glass design or the handy location in the heart of downtown Vancouver or even its enviable view—whenever the stubborn November clouds decide to part—of the North Shore mountains with a glimpse of ocean between.

But Detective Anson Chen does love his clothes. Will there be space for all his dress shirts, suits, and jackets once he moves in? Not to mention his extensive collection of Italian shoes and boots along with all his name-brand activewear.

"It's like you're running a Hugo Boss outlet out of your closet," Julie told Anson the night before as they cuddled in his bed.

"More like Armani or Balenciaga." He kissed her neck. "Boss just doesn't sit right across my shoulders."

"Why do I suddenly hear Carly Simon playing in my head?"

"Yeah, yeah, yeah. I'm so vain." He sat up in the bed. "This really about closet space, Julie?"

She considers the question again now as she eyes a row of dresses and skirts. But Julie doesn't feel as if she's getting cold feet. And she finds

Anson's meticulous attention to his attire—a hint of insecurity behind his otherwise impenetrably self-assured persona—kind of endearing. She is secretly proud of having by far the best dressed partner among her friends. But she hasn't lived with anyone for almost ten years. Maybe the closet does encapsulate her anxiety over trying again. Especially when she remembers how tragically it ended the only other time she did.

Julie is relieved when her mobile phone chimes and pulls her out of her First World conundrum. The day has been so quiet she almost forgot she's still on call for Poison Control. She hurries back to the kitchen and sweeps the ringing phone off the island counter. "Dr. Rees," she says.

"Julie, luv!" the man chirps in a singsong Yorkshire lilt.

"Hiya, Glen." She perks up, hearing the voice of one of her favorite nurses. "How are you?"

"Oh, just about five more pounds and ten extra blood pressure points away from a stroke, but otherwise tip-top. And you? How's that handsome detective of yours?"

"Get this, Glen." She can't help herself from sharing. "He's moving in with me."

"Oh, so many congrats! Stan will be thrilled. You know, we're going on twenty-eight years tomorrow ourselves? Of course, I never asked him to move in. He came over one night and just never left."

"Ha! You used that same line at your twenty-fifth anniversary bash."

"Can't repeat the truth enough, luv," Glen says. "Listen, I've got a doozy of a call on the other line. A real pickle."

"Tell me."

"An ER doc from your own backyard. Dr. Veljkovic."

"Goran?" Julie is surprised her friend and mentor—who's old school to the core—would even consult Poison Control. He possesses an encyclopedic knowledge of medicine, and what he doesn't know, he prefers to look up himself. "What's he got?"

"A thirty-six-year-old male bodybuilder with recurrent seizures. Possibly related to a new supplement the man has been taking. Oh, and apparently, his temperature is through the roof."

Julie's neck tightens as she thinks of her own similar case from the previous month. And how poorly it turned out. "Patch him through, Glen. Please."

A few seconds later, she hears the familiar deep voice with its slight Slavic clip. "Julija!" he says, pronouncing it as usual in the Croatian style, where each *j* sounds like a *y*. "Just the very person I sought."

"Hi, Gor," she says, all businesslike. "What's going on?"

"This patient, he will not stop seizing. We've loaded him with benzo-diazepines and Dilantin. But nada. No response. And he's an ox, Julija. At least two-fifty. Maybe two-sixty. No doubt steroids. But he's been tak-ing something else, too. Some pills a friend gave him. Oh, and his fever!"

"I was just going to ask—"

"It's over forty-one degrees Celsius! That's a hundred and six Fahren-heit, if you're averse to metric. He's delirious now but between convulsions he told us he took five capsules instead of the one he was instructed to."

"Did he tell you which capsules, Gor?"

"He has no idea. Why would you bother asking your friend silly ques-tions like what poison he is feeding you?" Goran snorts. "I'm thinking maybe it's an anticholinergic poisoning? Or a serotonin syndrome?"

Julie knows these are two of the most common types of overdoses that can cause fevers, seizures, and delirium, but she recognizes these symptoms as something else. "You've got to get his temperature down, Gor. Whatever it takes. Flush him with cold IV fluids. Ice packs to his armpits and groin. Soak him in freezing water and blast him with a fan. It's vital! Oh, and load him up with dantrolene."

"Yes, yes. I've already ordered it."

"And you can't fill him with enough benzos."

Goran's voice is suddenly soft. "What are you not telling me, Julija?"

"Those pills he was given." She takes a slow breath. "I had a case just like it last month. A DNP overdose."

"DNP? What is that?"

"2,4-Dinitrophenol."

"Never heard of such a thing."

"That's because it was never meant to be ingested. It's an explosive, Gor."

"*Explosive?* As in munitions?" His voice breaks. "What kind of mad-ness . . . ?"

"I'll be there in ten!" Julie says and disconnects without waiting for a reply.

CHAPTER 3

Over forty-five million Insta followers. Lorraine Flynn—known by most of the world as simply "Rain"—can't believe it herself. Five years ago, she would have been thrilled to hit ten thousand. Aside from the few dogged haters, Rain basks in the online love. It immerses her. Inspires her. Lifts her up. Her music is more visceral because of it, and her acting more intimate.

Most of the time, it makes up for how much she disgusts herself.

Rain raises her foot to step forward but freezes. She has already peed twice in the past hour. She hasn't touched a bite of food or a drop of liquid in almost fourteen hours. It's the perfect moment to get on the scale. But her stomach still rumbles, and despite how empty it is, she swears she's going to throw up as her big toe inches toward the scale.

There's only one way to do it. Fast. Like diving into a frigid lake!

Rain hops onto the scale with both feet. But her breath catches. And, almost involuntarily, her eyelids slam shut. Only after she steadies her breathing does she tilt her chin down and open her eyes. *How bad can it be?*

"96.4" the blue numbers glow.

The elation overwhelms her. More so than if she had found another ten million Insta followers. She prayed she would be under triple digits, but this is three pounds lighter than she dared to hope.

Rain has always been very public with her fans about her mental health struggles, especially her body image issues. She still can't shake the painful memories of all the low points—the lowest of all being the night of her fifteenth birthday when she felt so fat and ashamed that she had no choice but to swallow every pill she could find in her parents' medicine cabinet.

The whole world knows how much better Rain is doing since her troubled teen years. Dr. Markstrom reminds her of it almost every day. What a model she is for other kids out there who struggle with the same issues.

And Rain is happy to help. To show them what can be overcome.

She feels too contented to step off the scale. So instead, she stretches out a hand and pinches the bottle off the counter between her fingers. She taps out a single red-and-black capsule into her palm.

CHAPTER 4

Julie flies through the front door of St. Michael's ER and past the triage desk with a quick wave to the nurse behind it. There is the expected lengthy lineup of people waiting to register, including four sets of paramedics flanking patients on gurneys, one of whom is writhing in pain and another who appears to be unconscious. Two more nurses have already come out to the waiting room to assess both patients.

As Julie rushes down the hallway toward the resuscitation room, she picks up on the beeps, whirs, and voices of purposeful commotion even before she steps foot inside the expansive room. Only the first bay is occupied, but a flurry of activity encircles the hulking man on the stretcher. With an oxygen mask covering his face, he sits propped up as he picks at the air in front of him, exposing a rippled and veiny arm and shoulder.

The radiology tech beside him struggles to lean the goliath forward so that he can slide a chest X-ray plate behind the patient's back. One of the bedside nurses helps from the opposite side of the stretcher, and together they wedge the plate behind the man.

Julie has always considered Goran Veljkovic to be a bear of man in terms of size and hairiness. But even the sixtyish, Croatian ER physician looks small beside his patient.

As soon as Goran spots Julie in the doorway, he pads over to her.

"While they take the X-ray . . ." His gloved hand encircles her upper arm and gently leads her out of the room. Once they're standing in the corridor, he flashes a tired grin. "You didn't have to come, Julija. You could've saved the gas or electricity or rainwater . . . or whatever it is that powers that fancy new car of yours . . ."

"I wanted to."

Goran nods his appreciation. "No more seizures since we spoke, thanks God! But I just got his lab results. A real dog's breakfast. Not even. More like a rat's brunch. His kidneys have shut down. And his CK is through the roof," he says, meaning the blood level of creatine kinase, the biochemical marker for muscle enzyme breakdown. "As if his own body is trying to melt those tree trunks that pass for arms."

That's exactly what it is doing, Julie thinks.

"And did you notice the yellowing of his skin and around the eyes?" he asks.

She shakes her head. "I only caught a brief glimpse of him from across the room."

"I thought it must be his liver, but his bilirubin level is normal."

"DNP can leave a yellowish deposit under the skin, Gor," Julie says. "How's his temperature?"

"Won't budge. Still over forty."

She takes a deep breath. "Can I speak to him?"

Goran raises his shoulders. "He wasn't making a ton of sense the last time we spoke. He's in and out of delirium. But you can try. After the X-ray."

"Thanks."

His eyes bore into hers. "An explosive, Julija? For real?"

"Honest to God, Gor. DNP was first used in the First World War to manufacture howitzer shells," she says, still in slight disbelief herself, despite having confirmed it to be true after her own case last month. "The workers who touched and inhaled it in those French munitions factories would go into this hypermetabolic state. Fever, sweats, light-headedness. Eventually, they'd lose weight. The ones who survived, anyway."

"And from the trenches of France to my bodybuilder . . . ?"

"In the thirties, someone had the bright idea to turn DNP into a weight loss pill. And for a couple of years, it was all the rage. Until the dying started. Then it was banned by the FDA and other regulatory bodies around the world."

"And yet, here we are." He thumbs to the room. "Ninety years later."

"DNP has made a comeback online."

"Holy crap, Julija. Explosives!" Goran groans. "So how did you fix your patient with the DNP overdose?"

Julie tucks a few hairs behind her ear. "I didn't."

"He died?"

"*She,*" Julie says, fighting off the mental image of the terrified, middle-aged woman's gaunt face. She squeezes Goran's elbow. "Chances are, yours is going to as well, Gor."

His bushy eyebrows crinkle. "But he's still awake and speaking to us."

Before Julie can reply, a voice calls urgently from inside the room. "Dr. Veljkovic!"

Goran pivots, and Julie follows. The radiology tech has wheeled the portable X-ray machine away from the bed, and someone has lowered the head of the bed flat. As the patient glances wildly around the room, Julie now sees his yellowish tinge.

Sandy, the unflappable ER nurse who looks perpetually bored, motions calmly to the monitor above the bed. "His blood pressure dropped, and he just flipped into that." A red line rapidly oscillates on the cardiac monitor, indicating ventricular tachycardia, a potentially lethal heart rhythm.

"Get ready to shock him," Goran instructs the tall and wiry second nurse, James, who stands on the other side of the bed flushing an IV line with a syringe.

The patient reaches up wildly as if grasping for someone's arm. "*Shock me?*"

Goran hurries over to the bedside, but Julie forces herself to stay back, reminding herself she has come in her capacity as a toxicologist, not an ER doctor.

Goran catches the patient's flailing hand. "No big deal, Nicholas," he says soothingly. "We give you a little happy juice. Make you sleepy. And then . . ." He snaps his fingers. "A quick buzz to remind your heart to cooperate a little better."

Nicholas's head swivels toward Goran. "What's happening to me, Doc?"

"Those pills you took. They're not agreeing with you, Nicholas. Not at all."

"They're harmless! Tommy told me. He said they'd put me over the top for next month's competition."

"Tommy sold you a bill of a goods." Goran looks over his shoulder to Sandy. "Draw up ketamine for sedation."

"Tommy, Tommy . . ." Nicholas mutters, but then his head flops to the side.

Sandy's hand shoots up to his neck. "No pulse," she says.

Julie's eyes dart over to the monitor, where a chaotic wiggle of ventricular fibrillation has replaced the previous oscillation.

"We got v. fib!" James cries as he clasps his hands, one palm over the other, plants them on the center of Nicholas's chest, and leans his weight forward, pumping ferociously.

"Are the pads on?" Goran demands.

Sandy nods as she taps the toaster-sized defibrillator machine beside her.

"Charge to two hundred joules. And shock him."

Sandy hits the orange button and the machine whines in response, gathering its charge. No one has to tell James to pause CPR. He yanks his hands away from the chest the moment the defibrillator beeps its readiness.

"Clear!" Sandy says, and then, after a quick cautionary glance to ensure no one else is touching the patient, she presses the button. The jolt of electricity momentarily lifts Nicholas's back off the stretcher.

Julie's eyes dart to the monitor. The line is flat for a moment and then the squiggles recur. James lurches forward and resumes his compressions. The respiratory technician, a young new hire whose name eludes Julie, drops a triangular mask over the patient's face and secures it with her fingers stretched around his nose and jaw. She waits for James to pause his compression and then squeezes two breaths from the attached bag full of oxygen.

"Epinephrine one milligram now and draw up three hundred of amiodarone," Goran says. "Shock him again at two minutes."

The synchronized dance of the chest compressions followed by forced breaths makes time seem to pass faster. "Two minutes," Sandy calls.

Everyone stops when the defibrillator beeps again. Another shock arches Nicholas's back again.

Julie exhales as she spots the organized blips that replace the squiggles on the monitor.

"I've got a pulse," Sandy announces.

"And he's breathing," the respiratory tech adds without removing the mask from his mouth.

"Good." Goran catches Julie's eye momentarily before turning back to the patient. "Nicholas, are you with us?"

Only a garbled rumble emerges from his lips.

"What did you say, Nicholas?" Goran cranes his neck and leans closer to the bed.

Nicholas's face shoots up and smashes into Goran's cheek. As Goran jerks away in surprise, Nicholas begins to thrash on the stretcher. The floor seems to shake with the force of the contractions from his violent seizure.

"Ten of lorazepam now!" Goran commands. "And draw up the usual intubation meds. We have to paralyze him and get him on the ventilator."

James injects a series of preloaded syringes into the IV line, and after what seems like several minutes, but is probably less than one, Nicholas collapses back onto the stretcher, motionless again. The respiratory tech forces more breaths into him, as Goran assumes a position over the head of the bed.

He holds a curved metallic laryngoscope blade by its cylindrical handle and slides it along Nicholas's tongue. Goran lifts the handle and raises the jaw to see the vocal cords before he tries to snake the tube into the trachea. He struggles to feed the tube for several seconds before he gives up. "I can't visualize the cords," he groans.

Julie resists the urge to intervene as she would have with one of her learners after a failed first attempt. Instead, she watches as Goran repositions Nicholas's large head by extending his neck. On the next attempt, he passes the tube seamlessly and connects it to the ventilator, the old pro that he is.

Sandy confirms that the blood pressure and other vital signs have all stabilized—except the temperature, which still hovers in the low forties.

Once Goran seems satisfied with the connection and the ventilator settings, he steps over to where Julie is standing. He rubs the reddish mark on his right cheek where the patient unintentionally headbutted him. "If Nicholas can survive a shitstorm like that . . ."

"Yeah, maybe," Julie says.

But her mind drifts back to the comparable resuscitation she'd run the month before in the same room. She can still picture the incendiary fear burning in the eyes of her patient. Like Nicholas, Marcia Wildman had also argued from her stretcher that DNP must be safe. No one had told her as much, since Marcia had been skimming the capsules from her nineteen-year-old's private stash. But her daughter, Olivia, had never looked more radiant, healthy, or fit as she did in the weeks after starting those diet pills. Marcia was impatient for the same dramatic results. That was why she decided to swallow three of Olivia's capsules at once, shortly before she ended up in hospital.

"Promise me I'll make it off this thing, Dr. Rees," Marcia pleaded, moments before Julie slipped a tube down her throat and placed her on the ventilator.

"You need to focus on your breathing, Marcia. You'll be asleep soon."

"I have to wake up!" Marcia pawed at the air in front of her face. "I can't die. Not like this. Not from stealing my daughter's pills. What will she think of me?"

"You'll make it," Julie said, without meeting her eyes.

But Marcia didn't make it.

And neither would Nicholas.

CHAPTER 5

Cari isn't sure if it's the athletic trophies lining the bookcase, the old-fashioned bell mounted over the door, or the kids gathering on the bleachers outside the window, but the vice principal's office triggers unwelcome memories from her own high school days. Those feelings of self-doubt, disenfranchisement, and the unshakable jealousy over her little sister's effortless popularity seep back to her as she sits in the borrowed room.

Cari has come to track down Maya Townsend, a student whose name emerged during the search of Owen Galloway's room. The crime scene techs had almost overlooked the concealed bottles on their initial pass. Only after one of them flipped over the velvet ottoman did they discover the makeshift compartment hidden underneath. Inside, they found Owen's stash: a clear plastic bottle holding twenty-five red-and-black capsules along with a twenty-seven-ounce container of Miralax, and a vial of eleven Adderall tablets with Maya's name printed on the prescription label.

No one had recognized the unmarked capsules, but Cari had felt a chill at the sight of the other two medications. She was all too familiar with the combination of a laxative and a stimulant. Owen must have been struggling with an eating disorder, just as Cari's own younger sister had.

Involuntary thoughts of Lucia's losing battle flood back to her. And with them, the guilt. Dismissing the memories, Cari focuses on the twelfth grader sitting across the desk from her. "But the prescription was in your name, Maya," she says.

Maya's arms are firmly folded over her tightly fitting uniform blouse, and she has a look of pure defiance glued to her lips. "Then Owen stole the bottle."

"Stole it from where, Maya?"

"My nightstand. He was over a couple weeks ago. My parents were out, and we were kind of . . . fooling around."

"And afterwards? You never noticed your meds were missing?"

"I don't take my Adderall every day," Maya says. "Sometimes, I get ahead of my prescriptions. I had a couple old bottles with some pills left over."

"Owen never asked to borrow any?"

"No." She blows out her lips. "OK, maybe once a long time ago. But everyone does. They all know I've got ADHD. And they want Adderall to help them study for exams and papers and stuff."

"You think that's why Owen took them?"

"Yeah." Maya squints. "Why else?"

"Had you noticed that Owen had been losing weight?"

"I dunno." Maya uncrosses her arms. "I guess. He was running a lot. Training hard for a race."

"Which race?"

"No clue. Owen was a track star. Cross-country. He had some big race coming up. He always did."

"Maybe he wanted the Adderall to help train?"

"Uh-uh. No way."

Cari has little doubt that Maya gave Owen the bottle. But behind the girl's brave front, Cari can see that she's suffering. "It doesn't matter how Owen got the Adderall, Maya. The medical examiner says it wouldn't have killed him."

"It wouldn't?" She slumps in her seat.

"No. But he was taking other pills, too. And we don't know what they are."

Maya's eyes glisten and her lip quivers. "What kind of pills?"

"Red-and-black capsules," Cari says and then waits, but Maya's stare is blank. "Owen never mentioned anything about pills to help with weight loss?"

"He was so skinny," Maya croaks. "With his shirt off, you could see every rib. Owen told me it was from all the running, but . . ."

"What is it, Maya?"

"I never saw him eat. Like almost ever. If we went out, he'd just have a coffee or a Diet Coke. He told me he had a super-sensitive stomach, and he could only eat special food from home."

The excuse sounds painfully familiar to Cari. She thinks of those family dinners where Lucia wouldn't touch a bite, claiming that her gluten intolerance and array of other imagined food allergies were flaring up. "He might have bought them somewhere. On the street? Or online? Did he ever talk about ordering dietary supplements or anything?"

"Nah. Nothing like that." Maya sniffles, and the tears begin to flow. "But he was always ordering online. Some sketchball stuff, too."

"Sketchball?"

"Yeah. Like one time, he showed me this switchblade and pair of brass knuckles."

"Why would Owen order those? Was he in trouble? Being threatened?"

"No! Everyone loved Owen." Maya wipes her eyes. "He did it for kicks. To show that he could. He told me it was illegal to order those weapons online."

"Thrill-seeking, then?"

"I guess." Maya has to pause to get her voice to cooperate. "He was always the perfect kid. Top student. Awesome athlete. A prefect. He didn't hardly drink and wouldn't smoke weed. I think ordering that stuff was his way of rebelling or whatever."

"Against?"

"His mom. She's so fucking controlling."

Cari makes a mental note to check with the Computer Crimes Section again on the status of Owen's electronic devices and to ask them specifically to focus on his online orders. "Thank you, Maya." She stands, ending the interview. "I'm really sorry about Owen."

Maya looks up at her with imploring red eyes. "The Adderall . . ."

"Won't be an issue," Cari reassures with a small smile.

On her way out to her car, Cari checks her phone and sees two new texts, neither of which are welcome. The first is from her captain and reads: "Please come by my office ASAP." The second is from Mattias and says only "hi."

It has been six months since Mattias moved away. It was his idea to leave, and yet he has never been able to let it go. To let her go. Cari still gets random texts from him. At first, they were guised as follow-up on insignificant items he thought he might have left at her place. Soon, he dropped the pretense and began to send texts like "just checking in," "how ya holding up?" or, worst of all, "miss you."

Cari rarely responds. But they hurt to read. And they serve only, as her best friend Benny loves to point out, to keep her emotionally imprisoned. She wants to reply to each text with: "YOU LEFT!" But pride and common sense prevent her.

The midday traffic is manageable, and Cari reaches the modern glass-and-tile edifice of the LAPD Headquarters in under twenty minutes. She heads straight up to Captain Darren Taylor's office, strolling past his secretary, who waves her in.

Wearing a sky-blue pantsuit, Senator Galloway is already seated directly across from the captain. Her face is made up and shows little of the fatigue or raggedness Cari would expect to see in someone who suddenly lost a loved one, especially her own child.

"Ah, Detective. Perfect timing." The captain beckons her to the open chair. "You've met Senator Galloway, of course."

"Hello, Senator," Cari says as she lowers herself into the seat.

The senator shows her a tight smile. "Detective Garcia."

"I was just telling the senator how you have one of the highest case-closing records on the entire force, Cari," the captain says.

She knows the comment is purely for the senator's benefit. For the past five years, Cari has consistently been one of RHD's most efficient homicide detectives, in terms of murders solved, but the captain rarely lauds her for it and has never offered to advance her beyond the rank of detective class two. He does find it occasionally advantageous to show off his productive Latina detective. But mainly, the captain prefers to take credit himself for his officers' work.

"Have you figured out what happened to Owen yet, Detective?" the senator asks. "Or who was responsible?"

"With respect, Senator, we still don't know how your son died. Let alone if anyone else was involved."

The senator seems to ignore the remark. "And what have you learned about those pills they found in Owen's room?"

Cari isn't surprised that the captain shared the confidential finding with the senator, but she still has to bite her lower lip to stop herself from commenting. Her aunt taught her the trick after she kept getting into trouble in fourth grade for talking back to her teacher. It's become habit. But unlike in grade school, Cari doesn't have to count to ten anymore to avoid blurting something she might later regret. "We're working on that," she says evenly. "It's a top priority. But those red-and-black capsules in the one bottle are unmarked. They're not manufactured by any legitimate pharmaceutical company. We've sent them to the toxicology lab, but I still haven't heard anything."

The senator cocks her head. "Street drugs?"

"We won't know until the tox report comes back."

The senator turns to the captain. "That should be expedited, no?"

"It should," he agrees.

"We did identify the other two medications found in Owen's stash," Cari says. "One's a laxative and the second, Adderall, is a stimulant used to treat attention deficit disorder. Was Owen ever diagnosed with ADHD?"

The senator's nose wrinkles. "Owen was a prize-winning student. Top of the honor roll."

Cari wonders why the senator assumes that ADHD would have precluded Owen from academic success, but she doesn't comment.

"Someone must've given Owen the Adderall," the senator says. "Probably the same person who gave him those unmarked capsules. Do you have any leads at all?"

Cari remembers Maya's comment about the senator's controlling nature and wonders how it might have played into Owen's weight issues. She looks over to the captain, who nods his permission for full disclosure. "We're still waiting for the data from Owen's devices, but I went to the school this morning. I interviewed a few of his track teammates and other classmates. Including his girlfriend."

"You spoke to Maya?"

"I did."

"And what did she have to say?"

Cari can tell from the subtle change in the senator's tone that she does not approve of Owen's girlfriend, and she decides not to share the Adderall connection for the moment. "Maya didn't know what those capsules were. Or where he got them."

"Or so she says."

"I believe her, Senator. But she did mention Owen's weight."

"What about his weight?"

"Maya said that he was looking very thin lately."

"He was in training. A number of top colleges were actively recruiting him."

Cari can feel the captain's warning gaze on her. "Of course, Senator," she says. "As I understand it, laxatives and Adderall are sometimes abused in combination by people with eating disorders."

"Owen wasn't some vulnerable teenaged girl with anorexia!" the senator snaps. "Obsessing over online models, desperate to be as thin. No! He was a long-distance runner. A citywide champion. Lean is their *only* physique."

"I understand, Senator, but I have to ask. Was Owen ever diagnosed with an eating disorder?"

The senator glares at her for a few simmering seconds before suddenly breaking into a conciliatory smile. "We could discuss Owen's weight all day, Detective. But it's not relevant. The question you need to answer is: Who gave my son those capsules? And did they kill him?"

CHAPTER 6

*"C*hange Your Mind and Your Body Will Follow." The words are printed in sleek white cursive, right below the stainless steel MIND OVER BODY WELLNESS CENTER sign that hangs from the mahogany siding above the welcome desk.

Corny as it is, Gerard Martin still gets a kick out of the inspirational slogan that he originally coined. A placard also hangs in their office on Rodeo Drive, identical to this one at their location in Vancouver's trendy Yaletown district.

The idea struck him three years ago out of nowhere during an intense spin class. It wasn't only the motto that came to him as he sweated away on that bike. The whole concept hit him as an epiphany: one-stop wellness shopping. A total holistic approach that integrates mindfulness, yoga, anti-aging, aerobics, diet, and supplements. The inspiration came right when he needed it most, while his personal training business was stalled and the debts were mounting.

"Hey, Gerard. What about these?" Colby calls as he hoists the two heavy boxes off the wildly expensive beige rug in the foyer. "Ecru," the designer labeled it.

"Put them in the freezer," Gerard says. "You know the drill. *Carefully.*"

"We'll need a few bottles out front, *chéri*," Adèle Gagnon says as she bounds into the room from the yoga studio.

Who's the "chéri" in question? Gerard wonders. *Are you fucking that boy?*

But Gerard isn't allowed to ask. That's the agreement they have lived by for the past four years. Gerard rarely strays anymore himself. But it still hurts him to think of Adèle with anyone else, particularly Colby, that buff, sexually fluid, dense, twenty-one-year-old.

The slight Quebecois lilt in Adèle's voice alone—not to mention the glimpse of her lithe form in her clingy yoga wear—stirs Gerard. When it comes to Adèle, he can never distinguish love from lust.

She sidles up to him and runs her fingers lightly down his spine, but her luminous smile is aimed squarely at Colby. "You need help with those?"

"I'm good," Colby says with a happy nod as he toddles off toward the storage room.

Gerard gestures to the spray bottle and the towel in Adèle's hand. "Babe, aren't we a little past the point of cleaning the rooms ourselves?"

" 'Les petites attentions,' my *pépé* used to tell me back home."

He shrugs. "What about the little details?"

"Pay attention to those, and the big ones will take care of themselves."

Gerard can't help but chuckle. Adèle's grandpa filled her head with boundless folksy aphorisms during her childhood in Trois-Rivières. "Smart guy, your *pépé*."

"A genius, in his way." Adèle grabs Gerard by the back of his neck and smacks her mouth to his, parting her lips slightly as she flickers a sensual kiss. "Almost as smart as you, *chéri*. And you know how hot that gets me."

Gerard considers taking her right there in the lobby. Why not? It's after six o'clock and the door is locked. Adèle would be game. She always is. She would probably enjoy it if Colby were to walk in on them. But the idea of that douses his arousal. Besides, the office is for work, not play. Most of the time.

"You need to get changed now," Gerard says, as he pulls his face back from hers.

"Changed? For what?"

"Our celebratory dinner."

"And we're celebrating . . . ?"

"I just heard from the lawyer in San Francisco."

Adèle's expression lights. "We got it?"

"We got it! The lease is signed."

Adèle does a joyful pirouette, a residual move from her days spent as a dance hopeful. She often reminisces about her childhood ballet aspirations. But she never says a word about the pole dancing she was doing when they first met in that strip club in Montreal.

Adèle beams. "Our third gym in under two years!"

"Our third *center*," he stresses.

"We're sure we can afford to expand right now?"

"We almost can't afford not to." Gerard chuckles at his own awkward double negative. "You know what I mean. We can't keep up with the demand here and in LA."

She sweeps her hand toward the sign over the desk. "Babe, we've got the hottest act on the West Coast."

"We do."

Adèle isn't exaggerating. Mind Over Body is one of the most popular trends in two of the trendiest cities in the world, at least when it comes to health and fitness. The rich, the famous, and the elite are flocking to their centers in LA and Vancouver. And they keep coming, no matter how often Gerard jacks up the membership dues or adds new surcharges.

They are living the dream, and Gerard is not about to slow down now. He has already turned down two rich corporate buyout offers. Those heartless, big-box outfits wouldn't have offered him a dime if they could have figured out how to replicate his model. But they can't.

Every detail in his meteoric rise has been calculated to near perfection—even changing his name from Gerald to Gerard to better appeal to his entitled clientele—though, in retrospect, he could have called himself anything he wanted to and they would've kept flooding in.

The clients—those middle-aged paper titans, aging athlete-wannabes, botoxed MILFs, and all their entitled brats who expect to inherit the earth—are thrilled with the results. The boost in energy. The youthfulness. The aerobic fitness levels. The elevated mood. But mainly, the weight loss.

No one can believe how successful their method is at resculpting bodies.

Business is exploding.

CHAPTER 7

"**K**inda brazen," says Detective Theo Kostas as he stands under the gray drizzle that is so typical for November in Vancouver.

"You figure?" Detective Anson Chen motions to the row of storefronts standing beyond the uniformed cops, the media vans, and the fleet of first responder vehicles parked at every angle. "Middle of the morning in a crowded parking lot mall at the height of the holiday shopping season? A firing squad with automatic weapons. Rounds everywhere!"

"Not fifty yards from a toy store, too," Theo points out.

"A miracle no innocents were mowed down in the crossfire."

Theo nods to the shattered car window beside them. "Are you implying PG here wasn't innocent?"

"Not since about his eighth birthday," Anson says of the local gang leader. He leans his head through the hole where the black BMW sedan's driver window used to be. Parminder Grewal—or PG as he was simply known in the gang world—is slumped to his right, his lap covered in broken glass. Blood is caked on his neck, and part of his left temple is missing. His floral cologne competes with the smell of gunpowder residue and stale blood.

"Pretty safe to assume this was in reprisal for the Maddox hit," Theo says.

"No doubt."

It's accepted as fact within the Vancouver Police's Gang Squad and Homicide Unit that PG was responsible for Jamie Maddox's killing. The rival drug dealer was gunned down only six days earlier, while sitting on his Harley and waiting for his building's garage door to open. If PG hadn't pulled the trigger himself, which Anson considers the likeliest scenario, then he had ordered Maddox's hit. But as usual, finding a witness or definitive evidence has been proving almost impossible.

"How can we even keep up with them?" Theo asks.

"Keep up?"

"These domino murders. Like Maddox and PG here."

Anson can only shrug. It does seem that with each new gang hit, the lead suspect is knocked off in reprisal almost faster than the VPD can open a file on the original killing.

Theo's shoulders dip lower than even usual. "This turf war has spiraled way out of control."

In his baggy brown suit and loosely knotted tie, Theo looks more like an exasperated accountant or a burned-out college professor than a cop. But he's a distinguished detective with an impeccable record who once survived a spectacular car crash after a high-speed chase that killed his previous partner and left him with a permanent limp. The father of five lovable boys, Theo has been with his childhood sweetheart, Eleni, for almost thirty years. And he's one of the wisest, kindest, and most observant cops Anson has ever met. Anson knows he's lucky to have Theo as a partner, but he wouldn't tell him that. It would only embarrass them both.

"Yeah, well, I guess profits from fentanyl are just too rich to share these days," Anson says. "Besides, what can we do to stop these gangs from culling each other's herds?"

Theo points to the nearest media van. "The press is going to rake us over the coals for another public hit in broad daylight."

"And the deputy chief's going to lose her shit altogether. Can't wait for *that* staff meeting."

Anson feels his phone pulsating and recognizes the caller by the distinct vibration. "It's Julie," he says to Theo, as he steps away from the car and answers his phone. "Hey."

"Hi, you," Julie says. "Got time for lunch?"

Anson glances over to Theo, who is now extending both arms and pointing an imaginary gun at the open window, trying to establish the angle the killer fired from. "I'll make time," he says to Julie. "Where?"

"The usual?"

"Absolutely." The usual is Pete's Brunchery, the hole-in-the-wall diner on Granville Street that has become their favorite casual spot for breakfast or lunch. "Can't get enough of their eggs benny."

"What would your grandma have to say about that?"

"That Western food is dog food," he says, translating one of the feisty ninety-two-year-old's frequent Mandarin sayings.

"And Western girlfriends?"

"Well . . . the fact you're a doctor makes you almost palatable to her."

"Almost!" She snorts a laugh. "Can you meet me there in fifteen?"

"I'll try." After he disconnects, he glances back over to the shot-up sedan. The white-clad crime scene techs have swarmed the car now, while Theo stands a few feet back. "I'm going to grab a quick bite with Julie. Meet back at the office?"

Theo feigns disappointment. "I don't make the cut?"

"Not even close."

"Give the good doctor a hug for me." Theo shakes his head. "How you hit it so far out of your league . . ."

"Yeah, yeah," Anson says, as he heads to his car.

A uniformed officer lifts the crime scene tape for Anson to drive under. The parking lot is crowded with shoppers, looky-loos, and several reporters and cameramen. He sees two South Asian women standing behind the tape, one sobbing against the shoulder of the other.

Anson's jaw clenches as he rolls past them. "Brazen" doesn't begin to do the shooting justice or describe the risk the killers took with all the innocent lives in the vicinity.

The traffic is light, and Anson reaches the restaurant in just over fifteen minutes. Julie is already waiting at a table by the window. He slides into the chair beside her and kisses her cheek. "You still battling your existential closet crisis?" he asks.

"Depends." Julie flashes one of those disarming half-grins, where her lips hardly move but her forest-green eyes shine, somehow lightening their hue. "You still battling a clothes-hoarding crisis?"

"There's no urgency to me moving in, Julie."

"Says the man who's already given up his lease."

"Yeah, but there are some perfectly good bridges I could sleep under."

"That'd be murder on your nubuck shoes."

"There is that."

Julie slides her hand across his neck and massages it. "I want this as much as you do, Anson."

He realizes that now would be an ideal moment to mention his recurring dreams. But instead, he lays his hand over hers and gives it a squeeze. "We're sticking with Sunday, then?"

"By Monday, we'll be like an old married couple."

Anson chuckles, but he shifts in his seat. Marriage is a delicate subject between them, considering each of their past experiences.

Julie pulls her hand from his neck. "Hey, I had a tough call last night on Poison Control."

"Tough how?"

"Remember that woman I told you about? Last month? The one who died after taking the diet supplement?"

Julie doesn't often bring her work home with her, and he distinctly remembers how much the case upset her. "Her daughter's diet pills, right?" he asks.

"Yes. And last night's call was basically a replica," she says. "A patient of Goran's."

"Diet pills again?"

"This guy was a bodybuilder. He took it to bulk up his muscles."

"Was?"

"He died in the ICU this morning. From the same super-poisonous crap, Anson. DNP."

"You told me the stuff has been circulating for a while now."

"Globally, yes. Not in Vancouver. Up until recently, we only had a handful of reported poisonings and one death. But Goran's patient is the third fatality in the last two months."

"There was another one?"

"Yup. I confirmed it with Poison Control. There was a case at Vancouver General a few weeks ago. A competitive gymnast." She sighs. "Someone must be spreading DNP around town."

"Three deaths in two months is a pattern. No question. But I doubt it's being peddled locally."

"Online?"

"Probably. A bodybuilder, a competitive gymnast, and a middle-aged mother? What would link them? Chances are they heard about it online. God knows where they might've ordered it. Could be coming from anywhere on the planet. And each victim could've ordered it from a different supplier."

She traces her fingers over his knuckles. "I'm sure some brilliant detective could figure it out in no time."

"Don't even, Julie."

"You could maybe speak to the victims' families? See if they know where the DNP came from?"

"Whoa." Anson pulls his hand from hers and holds up his palm. "We don't choose our own cases. Homicide doesn't work that way. Besides, it would fall to the Drug Unit to check this out. They're probably already on it."

Julie's gaze drifts down to the table. "I basically lied to my patient, Anson. Told her she was going to be OK." She swallows. "Then . . . afterwards . . . I had to break it to her daughter that the illegal pills she ordered killed her own mother. If you could've seen the kid's face . . ."

Anson stares at Julie for a long moment, realizing that he's about to cave but not quite ready to admit it. "One or two calls," he finally says.

Her face lights up. "You will?"

"A call or two. To see if anyone in the VPD knows where the victims got their supply. Nothing more."

Julie presses her lips to his. "Clotheshorse or not, I love you, Detective Chen."

CHAPTER 8

As Cari steps into the elevator of the Hertzberg-Davis Forensic Sciences Center, she tries to recall another instance when the LAPD's crime lab ever reached out to her proactively, but comes up blank. And she has been a cop for over sixteen years, eleven of them as a detective. Most times, she has to badger the lab for DNA, ballistics, or toxicology results, which can take forever thanks to their perpetual backlog.

Then again, Owen Galloway is no ordinary victim, Cari reminds herself, as she steps out of the elevator and into the stark white hallway. She follows the signs down to the Toxicology Unit and eventually reaches the door with the placard reading: WINSTON PARK, PHD, DABCC. She knocks and a voice from inside chirps, "Come, come!"

Cari opens the door and steps into a compact, windowless office where three prominent computer screens stand on the desk. A smallish man in an oversized but immaculate lab coat springs up from his seat. "Detective Garcia? Correct? I am Dr. Park, yes."

"Good to meet you, Dr. Park."

"Yes, yes. Thank you for coming."

"Assumed it must be important."

"Well, I thought so, yes."

The comment hangs between them in an awkward silence. "Can you elaborate?" Cari finally prompts as she lowers herself into the seat across from him.

"Fascinating case," Dr. Park mutters, as he also sits down. "Then again, I don't often get requests from the director of the institute herself to fast-track a simple pill analysis. As in, never ever."

"Not my call," Cari says, thinking of the senator. "The pressure is all coming from above."

"Yes, yes." He arches an eyebrow conspiratorially. "Senator Galloway's son. I read about it. Tragic, isn't it? Is something going on there?"

Cari is wary of being drawn into gossip around any case, let alone such a high-profile one that she is not convinced is a homicide. "Is that what you meant when you said 'fascinating case'?"

"Oh, no, no," he says with pinched lips. "It's what I found inside those capsules!"

"What did you find, Dr. Park?"

"The Adderall tablets and the Miralax powder are legitimate. Just what you would expect to see on analysis. Probably a case of anorexia or bulimia. Yes, Detective?"

"Possibly. And the capsules?"

"Not what you'd expect at all!" Dr. Park whistles as he spins the nearest screen out to face her. He clicks his mouse and the screen displays a linear graph with numerous colored spikes along the horizontal axis. A look of deep satisfaction crosses his lips as he leans back in his chair.

"I have no idea what I'm looking at, Dr. Park."

His expression turns grave. "This is a total ion chromatogram." He waits, as if that were explanation enough.

Cari only shrugs.

"From the gas chromatograph-mass spectrometer, yes? The biochemical fingerprint is unmistakable."

A familiar buzz of expectation grows inside her. "Unmistakable for what?"

"The yellowish powder inside those capsules. They contain pure 2,4-Dinitrophenol."

Cari realizes the discovery is significant, but the words are gobbledy-gook to her. "What is that? In layman's terms, if you don't mind, Dr. Park."

"DNP. A hundred milligrams—give or take—per capsule, yes."

"DNP?" She leans forward, sensing that this will change the whole slant of her investigation. "Does it have a street name?"

He frowns. "Did you not read the exposé in the *Times* last month?"

"No."

"DNP has been gaining popularity in the bodybuilding world for the past decade or two. And now people are abusing it for weight loss, too, yes."

It all fits. "It can't be legal, can it?"

"As a fertilizer or a pesticide, yes. Or even as an explosive—which is what it was created for."

"But as pills?"

"*Capsules*," he corrects. "And no. Of course not. It's illegal for human consumption. DNP is toxic."

"How toxic?"

"Extremely. The lethal dose has been reported to be as low as three or four milligrams per kilogram of body weight. Even the slightest overdose can kill a person. Two or three pills could prove lethal to someone who wasn't very heavy, yes? People have died following the exact dosage recommended on the instructions."

Who would ever recommend it? "Where do these capsules come from?"

"The dealers order the industrial chemical in bulk from legitimate suppliers in India or China, for pennies on the kilogram, yes, then load it into capsules and sell them online at a massive profit."

"You're certain this DNP killed Owen Galloway?"

He whistles again. "We'll need to confirm it with the victim's blood and urine toxicology. But yes, I expect his death will be another case of DNP poisoning."

For a split second, Cari feels relieved that DNP wasn't as prevalent when Lucia was struggling with her condition and abusing anything and everything she could get her hands on to shed weight she didn't have to lose. But it's an illogical thought. Even without DNP, the outcome would have been the same for her sister.

"Another?" Cari cocks her head. "You've seen more cases, Dr. Park?"

"It would be the eighth death this year alone attributable to DNP, yes."

"In the US?"

He grimaces. "Here. In LA County alone."

CHAPTER 9

It's not illegal or even against the hospital bylaws, but Julie wonders if her current search is ethical. After all, unless a doctor is reviewing a chart for medicolegal purposes or to perform quality improvement rounds—neither of which applies to her current endeavor—then there's no reason to access a patient's record a month after her death.

But yesterday's poisoning reignited Julie's insatiable curiosity over the patient she lost to DNP last month. *What would push a mother to steal her daughter's diet pills?*

The scene in the ER that day was so chaotic that Julie never had the chance to ask her patient. Amazingly, the woman had driven herself in to the hospital. But within minutes of being rushed into the resuscitation bay, Marcia Wildman had collapsed into a protracted seizure known as *status epilepticus.* Even after the medications finally controlled her convulsions, nothing would tame her raging fever. When conscious, Marcia was desperate for reassurance. Seeing the fear in her eyes, Julie thought it only merciful to assure Marcia that she would survive. But Julie regrets making a promise she couldn't keep.

Scouring the electronic record for clues to Marcia's motivation, Julie comes across a consult note written by Dr. Leanne Melnyk. She doesn't have to open it to confirm Marcia's underlying diagnosis. Leanne, a close friend of Julie's from med school, runs St. Michael's Eating Disorders Clinic.

Julie texts Leanne to ask when she might be free to chat and is surprised to get an immediate response saying that her most recent appointment is a no-show and she is free right now. They agree to meet at the café across the street from the hospital that, convenience aside, is known within the hospital for its mediocre coffee and less than fresh pastries.

Julie spots her friend standing at the café's counter. Leanne was popular in med school for her fun-loving personality, Slavic good looks, and, especially among the male students, her voluptuous figure. She has grown even curvier since, having had three kids in close succession, and Julie appreciates that Leanne has only become more attractive with time.

"How are you, girlfriend?" Leanne cries, waving the two cups in her hands. "Got us tea. I wouldn't serve the coffee here to my pup."

"Hi." Instead of a hug, Julie brushes the back of her hand along Leanne's smooth cheek.

Leanne leads her to a waiting table, tucked in the back corner. As soon as they're seated, Julie asks, "How are the kids?"

"Good. Great. This is the first year all three tykes are in school the whole day." Leanne chuckles. "Feels like getting sprung from maximum security or something."

"When do I get to see them again?"

"Soon as you want. Why don't you take them for a sleepover? Like maybe until about Christmas?"

Julie grins. "How about I take them to the aquarium or Science World next week?"

"Yeah, they'd love that. They still haven't shut up about their pizza night with Auntie J." Leanne exhales. "And you? Has that cop put a ring on your finger yet?"

Julie sticks out her tongue. "What is this, Lee, 1954?"

"It's been a year or two already, hasn't it?"

"A year and a half. Matter of fact, Anson is moving in this weekend."

Leanne taps her teacup to Julie's. "There you go. Progress."

"Progress? What ever happened to female empowerment?"

"It doesn't flourish in my Ukrainian gene pool. I'm afraid it's marriage or bust as far every woman in the Melnyk family is concerned."

Julie laughs. "I've missed you."

"Me, too. I'm proud of you, Julie."

"For what? Finding a guy to live with me?"

"Well, that, of course." Leanne winks. "And for how far you've come."

From anyone else, Julie might have read condescension into the comment. But like Goran, Leanne was there for Julie when she hit rock bottom, ten years earlier. Even after she fell deep into opioid addiction and her fiancé—their mutual classmate Michael—overdosed in the bed beside Julie, Leanne stuck by her friend. Leanne even attended a couple of Narcotics Anonymous meetings with her, joking that she only showed up for the chocolate chip cookies.

Julie takes a sip of her tea, wincing at its weakness. "We need to go out for dinner. And soon."

"No kidding. I'd kill for a grown-up girls' night."

Picking up on her friend's fatigue, Julie asks, "You managing, Lee?"

"Yeah. Just perpetually exhausted. Kids!" Leanne runs a hand through her thick hair. "But you probably didn't reach out just to hear me whine."

"Actually, I wanted to ask you about a patient of yours."

"Oh? Which one?"

"Marcia Wildman. I saw her in the ER after her DNP poisoning."

"That's right. I saw your resuscitation note." A pained look crosses Leanne's lips. "Poor Marcia. I never thought she was going to turn out to be one of them."

"One of them what?"

"A SEED."

"What's that?"

"An acronym for severe enduring eating disorder," Leanne says. "It's the chronic form of anorexia. The incurables of my profession. About seventy-five to eighty percent of patients with eating disorders get better or at least go into remission. But the SEEDs never do. Some live their whole life in a state of starvation. And others . . . like Marcia . . . they die."

"She was only in her late forties."

Leanne shakes her head. "It's not as uncommon as you think. Many people live with anorexia for decades. I mean, eventually, the starvation catches up to them—kidney failure, bone collapse, and so on. But they can function in that state for ages."

"Marcia did?"

"Not that long, really," Leanne says. "That was the unusual part. Marcia had a late-onset eating disorder. She was well into her thirties and post-kids before she became truly symptomatic. Her biggest thing was the compulsive exercising. She would ride up to a hundred miles a day on her road bike. Or, in the cold and rain, she would spin indoors for three or four hours at a time."

"She was skin and bones the only time I ever saw her."

"Marcia could never be thin enough."

Julie shakes her head. "Body image delusions always accompany eating disorders, right?"

"Always. Body dysmorphia. An obsession with perceived but nonexistent body flaws."

"And they never recognize how skinny they've become? How unhealthy it is?"

"Not patients like Marcia," Leanne says. "With them it's absolute. They can be seventy pounds and still think their arms look flabby or their butt is too big."

"I guess that's what drove Marcia to steal her daughter's diet pills."

"Yeah, heartbreaking. Marcia is the first patient I've lost to DNP. At least, I think she is."

"But she's one of three DNP deaths in the past two months alone. It's circulating in Vancouver now." Julie eyes her friend steadily. "Do you know of any other patients who are taking it?"

"No." Leanne takes another sip of tea. "But it's painfully common for anorexics to abuse drugs to lose weight, or at least to help them to keep it off."

"Like laxatives?"

"Laxatives and purgatives don't do much for weight loss. They don't stop the absorption of calories. They're more often abused by patients with bulimia."

"What other drugs then?"

"For starters, a lot of anorexics abuse diuretics."

"But that's not real weight loss either."

"Yes and no. It might be temporary, but it's immediate, in the form of fluid loss. The dehydration makes them feel thinner." Leanne pulls a face. "But it can be murder on their kidneys and electrolytes, as you know. And it can even cause sudden death. Especially if their potassium plummets."

Julie nods. "I've seen a few close calls myself."

"Oh, and in the last couple years, that diabetic medication, Ozempic, has been increasingly used and, frankly, *abused* for weight loss."

"You need a prescription for that, don't you?

"You do," Leanne says. "But if I'd had to predict a drug for Marcia to abuse, Ozempic would've been my bet."

"How come?"

"It totally fits her demographic. A lot of middle-aged women on the Westside—many of whom are already underweight—go on it after gaining a few pounds during menopause. There are some private physicians in town who give it out like candy. Pardon the pun."

"That's depressing."

"It's out of control, is what it is. Not to mention highly unethical." Leanne runs a finger along the rim of her cup. "But the fact is, the most popular drugs of abuse among the eating disordered are still the illicit ones."

"Like cocaine?"

"Coke and crystal meth, for sure. Also, prescription stimulants like Adderall. Because they're all such effective appetite suppressants."

"I guess that makes some twisted sense. After all, an eating disorder is a form of addiction, right?"

"Very similar to one, anyway," Leanne says. "And those street drugs make anorexia an even more lethal disease."

"But they're mother's milk compared to DNP."

"It's that toxic, Julie?"

"Goran's patient—who weighed well over two-fifty—died after taking only five capsules. And DNP's toxicity is based on weight. The lighter you are, the more susceptible. Some people overdose on a single pill."

"Poor Marcia never stood a chance." Leanne closes her eyes momentarily. "If DNP were to circulate among the rest of my patients . . ."

"Which is exactly why someone better find out how and where the victims got their supply."

CHAPTER 10

"And that's a wrap, folks," Gerard says as he lets the pedals come to a rest and grabs his water bottle.

"Jesus! You nearly killed us this time." Lloyd Hunter pants heavily as he reaches for his towel. He looks as if he just stepped out of the shower, and his spin bike continues to drip sweat onto the mat even after he dismounts.

"Absolutely brilliant, Ger!" Lloyd's wife, Cecilia, says in her clipped, upper-crust English as she climbs off the bike beside her husband's. "Love when you punish us so."

"I'm with Cecelia," Adèle says as she wipes down her own bike. "What's the point if it doesn't hurt?"

Cecilia glances over to the other woman. "True of most things in life, *n'est-ce pas*, gorgeous?"

Gerard ignores the suggestiveness in Cecilia's tone. "You'll thank me later, Lloyd. You really will."

"Oh, probably." Lloyd chuckles. "But let me hate you for an hour or two."

Gerard finds these sessions with the Hunters demeaning. They remind him of a life he has outgrown. Gerard hasn't taught a spin class for anyone else in over two years. But he has to make an exception for his silent partners, whenever they're in town. After all, they gave him and Adèle the seed money to launch their first Mind Over Body Wellness Center. And the Hunters still own forty-nine percent of the business, despite how hard Gerard has tried to buy them out.

They leave the bikes and gather around the long table that boasts a row of fancy glass water dispensers. Today, slices of orange, lime, strawberry, and cucumber each float in one of the containers. Cecilia refills her bottle with the cucumber-flavored water while Lloyd, predictably, opts for the strawberry—no doubt for the extra sugar, even if it's only a trace.

Gerard first met the Hunters when he was running his spin studio and struggling to keep up with the bloated lease payments. They weren't his only wealthy clients. Based on the rows of luxury model Range Rovers, BMWs, and Teslas parked out front alone, affluence was the rule, not the exception. Some were richer than the Hunters. And on a personal level, Gerard was closer to other clients. But when he went looking for a financial backer for his new business, Lloyd was the first one he approached. Something about the fifty-five-year-old mining company CEO's dedication and intensity in class convinced Gerard that Lloyd would make a committed partner. And he sensed an uncanny savviness behind the man's bland exterior.

It still amazes Gerard that despite all the energy and focus Lloyd invests in his fitness training, he has never been able to lose his spare tire. His sweet tooth is too strong, and his willpower and metabolism are too weak. It's another reason Gerard doesn't want Lloyd associated with their brand any longer, even as a silent partner.

"We're full steam ahead on San Fran?" Lloyd asks, as he wipes his dripping brow.

"According to the lawyers," Gerard says.

"Like they're never wrong."

"We've signed the lease. Permits approved. Just a few lipstick renovations, and it's done, Lloyd. Our doors will open in just over a month."

"Good. But we can't rest on our laurels now, Ger. You should already be thinking about expanding to the East Coast. And UK and Europe soon after!"

The last thing I want is your advice. "Isn't it too soon?" Gerard asks, pretending to care.

"If you're not growing, you're dying, my friend."

"Well, I for one, think a San Francisco site is bloody thrilling!" says Cecilia, who, unlike her husband, has the physique of a gymnast. "Let's get out of this grim Vancouver rainfall and go survey our new site, shall we? We'll take the company jet. It will be absolutely brilliant. Ibiza all over again."

"Ibiza! Oh, my god. What a blur." Adèle runs her hands through her hair. "That would be wild."

But her quick glance sends Gerard a very different message. He thinks of their week in Ibiza and the times Cecilia wound up in bed with them after Lloyd passed out from over-partying. And how Cecilia was the one who always invited herself there.

Gerard knows Adèle has no interest in revisiting that arrangement. "We definitely should," he says. "We're committed in Vancouver for the next few weeks, but we should see if we could squeeze in a time before the opening."

"Which is going to be off the freaking charts!" Adèle says.

"If Vancouver and LA are anything to go by," Lloyd says.

"They're everything, love." Cecilia turns to Gerard. "Did I mention my friend Madeline is convinced you're some kind of witch doctor."

Gerard grimaces. "A witch doctor?"

"The poor soul has tried everything since her babies. Diets, fasts, liposuction . . . Nothing would touch those last few stubborn pounds. Then she discovered Mind Over Body, darling. And voilà, she's skinnier than she was before children."

It's all about the secret sauce, isn't it? But Gerard isn't about to discuss that with these two. "And you're surprised, Cece?" He throws in the nickname, knowing how it grates on her.

"On the contrary. I would have been shocked if your magic didn't work." Cecilia brushes imaginary crumbs off her damp tank top. "My point is, darling, the only thing you are going to struggle with in the Bay Area is keeping up with the demand."

Gerard can't help but smile. "That's a struggle I can live with."

Cecilia winks. "Careful what you wish for."

CHAPTER 11

Cari sits beside her friend Benny Jones on one of the white bucket chairs perched on the sidewalk outside the café at the corner of Sunset Boulevard and North Gower. The bright sun reflects off the windows of the building across the street, forcing Cari to put on her shades. But the glare doesn't seem to bother Benny, whose sunglasses rest on the table. As Benny sips his nitrogen-infused iced coffee, Cari notices how his form-fitting pale blue jacket and light beige T-shirt set off his dark ochre skin tone.

Platinum & Gold is the only coffee shop in Hollywood where Benny will deign to meet her. He likes to refer to himself as a "caffeine sommelier," while Cari just calls him a "coffee snob." But he is her most loyal friend and has been since the eleventh grade, when he came out of the closet while they were still dating.

Benny lowers his glass. "Robert was devastated."

Cari views him sidelong. "Over a canceled blind date?"

"He'd already fallen in love with you based on the photos I shared. They all do, Caridad. I mean look at you! Cheekbones that would cut diamonds. Perfect complexion. And those huge brown eyes! A fellow could practically drown in those."

"Enough, Benjamin!"

"What am I supposed to do with you? You won't go online—"

"Absolutely not."

"And you keep breaking the golden rule."

"I do not keep—"

"Mattias, Vicente, Isaac, and what's-his-face?" He lists the names off with his fingers as he speaks.

"Nate. And that was nothing but a rebound fling. Isaac wasn't much more. Besides, Vicente and I met in the Academy. That hardly counts."

"Yeah, and Mattias was your partner in Homicide," Benny says. "Your *married* partner."

Cari holds up a hand. "Not again. Not now."

"It's just so basic, Caridad. *No cops!*"

It wasn't as if she had intended to fall in love with Mattias. A husband. A father. And her own partner. She still can't believe it happened. It didn't hurt that he was six-two, trim, and dimpled, or that his gray-blue eyes were as expressive as any pair she had ever seen. But it was the intense laughter and easy intimacy they shared that made Mattias so irresistible.

Benny has heard it all before, so instead she says, "He keeps texting me."

"Uh-uh." Benny shakes his head. "Mattias has no right. None whatsoever. He pulled you into that mess and then just up and leaves?"

"I'm just as responsible for that mess."

"Don't buy it, Caridad. Messes are my specialty, not yours." He sighs. "Speaking of, Lawrence and I are done. For good."

"How many times have I heard this before?"

"No, he's moving out," Benny says of matter-of-factly. "Two musicians. Not much better than two cops."

Despite his lighthearted tone, Cari picks up on the hurt buried in it. Benny and Lawrence have had a volatile relationship since the day they met, competing for the same open violinist spot in the orchestra. But theirs is the longest relationship Benny has ever been in.

Cari strokes her friend's arm. "You OK?"

"Yes. Honestly. My God, we all know it's for the best."

"You sure?"

"Hundred and ten percent," he says, maybe a little too enthusiastically. "Besides, I've been dating again. Unlike you, online suits me just fine."

"You'll give yourself a bit of time to process it, right?"

"It's just dating." He eyes her knowingly. "I'm certainly not going to hibernate for six months."

"You and I work at different speeds."

"You mean warp versus glacial?"

"Sounds right." She takes a sip of her latte. "I've been thinking a lot about Lucia lately."

Benny frowns. "Why now?"

"This victim I've been working . . . a teenaged kid . . . he had an eating disorder."

"Ahhh." He nods. "Triggering, huh?"

"Yeah, I'm breaking my old instructor's rule."

"Of course! Your golden rule." He chuckles and then lowers his voice to a growl, aping his best version of a grizzled TV detective. "Never let a case get personal, doll."

She doesn't join in on the levity. "Luci was just a kid when she died, too."

"A kid at twenty-three? I suppose." He pauses for a sip of coffee. "But if so, a wildly self-destructive one."

"I could've done more for her, Benjamin." She looks down and adds quietly, "I should have."

"No, no, no." He tsks. "You don't always have to load the whole damn globe on your shoulders."

She is about to respond when her phone chimes, and she glances at the text from the captain that reads: "Computer Crimes have preliminary results." Realizing it's almost four p.m., Cari gets to her feet, concerned the forensic computer techs might soon leave for the day.

Benny looks up without moving. "Duty calls?"

"As usual." She bends forward and pecks him on the cheek. "Let's pick this up soon. Over dinner Thursday?"

He flicks her away with the back of his hand. "Go. Go save the world."

Cari hurries out to her car. Twenty-two minutes later, she is back at the Hertzberg-Davis Forensic Sciences Center, this time on the third floor, seated at a cubicle inside the Computer Crimes Section.

Zach Brenner, the wiry, bespectacled technician beside her, looks like a young Jeff Goldblum and smells faintly of fabric softener. But Cari has worked with the computer crimes specialist before and seen firsthand how capable he is.

"The warrants for the victims' devices came through," Zach says.

"For Owen Galloway?"

"For all of them."

"All of whom?"

"The known DNP deaths," Zach says. "Someone pulled some serious strings."

Of course she did!

Earlier in the day, only minutes after Cari had reported the lethal levels of DNP found in Owen's system to the captain, the senator called her. "Who gave it to him?" were the first words out of her mouth.

"I'm working on that, Senator," Cari said. "Getting access to his electronics might be key."

"I'll see what I can do," the senator said. "Eight deaths in LA County alone. That's more than murder. It's bordering on a conspiracy."

"Maybe," Cari said, resisting the urge to tell the senator that she was getting way ahead of herself.

"Go find out, Detective. Whoever did this to my Owen has to pay."

Cari suspected that the senator's thirst for retribution was not only driving her but also keeping her sane. And she saw no point in arguing. "They will, Senator."

Brushing off the memory, Cari turns back to Zach. "What did you find out?"

"I haven't cracked the victim's phone yet," he says. "But his laptop was child's play. And it tells a story."

Cari leans forward in her seat. "Which is?"

Zach taps at his keyboard, and an image fills the screen closest to her. The website's banner reads: "Dr. Muscles Pharmaceuticals." The layout reminds her of any generic online ordering page, but her eyes are drawn to the testimonials in boldface along the left-hand side border. "Dropped twenty pounds in twenty days!" writes Steve M. from Vancouver. "Added four inches across the pecs and two over the biceps!" raves Kevin R. from Oakland.

Cari points to the site's logo—a cartoonish rendering of a flexed arm with bulging biceps—at the top of the screen. "This is where Owen ordered his DNP?"

"Looks like. Found it in his deleted junk folder. Receipts from two different orders. And he wasn't the only one ordering from this site."

"The other victims? They ordered from here, too?"

"At least two of them."

"There are eight so far, right? What about the other five?"

"I only have access to the device from one other victim. And I haven't gotten through her files yet. But get a load of this." Zach scrolls down the screen where, in smaller font, a warning label reads: "Not recommended for human consumption." He shakes his head. "That's some gall, huh? To list that right below the testimonials!"

"Unbelievable." But Cari warms with the familiar buzz of anticipation. "Where is this Dr. Muscles located?"

"No idea." Zach highlights another phrase on the screen that reads: "Discreet shipping guaranteed." "Seriously, the gall!"

"You couldn't track down their IP address?"

Zach grimaces. "The site is a ghost, Detective. Gone. Hasn't been active for weeks. I only found it in a cloud cache."

"But there must be a trail, right?"

"This is what dealers do. Move from website to website and server to server. Or just use third-party platforms and anonymous forums or chat channels. Then they redirect people from public to private forums. Ping-pong back and forth between the regular and the dark web. That's how these rogue internet pharmacies run. We see the same thing with online sales of other illicit drugs like fentanyl, meth, you name it."

"There's nothing to glean from this website?" she asks as her hopefulness dissipates.

"I didn't say that."

She perks up again. "I'm all ears . . ."

"I was able to track their payment system. Up to a point. The deposits are routed through a bank in Iceland to Belarus. But from there, the trail gets murky. The funds are converted into crypto."

"Sounds like some high-tech international subterfuge."

Zach shrugs. "Actually, it's fairly standard operating procedure for these black-market sites."

"It doesn't help much if we don't know where the money wound up."

"I think Dr. Muscles might be operating out of Canada."

"What makes you say that?"

"When I look the site up on ICANN—"

"ICANN?"

"Internet Corporation for Assigned Names and Numbers. One of the major entities that offers domain name registration services to generic top-level domains."

Cari holds her palms out, helplessly. "You're losing me, Zach."

"ICANN regulates the companies that provide the website domains. In theory, anyway. Dr. Muscles Pharmaceuticals appears under a Canadian registrar. And so do a few of the previous iterations of the same website with their dumbass names like Dr. Slim Pharmaceuticals or Dr. Beefcake Pharmaceuticals."

Cari considers it. "If the seller is based in Canada, how do they ship past US Customs?"

"Dead easy," Zach says. "They could mislabel the DNP as a vitamin or whatever. And then just mail it internationally. Even if it happened to be intercepted by the US or Canadian postal authorities and they did figure out what was inside, they'd still have no clue who sent it."

"Are you saying the website is a dead end?"

"Maybe, maybe not. It's sophisticated stuff, Detective. Designed for one purpose: to hide the seller's identity. I'll do more digging. See if I can find their latest pop-up shop. But we're far more likely to find the source by following the money. Not the product."

"Thanks, Zach. Really good work." But Cari still feels a bit deflated as she gets to her feet. "Keep me posted?"

"Always," Zach says, still staring at his screen.

As Cari heads out to the elevator, the vision of Owen sprawled at his mother's feet pops to mind. Thanks to whoever is behind this Dr. Muscles Pharmaceuticals site, Owen—and at least two others in LA alone—have ended up dead.

CHAPTER 12

"Thanks for agreeing to meet," Julie says to Olivia Wildman, Marcia's daughter, as they stand off to the side of the entrance of the drugstore where the nineteen-year-old works. Olivia is bundled in a down coat, and Julie regrets not wearing a thicker jacket herself. It's almost six p.m., the sun has already set, and there's a penetrating chill in the damp breeze.

"Sure," Olivia says. Despite her overly made-up face, Olivia looks almost as hollow-eyed as she had the last time Julie saw her in the ER, only minutes after her mother died. "The nurse, she told me you almost . . . saved Mom. That no one could've done more for her."

Julie's stomach sinks. The compliment only makes her feel guiltier. She has no professional reason to be talking to Olivia about her mother's death. And Julie can only imagine how Anson will react. But she just hasn't been able to let what happened to Marcia go. "How are you holding up?"

Olivia shrugs. "Better than Dad, I guess. He's kind of a mess."

"Can't imagine. I'm so sorry for your loss." Julie clears her throat. "You're probably wondering why I reached out?"

Julie is rarely active on social media—she never posts herself—but she does have accounts across the major sites. She easily tracked down Olivia's Instagram account, and despite that it was set to private, Olivia responded immediately to her direct message requesting to meet.

Olivia stares down at her feet. "It's about those pills, right?"

"Yes."

"They're gone. I flushed them down the toilet."

"Did you throw away the bottle and packaging, too?"

Olivia nods. Her cheeks redden, but she still doesn't look up.

"How did you even hear about DNP?"

"I saw this post," Olivia says quietly. "On TikTok."

"Can you tell me about it?"

"Some random chick screaming about how effective these weight loss pills were. She had all these before and after shots in a bikini . . ."

Olivia goes quiet, but Julie senses that it's best to let her tell it in her own time.

"I . . . I wasn't even looking or anything. Not really." Olivia's voice thickens as she finally looks back up. "After I started university last year, I wasn't exercising or eating very well. And I'd kinda packed on the freshman fifteen. You know?"

"I remember it well from my college days. Are you still in school?"

"Yeah. Or . . . not right now. After Mom . . . I decided to take the year off."

"Understandable," Julie says. "Do you remember who posted the clip, Olivia? Or if it was an ad?"

"Don't think it was an ad. It didn't have a sponsor badge. And the production value was kind of cringe. On my FYP, I think."

"FYP?"

"For You Page," Olivia explains. "It's like where TikTok finds you posts it thinks you'll like. But they're supposed to have this badge telling you if they're an actual ad."

"Ah, I get it," Julie says. "And this clip convinced you to give the capsules a try?"

Olivia breathes harder. "I didn't have Mom's self-discipline. Plus, with school and all, I had no time to work out!"

Julie smiles sympathetically. "And this girl on the video. She must've made it sound like DNP was some kind of wonder drug, huh?"

"Totally! The chick said she tried *everything*, and this was the only thing that worked. So easy. So cheap." Olivia swallows. "So safe."

"How did you get the pills?"

Olivia closes her eyes. "At the end of the clip, she listed this site where you could order from."

"Which site?"

"Dr. Slim Pharmaceuticals." Olivia shudders. "I should've guessed by the ridic name what a scam it was."

"No doubt it was extremely convincing, Olivia. And I bet lots of people fall for it."

"I read they can be dangerous if you take too much, but . . . but . . ." Olivia's shoulders shake, and her voice dissolves to sobs. "I never . . . not in a million years . . . thought Mom would steal them from me . . . That was so not her."

Julie is close to tears herself. She knows exactly what it's like to feel responsible for a loved one's death—after all, she slept through her fiancé's fatal fentanyl overdose. She resists the impulse to hug the young woman. Instead, she says, "Thank you, Olivia."

Her gaze glued to the ground, Olivia continues to tremble.

"What you just told me could help prevent more unnecessary tragedies. Honestly."

Olivia's shoulders finally still and she wipes at her eyes with an arm.

"Do you still have the email confirmation of your order from Dr. Slim Pharmaceuticals?" Julie asks.

"Maybe." She swallows. "Probably."

"Can you forward it to me?"

Olivia nods.

"Great. Thank you."

They exchange email addresses and then Olivia hurries back into the store.

Julie finds little satisfaction in having tracked down the name of the DNP supplier responsible for Marcia's death. Anson is right. The product could have been shipped from anywhere. As best as she can tell from her own limited research, no one person or place has a monopoly on DNP distribution. Maybe the other victims got suckered into ordering from the Dr. Slim Pharmaceuticals site by the same promotion as Olivia did, or maybe they ordered from a different place altogether. Maybe the city is only beginning to see the collateral damage from a deadly new weight loss trend that's on the verge of going viral.

After Julie gets back into the car and cranks up the heater, she checks her phone and sees four texts from Anson. For an irrational moment, she worries he might already have gotten wind of her meeting with Olivia. But Julie opens the texts to find four photos of a meal in various stages of preparation. She assumes he's making a stir-fry, but she can't be certain. She smiles to herself. Her partner might not be the best cook, but he's an enthusiastic one, and whenever he does cook, he loves to make a production out of it.

The scent of sautéed garlic and ginger wafts to her as she steps through the doorway to her home. The dining table is set with wineglasses, burning candles, and a bouquet of fresh flowers. Anson has even managed to hunt down peonies—her favorite flower—in pink, no less—despite that they are out of season.

Wearing an apron over his blue button-down shirt, he approaches with an open bottle of red wine in hand. He nods to the table. "Not bad, huh?"

"Downright impressive."

"I copied it off an online image. From this site that's dedicated to domesticating men."

Julie chuckles. "Fake it till you make it, huh?"

"Exactly," he says, as his kisses her tenderly, leaving a hint of ginger on her lips.

"Hey." She shifts her weight from one foot to the other. "You remember that poisoning case?"

"Let's just have dinner, Julie. Work can wait."

She would love nothing more than to forget about everything else and just enjoy the dinner. But she decides it's better to get it off her chest now, as it will only get harder to tell him as time passes. "You're not going to be happy with me."

He lowers the wine bottle to his side. "Oh?"

"I went to see Olivia Wildman."

He frowns. "Who?"

"Remember my patient from last month? The DNP death? Her daughter."

Anson rubs his temples with his free hand. "I told you I was going to look into it, Julie. I've already got a call into my friend, Rahim, in the Drug Unit."

"I know. And I totally trust you to. It was just . . . gnawing at me."

"You've got give me a bit of time. I'm absolutely swamped with these whack-a-mole gang hits. If I don't hear back from Rahim tomorrow—"

Julie holds up a hand. "I get it."

"Do you, though? It's like those carfentanil poisonings last year. Lines were crossed, Julie. God knows you mean well, but you just keep pushing."

"You're right. I'm sorry. But Anson, we have at least three unnecessary deaths related to this deadly poison. And if things don't change soon, we both know there are going to be more."

He eyes her for a long moment. Then he turns to the table and fills both wineglasses well past the midpoint. He puts down the bottle and picks up the glasses, handing one to her. "What did the daughter have to say?"

CHAPTER 13

Rain's penthouse condo does look "beyond fucking brilliant," as her friend the British rapper TKT had gushed minutes before disappearing into one of the guest bedrooms with someone else's wife.

The party planners have outdone themselves with the chocolate fondue waterfall and the two levitating bars that appear to defy gravity, suspended as they are by thin steel cables that are invisible in the dim light. And on this rare clear November night, the Vancouver skyline plays the perfect backdrop for her event. A warm glow emanates from the vessels in the harbor, and the lights lining the chairlifts on Grouse and Cypress Mountains, on the other side of the inlet, make them also appear to float. No wonder so many film and TV productions flock to this northern metropolis.

Tonight, Rain's penthouse could pass as the location for a Grammy or even Oscars after-party. Celebrities are everywhere. The streaming series that she has come to Vancouver to shoot boasts a twelve-million-dollar-per-episode budget and two Emmy Award–winning actors. Despite all that star power, Rain still tops the bill on the show, which, as best as she can tell, can't seem to decide if it's a thriller or a comedy.

Rain has every reason to celebrate. But how can she as long as Braden is here?

She owes her career to her manager. Braden Hollands plucked her out of relative YouTube obscurity and engineered her stratospheric rise. Without Braden, there would be no platinum albums. No endorsement deals. No starring roles. And none of the six luxury properties she owns across the globe.

But without him, there might be more joy and certainly more freedom in her life. Also, maybe her heart would be whole again. As much as Braden has given Rain, it often feels as if he has taken even more.

"Don't fall in love with that man," her mom cautioned the day before Rain left Denver for her first tour, a West Coast swing. At the time, the then eighteen-year-old Rain thought it weird that her mom had specified love and not sex. Plus, she was grossed out by the thought of it. As the last virgin among her friends—at least, if they were to be believed—the idea of having sex for the first time with a man three years older than her own dad was beyond imaginable. But as usual, her mom's instincts proved right. Within four months of leaving Denver, Rain was not only madly in love with Braden, but she was also basically living with him. They were inseparable for the next thirteen months, until Braden did what it turned out he always does and summarily dumped Rain for the next year's model—in this case a literal one, a Spanish swimsuit model named Paloma.

But Braden didn't allow Rain's heartbreak to affect their bottom line. He insisted on remaining her manager. And it sickens Rain to admit to herself that she was so desperate for any form of his presence in her life that she eagerly accepted the arrangement.

Four years later, the sting of that rejection has lessened, but Rain has never been able to stop loving Braden. And her disappointment tonight feels as crushing as it did the day he left. After all, a big part of the reason she threw the party was to impress him. She assumed he was single again after having broken up with Paloma's replacement only weeks before. But he showed up tonight with a date—a willowy Nordic beauty named Anya, who is overdressed in a silver slit gown, as if she were on her way to attend some major gala. Braden has taken care not to show Anya too much attention, but Rain can tell by the bounce in his step how infatuated he is with his new girl.

Anya's lean, statuesque figure only makes Rain feel worse about her own body. Especially today, which was supposed to be a triumph of self-esteem. Rain finally got up the nerve to share her photos from a recent boat trip in Laguna Beach. Instagram is abuzz over the first bikini shots Rain has ever posted. But all she can focus on is the one comment that reverberates inside her skull. Rain never reads through the comment section—she knows better than that—but somehow her eyes just fell on one entry. "Looking skinny, bitch. Too bad about the cankles," @nights-fordays66 had written.

They are cankles! Rain thinks with disgust about the thick calves that she inherited from her mom. Even her miracle capsules can't do anything about them. But that didn't stop Rain from trying. Soon after Braden and his latest plaything showed up, she slipped off to her bathroom and downed three more capsules with half a glass of vodka.

Rain can't tell if it's the vodka, the empty stomach, or those three pills that are making her feel so loopy. She also can't believe how warm the penthouse is, even with the balcony doors wide open. It's embarrassing. Other guests might soon start to feel as light-headed as she does. She needs to address it.

"Excuse me, I have to speak to the caterer," Rain says as she turns away from her series' showrunner, who is standing too close and droning on too long.

She weaves her way through the throng of guests to the kitchen in the search of the caterer, stopping for quick chats, hugs, and a few selfies on the way. Her friend Maleeka Khan blows her a kiss from the couch where she has wedged herself between two buff young actors. "Boo, this partizzle is way O.T.T.!" cries Maleeka, who practically speaks in emoji.

Maleeka was a backup singer on Rain's first tour and has traveled with her ever since. They bonded from day one—two young women, both out of their element, each suffering from deep insecurities. Rain's centered on her body image, while Maleeka has never felt worthy of love, which makes her pursue it that much harder. Rain is growing tired of Maleeka's nonstop partying and endless need for male attention. But she's one of the few true confidantes Rain has her in life, and Maleeka, of all people, understood how devastating it was when Braden dumped her.

Rain blows a kiss back to Maleeka but keeps moving. By the time she reaches the kitchen, she feels unsteady on her feet. She braces herself with a hand to the countertop.

Someone grips her tightly around her other arm. "Your face, Lorraine! It's beet-red. You OK?"

Not now. She refuses to turn her head. She can't face those pale penetrating eyes. "All good. Just so effin' hot in here."

"Hot?" Braden says. "I haven't even taken my jacket off yet."

She wriggles free of his hand. "Guess I've been rushing around too much. Hosting and all."

"How about I get you some ice water? That might help."

"I'm good."

"Come on, Lorraine. It's me. Something's off."

Rain finally turns to him. It pains her to see him looking so handsome with the thick, salt-and-pepper stubble lining his cheeks and a shirt that's darker than his casual blue jacket. "I'm good, Braden. Go check on your date. She's probably looking for the silent auction or whatever."

He chuckles. "Anya's from the East Coast. She's used to more formal cocktail parties."

Fuck Anya! Rain thinks as the floor sways beneath her. "She's an eleven out of ten. She seems great. Can't wait to get to know her."

He squints at her. "Let me go get Dr. Markstrom."

She forces a lighthearted laugh. "What's he going to do? Analyze me into feeling cooler?"

"At least let's go out on the balcony and get some fresh air?"

He reaches his hand out again, but she recoils, almost stumbling in the process. "I got a better idea," she says. "I'm going to splash myself down with some cold water."

Rain swivels on the spot and heads for her bedroom. She hears someone calling her name, and the voice echoes as if in a cave, but she keeps moving. Her face is on fire, and she's aching for privacy. She almost reaches the door to her room, but the man catches up to her. "Hold on there, Rain," Dr. Markstrom says.

Rain reluctantly stops. "Oh, hey," she says. "Having a good time?"

The short, balding man in the bow tie views her silently for an uncomfortably long moment. Rain can never tell if she sees sympathy or judgment in those owl-like eyes of his. Sometimes she thinks he likes it that way. To keep her guessing. To maintain his control. "You're so flushed, Rain."

"Been running nonstop since before the guests got here." She gestures to the bedroom. "Going to cool myself down with some cold water."

Without warning, he reaches out a hand and rests the palm of it against her forehead. "You're burning up."

Fighting off a swoon, Rain pulls her face back from his hand, which smells of scented soap. "I might have another bladder infection. Been peeing razors again. If you must know."

"Rain . . ."

"I'm OK."

His stare is unrelenting. "How much did you take?"

"Just what I'm supposed to."

"Nothing else?"

"A couple drinks. No coke or Adderall, if that's what you're wondering."

Dr. Markstrom's gaze is skeptical. "Let me take you to a doctor who can sort out this 'bladder infection' of yours."

He reaches for her arm, but she shrinks from his touch. "I'm a fucking adult!" she snaps, surprising herself with her defiance.

"Then be an adult," he says unperturbed. "And go see a doctor."

What the fuck are you supposed to be? The lightheadedness intensifies. It's all she can do to stay upright. "I'm going to my room."

Rain hurries away, thankful it's only a few more steps to her bedroom. As soon as she's inside, she slams the door and locks it behind her. She lurches to the bed and collapses on top of it. Her whole body is on fire. But she doesn't have the energy to get up to go to the en suite bathroom and soak a towel over her head as she intended.

The party is a disaster. The man she loves, and always will, has moved so far on from her. And no matter how hard she works or how much she deprives herself, she will never shed her cankles.

Will I ever be happy? she wonders, just as her torso jerks violently.

Rain tries to sit up, but her body won't cooperate. Her throat tightens with sudden fear. *What's happening?*

The world starts to tunnel. And in the instant before everything goes black, she feels her limbs flail involuntarily against the bed.

CHAPTER 14

Anson can't hear what Nicole is saying, but her face is contorted with worry. He's desperate to reach out to her—to hold her—but his arms won't cooperate. She is only a few feet away, but the ear-piercing ringing drowns out her words. *What's wrong, sweetheart?* he wants to scream.

But then she's gone.

Dark as the room is, Anson realizes he is in Julie's bed. He assumes it must be her phone that is shrieking. Ignoring it, he lets himself drift back into sleep, hoping to reconnect with his dead wife. But someone shakes his shoulder, and the moment is lost.

"Anson," Julie says groggily. "Your phone. It's the second call."

He reaches out and pats the nightstand blindly until his fingers wrap around the device. Once he lifts it to his face and sees "DC" on the caller ID, he wakes more fully, noticing the "03:11" time stamp on top of the screen.

He brings it to his ear. "Hello," he mutters.

"Detective Chen," Deputy Chief Gina Brower says in her gravelly voice—a permanent reminder of the time a perp who was wired on crystal meth broke her larynx with a vicious elbow chop. "Sorry to have to wake you."

"No problem, DC," Anson says, clearing the rest of the mental cobwebs as he sits up and throws his legs over the side of the bed. "What's up?"

"Rain Flynn is dead."

"The singer?" His voice rises. He assumed the deputy chief would be calling to advise him of another gang hit.

"The very same. She was found dead in her condo in Coal Harbour an hour or two ago."

Like almost everyone in Vancouver, Anson had heard Rain was in town filming for the past month. "Any signs of a struggle?" he asks.

"No. Nothing like that. She was hosting a big bash. A real who's who of A-, B-, and C-listers. Apparently, she went into her bedroom around midnight and locked the door behind her. When she didn't come back out, her friends got worried. They eventually broke the door in and found her pulseless on her bed. One of the caterers tried to perform CPR, but she was very dead by the time the paramedics got to her."

"Drugs?" Anson asks.

"Probably," the deputy chief says, and Anson can feel Julie stirring in the bed beside him. "How else do young Hollywood stars die these days?"

"Not just Hollywood," he says. "Overdose now tops all causes of death in the under forty set in our little metropolis, too."

"Yeah, I've seen those uplifting stats."

"I don't get it, DC. Why Homicide?"

"Word is out. Social media is on fire. You woulda thought a comet smashed into the planet. And VPD Comms is absolutely blowing up. I've already had calls from the chief and the mayor. Doesn't sound like a homicide. But I sure as hell don't want us to be caught with our pants down."

"Yeah. I hear you."

"Can you and Theo go to check out the scene? I'll text you the address." She exhales. "Please go put my mind at ease, Anson. We don't need to be involved in what's already shaping up to be the shit show of the century."

"I'll update you later in the morning," Anson says as he hangs up.

"What's that about?" Julie asks from the darkness behind him.

He doesn't see any need to protect confidentiality, based on what the deputy chief told him, so he says, "Rain was found dead in her room."

"Dead?" Julie croaks. "Here? In Vancouver?"

"Yeah. At a condo in Coal Harbour. The deputy chief wants us to go check it out. Make sure there's no funny business."

"Rain . . . dead," Julie mutters in disbelief. "She wasn't even twenty-five, I don't think."

"Which is a prime age for a fentanyl overdose."

"True. But what a loss." Julie clicks her tongue. "'Can't Go Back' is the top song on my current workout playlist."

"Yeah, well, apparently that song just got a lot more meaningful." He leans back and brushes his lips over her cheek. "I'll see you later."

After Anson brushes his teeth and steps into a slate-gray suit, he dials his partner on speakerphone. Theo answers, sounding as if he's already been awake for some time. Anson explains the situation, and Theo asks no questions except whether Anson would mind swinging by to pick him up since his wife's SUV is in the body shop, and she needs to borrow his car in the morning.

Less than fifteen minutes later, Anson pulls up in front of Theo's house in the quiet Main Street neighborhood, where his partner is already standing at the curb.

After Theo buckles his seatbelt, he shows Anson a clickbait headline on his phone screen. "RAIN IS GONE!" it screams. The tasteless pun is written in all caps above an unflattering photo of the superstar on the dance floor of some nightclub with a cocktail glass in each of her hands. "Wonder if this will turn out to be one of those 'what were you doing when you heard the news . . .' moments?" Theo asks, as they drive off.

"Not for me." Anson is familiar with Rain and her ubiquitous cultural footprint, and he even finds some of her music catchy, in an inconsequential way. But news of her passing doesn't resonate with him like the sudden deaths of certain other celebrities did. "Ask your sons. Or better still, their girlfriends."

"No doubt it'll be the talk of the Kostas dinner table."

The skies open and rain pelts the windshield as they cross over the Cambie Street Bridge, passing only the occasional car and early morning delivery truck. But as they drive through downtown, the traffic begins to build. And once they reach Coal Harbour and turn onto Cardero Street, pedestrians join the cars lining the street, all heading in the same direction they are driving.

Theo points to the building at the end of the block. A large crowd has already formed an impromptu vigil. Several people hold candles in front of the row of police cruisers, ambulances, and other official vehicles. Media vans are parked on either side of the street. "Not sure our city needs this kind of attention," Theo says.

"Very sure it doesn't," Anson grumbles. "But need it or not, it's going to be with us for a while."

Anson drives as far as he can on the street and then pulls over, double-parking beside one of the media vans. They climb out into the cold rain and flash their badges as they weave through the throng and into the lobby of the building. A young constable escorts them into the elevator and uses a security fob to light the button for the top floor.

The doors open inside a sprawling penthouse suite with an open floor plan. The floor-to-ceiling windows offer a 360-degree view of the city, which is shrouded in angry clouds. Remnants of a party are everywhere, from the floating bars to the half-empty trays of food and glassware scattered around the room.

All kinds of uniformed attendees—police officers, paramedics, firemen, and crime scene techs—mill around. There are far more first responders than Anson would expect to see at the scene of a typical sudden death, but he's not surprised. The victim is the antithesis of typical. Anson flashes his badge to the turbaned police sergeant who appears to be in charge. The sergeant gestures to the bedroom at the far side of the unit.

On the way there, Anson spots the chief coroner, Desmond Wilson, in the far corner of the room, speaking to another man who's as short and bald as him but more formally dressed in a suit and a bow tie. "When was the last time you saw Desmond at a crime scene?" he asks Theo. "Especially after hours."

"Never," Theo says. "But that guy hasn't met a microphone he didn't love. And this case is going to bring him a boatload of those."

They walk through an open door into an expansive bedroom. Rain is on her back in a short black dress, lying on top of a twisted duvet with her arms straight by her sides. She could almost pass for someone resting in bed, were it not for her vacant gaze or the lacy lividity in her cheeks and arms. Anson is struck by her scrawniness. He could almost wrap one finger around her wrist. But while she might have a build compatible with hardcore drug use, the skin on her arms is smooth and bears no track marks.

One of the crime techs circles the bed, snapping photos. Anson has full trust in the professionalism of the VPD forensic team, but he still wonders how much those photos would be worth on the open market if someone decided to sell them.

"No sign of a rig or pill bottles or any other drug paraphernalia?" Theo asks the tech, motioning to the nightstand.

"Nada," the tech replies, without lowering the camera. "Not even a water glass by the bed."

"You don't mind if I check out the bathroom?" Theo asks the tech, who only shrugs in response.

Anson kneels by the bed and studies Rain's head and neck, scanning for the usual signs of trauma: broken blood vessels in the whites of her eyes, blood at the lips or nostrils, or bruising around the neck. But all he sees is the unblemished face of a woman who has died far too young. The face is both foreign and familiar to him. He's seen it plastered across screens for the past four or five years. This close, the gravity of her death sinks in.

"Partner," Theo calls from behind him.

Anson straightens and heads over to the en suite bathroom, noting its huge soaker tub and double-sink vanity with marble countertop. He inhales a whiff of incense as he steps over to where Theo stands beside a stocky crime tech in front of an open mirrored cabinet. The gloved tech is cataloguing the names of the pill bottles on his tablet computer.

"What have you got?" Anson asks.

"Plenty of over-the-counter vitamins and supplements," Theo says. "But in terms of prescription meds, only Wellbutrin and Vyvanse. Both prescribed in LA."

"Wellbutrin is an antidepressant, right?"

"Yeah, that or to help someone quit smoking. And Vyvanse is apparently for ADHD, right?" Theo asks the tech, who flashes a thumbs-up. "Both bottles are almost full. Doesn't look like she could've overdosed on either."

The tech raises what resembles a capped fountain pen. "There's also this," he says. "No name or prescribing doctor on it, but it was together with her other meds."

"What is it?" Anson asks.

"An Ozempic self-injector."

"OK . . . What's it used for?"

"Diabetes, usually."

"As in insulin?" Theo asks.

The tech shakes his head. "It's for the adult-onset type. The heavy folks. My doc was considering prescribing it for me." He pats the bulge over the front of his white forensic bunny suit. "I don't have blood sugar issues, but apparently it's also magic for weight loss."

"Weight loss?" Theo grimaces as he thumbs to the bedroom. "Did you get a load of our victim?"

"Skinny one, wasn't she?"

Theo thanks the tech and they head back out into the living room. "No evidence so far of any drugs, illicit or prescribed, to explain her death," he says.

"Doesn't mean much," Anson grunts. "Anyone could've brought drugs to the party. Rain could've swallowed, smoked, or snorted them pretty much anywhere in this giant pad."

"Agreed. I'm just saying," Theo says. "And that diabetes injector doesn't make a whole lot of sense."

The middle-aged man in the bow tie who was talking to Desmond earlier approaches them, his face set in a look of sheer determination. "Are you detectives?" he asks.

"Yes," Theo says. "Detectives Kostas and Chen. And you are?"

"Dr. Anders Markstrom," he says. "Rain was my client."

"Your client? What kind of doctor are you?"

"A clinical psychologist."

Anson tilts his head. "And were you at her party?"

"I traveled up here with Rain from LA for the filming. I am staying just a few floors down."

"Did she usually travel her with her therapist?"

"Sometimes. It would depend on how long she was traveling for. And so on."

"And so on?" Theo prompts.

"Her state of mind and such."

"What about her state of mind? Did she suffer from mental health issues?"

"I'm really not at liberty to discuss those details."

"We found antidepressants and ADHD meds in her vanity," Anson points out.

"I am bound by therapist-client privilege," Markstrom says. "But Rain has always been very open with her fans about her struggles."

"Which struggles, Dr. Markstrom?"

"Her battles with an eating disorder. And how she came very close to dying from an overdose when she was only fifteen."

"Overdose?" Anson says. "As in deliberate or accidental?"

"Deliberate. She swallowed several bottles of her parents' medications. But that was eight years ago. She has been very stable on her medications and, of course, with therapy." Markstrom points to the bedroom. "There's no suggestion of an overdose this time, is there?"

"We can't say without toxicology results."

"But her pill bottles?"

Theo glances at Anson before answering. "Were not emptied."

Markstrom nods, satisfied. "That poor girl," he says emotionlessly. "Her parents are going to be devastated."

"Did Rain have diabetes?" Anson asks.

"Diabetes? No." He frowns. "Why?"

"We found a diabetic medicine in her bathroom. Ozempic."

Markstrom doesn't react.

"It's a medication that some people also use for weight loss," Theo says. "Did you know Rain was taking it?"

Markstrom folds his arms across his chest. "I have a PhD in counseling. I do not prescribe medications. You'd need to discuss those with her medical doctors."

"We will," Anson says. "But you just told us how stable she was on treatment."

He sniffs. "She was."

"But she still brought her therapist on location?" Anson nods to the bedroom. "And to me, she looks like she was on the verge of starvation."

Markstrom eyes him for a long cold moment. "Stable is a relative term, Detective."

CHAPTER 15

As Gerard sits at his desk with a cup of espresso in his hand and reads the online article about Rain's death, he makes a mental note to send Adèle a bouquet of lilies. He got tied up so late at work last night that he ended up crashing in one of the spare rooms that he has claimed as a makeshift bedroom. He hasn't heard from Adèle this morning, which means she either slept in with someone else or is too devastated by the news of Rain's death to get out of bed. He hopes it's the latter.

They saw Rain perform from a VIP box at Coachella last spring. Gerard even called in a favor with one of his celebrity clients in Beverly Hills, a major music producer, who arranged for Adèle to meet her idol at the after-party. Gerard had never seen his girlfriend so giddy or starstruck. He was underwhelmed, both by Rain's performance and her presence. She struck him as a scared girl who was playing way out of her league.

Gerard closes the browser and opens his inbox instead. There are over a hundred unread emails waiting. He has just begun to wade through the first few when the office door whooshes open.

"There are you, darling!" Cecilia says, as though she has discovered his secret hiding spot, as she sashays toward his desk in a yoga unitard that highlights her perky nipples.

"Morning, Cece," he says, annoyed but not surprised by the presumptuous entrance. Boundaries are not much of a thing for Cecilia. "You heard about Rain, huh?"

"You'd have to be a hermit monk living in some skete not to have!" Cecilia cries. "Even *those* monks have probably heard."

"It did happen here in Vancouver. That's a big deal."

"Is it? Why, darling? Is there anything more tiresome than another dead young celebrity?"

"She was Adèle's favorite."

"Aw. Now I am heartsick." She fingers the gold chain around her neck. "We should really try to cheer up that French Canadian beauty of ours."

He smiles half-heartedly. "We should."

Cecilia arches an eyebrow. "As it happens, Lloyd is leaving town a day earlier than me at the end of the week. Perhaps the three of us could have a quiet night in?"

"Yeah, maybe," he says vaguely. "Was there something else you wanted to talk about?"

Cecilia eases herself into the chair across from him. "As a matter of fact, there is."

When she doesn't elaborate away, he says, "And that would be . . ."

"I am hoping for more of your witchcraft, darling. A particularly strong spell this time."

He doesn't have time for her games or riddles. "What are you talking about?"

"Lloyd."

"What about him?"

"You saw him at the spin class yesterday. He does not exactly cut the figure of an Adonis."

Gerard frowns. "Has he ever?"

"Of course not! He can't even whittle himself down to the level of a dad bod. Although not from lack of trying, darling."

"Some people just don't have the necessary metabolism."

"Or the willpower. Especially when it comes to keeping his paws out of the honey jar. Or the liquor cabinet." Cecilia absentmindedly wraps a few strands of her hair around a finger. "But the poor man agonizes over it. And, to be frank, I have to sleep next to that gooey body most nights. So . . ."

"Not sure what to tell you." Gerard shrugs. "I've trained him personally. We've maximized every modality from diet to meditation."

"I'm thinking more of your supplement."

Gerard sits up a little straighter. "Does Lloyd not follow the regimen?"

"Oh, he does. Religiously."

"Then I don't see what else—"

"When I consider all your other success stories . . ." Cecilia waves a hand over her upper torso, letting it linger at the level of her breasts. "Like Madeline. And the others I see coming through the doors of our wonderful establishment."

"No method is foolproof. We can't guarantee success."

"Perhaps not. But you can always load the dice a tad more."

He rubs his forehead in exasperation. "I'm not following, Cece."

She flashes him a big smile, and despite the perfect teeth, angular cheeks, and Mediterranean blue eyes, he finds something ugly about her. "What I would love, Gerard, is for you to increase the potency of Lloyd's supplement."

He tenses. "The supplement is premixed. Besides, it's a tried-and-true balance of vitamins B and D, magnesium, green tea extract, iron, and other minerals to promote metabolism. It's not like we can just increase one of those components by fifty percent and double the weight loss all of a sudden."

She tilts her head and eyes him for a few seconds. "Can't you though, darling?"

"You have no idea what you're talking about."

"I've been around fitness and weight loss programs my entire life. None can hold a candle to the results of yours."

"Exactly."

"But, darling, I also wasn't born yesterday. It's not the green tea extract or the extra ten minutes of meditation that reshape bodies like your system does. There must be a little something more to your supplement."

She rises lazily to her feet. "I'm not asking you to tell me what that is. In truth, I'd prefer not to know. I'm simply asking you to tailor a more potent supplement for my husband."

Gerard stops himself from gritting his teeth. "I'm not sure that's possible."

"Anything is possible," Cecilia says as she turns away from the desk. "And don't worry, darling. Your secret is safe with me."

CHAPTER 16

The heavy bass from the nineties hip-hop song vibrates the floor beneath Cari's feet as she stands at the welcome desk of Fitter Tomorrow. The bubbly young receptionist with piercings through both nostrils and a name tag that reads "Hi! I'm Mysti!" promised to be back "in a shake." Waiting for her to return, Cari glances around the cavernous gym that is filled with cardio and weight machines, not many of which are occupied. The black walls are adorned with inspirational workout slogans written in fake chalk as if they had just been scribbled on recently. And the ceiling is unfinished, with all the venting and plumbing exposed. The whole package strikes her as cliché.

"Found him!" Mysti chirps as she bounds back to the desk.

Behind her struts a tall man with a shaved head. He's wearing a black, long-sleeved workout shirt and leggings that are tight enough to highlight his sculpted musculature. "Hello there, I'm Aiden." He extends a meaty but manicured hand and flashes snow-white teeth. "I understand you're looking for me?"

Cari meets the firm handshake. "Yes, I am. Thanks."

"Are you interested in individual or group training?" Aiden Cowell asks.

"Neither."

"Um . . . OK. How can I help you then?"

"I'm Detective Garcia with the LAPD," she says. "I've been trying to reach you, Aiden."

His smile falters. "Yeah, yeah. I was going to get back to you right after work."

"Can you talk now?"

Mysti eyes Aiden with interest as he makes a show of consulting his watch. "My next client will be here any sec . . ."

"It won't take more than five or ten minutes."

"OK, fine." Aiden steps away from the desk and heads over to the corner of the room, tucking himself away behind a row of lockers.

Cari follows him there. "I was hoping to ask you about Katie Lashley," she says.

A pained look creases the trainer's face. "I don't like talking about that."

"Must be hard. I'm sorry." Cari sighs. "You and Katie were living together at the time, right?"

"We were engaged," he murmurs.

"Oh, I'm sorry," Cari says. "About that weight loss drug she was taking—"

"All those stupid supplements!" Aiden's thick shoulders shudder. "Katie was obsessed with competing."

"Competing in . . . ?"

"Fitness and figure competitions." He sighs. "It's like bodybuilding, except the emphasis is all on muscle definition, not size."

"Oh, yeah." Cari pictures the Instagram models in her head—all those over-the-top smiles and oily poses in tiny bikinis.

"Katie would've swallowed radioactive swamp water if she thought it would help her on competition day," Aiden says. "This one time, she fainted from all the diuretics she was downing."

Cari suddenly remembers the morning after she had agreed to let Lucia move in with her again, when her little sister collapsed in the kitchen. They had been arguing at the time, and Cari just assumed Lucia was faking it.

Cari hovered over Lucia without offering to help her up. "What are you? Five years old?"

"I'm dizzy, sis."

"Are you, though?"

"Whatever." Lucia made a show of holding on to a chair to try to pull herself up before dropping back to the floor.

Cari could see the sharp outline of the bones in Lucia's forearms. "Why do you do this to yourself?"

"You're blaming me for fainting, now? Jesus!"

"I meant starving yourself."

"Maybe I just don't want to be fat like Mom and . . ."

"Me, huh?" Cari said, swallowing the hurt. "Mom's not fat, and neither am I. We're curvy. It's in our genes. It's what makes us attractive."

Lucia snorted a laugh. "You keep telling yourself that."

"Get off the goddamn floor!" Cari barked.

But when Lucia finally managed to stand up, she was ghostly pale. And she would be dead within the month.

Shaking off the painful memory, Cari asks Aiden, "When did Katie start using DNP?"

"No idea." He folds his arms. "Didn't even know she was. I'd never heard of the stuff until after she died."

"Is that right?"

Suspicion creases his eyes. "Yeah."

"Aiden, I saw the texts between you two."

His eyes narrow even more. "What texts?"

"We have her phone records. From your chats, it sounded as if Katie was ordering the DNP as much for you as for her."

"What the fuck? You're allowed to read her texts?"

"With a warrant, yes."

"This isn't right!"

"Can you tell me anything about the website Katie ordered from?"

Aiden abruptly steps around Cari, brushing her shoulder. "My client must be here by now."

"There have been eight deaths related to DNP in LA alone. If you know anything, Aiden . . . or if you're still using it yourself . . ."

"Nothing to do with me," he says as he strides away. "Katie ordered that shit. I already lost her. I'm not taking the hit for that, too."

Must be convenient to be able to blame your dead fiancée. But Cari
bites her lip before saying it aloud and instead calls after him, "I'll be in
touch."

She has just gotten back into her car when her phone rings and "Captain Taylor" flashes across the call display.

"Hello, Cari," the captain says with a friendliness that puts her on
edge. "Got a minute?"

"What's up, Captain?"

"I was hoping to get a quick update from you."

"Sure. We're still trying to hunt down the location of the website
where Owen Galloway ordered the DNP," Cari says, quickly summariz-
ing what she learned from Zach at CCS. "I've followed up with the other
two victims who are known to have ordered from the same site. No luck
on the first one. A Gisele Santoro. She was from Brazil and had only been
in LA for six months before she died. I haven't found any contacts for her
yet. At least, ones who know anything."

"And the second?"

"Katie Lashley. I just spoke to her former fiancé." She chooses her
words carefully. "That lead's a bit more promising."

"Good," the captain says. "But eight victims. With sales on the dark
web coming from Canada. *Maybe.* For all we know, the pills could be
coming from Tonga. That's a lot of legwork for one investigator."

By her own choice, Cari hasn't had a new partner since Mattias
abruptly left both her and the LAPD. She asked Lieutenant Greene,
who's less ambitious and a more empathetic boss than Captain Taylor,
not to pair her up immediately. Over the past six months, Cari has been
investigating cases on a one-off basis with temporary partners or on her
own. It has worked out up until now, but the investigative load from this
case is more daunting. "I could use a bit of help," she admits.

"That's why I've decided to set up a task force."

"A task force?" she blurts. "Really?"

Cari hears someone clear his or her throat in the background. *Of
course. The senator is listening in.*

"Eight dead and counting. We need to get to the bottom of this thing
before more bodies pile up." The captain lowers his voice, as if he's about

to let her in on a secret. "After that *Times* article and, of course, the senator's son . . . the press is already sniffing around."

The senator and the media. Two factors that have an influence over the captain's career. Now it all makes sense to Cari. "How big a task force?" she asks.

"Something lean and nimble. A few detectives and support staff."

Cari catches her own skeptical reflection in the rearview mirror. "Who will lead it?"

"I will, of course," he says. "You'll be the lead investigator. But we'll need to recruit a few detectives from RHD for support."

"OK," Cari says, hoping the reluctance in her tone isn't too obvious. She can certainly use the help, but the idea of being a pawn in the captain's latest professional advancement scheme doesn't sit well.

"I'll see you in my office tomorrow," the captain says. "At nine."

Cari is about to pull out of the parking lot when her phone buzzes again with a text from Zach at Computer Crimes asking her to call. She dials him immediately.

"Dr. Chiseled Pharmaceuticals," Zach says by way of greeting.

"What's that?" Cari asks. "Another rebrand of the Dr. Muscles site?"

"So it seems."

"Did one of the other victims order from there?"

"No," Zach says. "Dr. Chiseled Pharmaceuticals is their current pop-up site."

The exhilaration rushes through her. "Can you pinpoint their real-world location?"

"No can do. The site is buried beneath a mountain of firewalls and redirects. Dark web protocols. Sophisticated stuff."

"But?"

"It's live right now, Detective."

She laughs, suddenly realizing what Zach is getting at. "Time for us to order some DNP?"

"Who doesn't love a good old-fashioned online sting operation?"

"And then we follow the money?"

"Bingo," Zach says. "And with any luck, our shipment will arrive postmarked, too."

CHAPTER 17

Julie sits at her laptop in the spare bedroom that doubles as a home office. Her earbuds are in as she listens to Rain's first album, *Cloudburst*. Though she's aware how cliché it is, Julie can't help reading more into the melancholic lyrics, considering the singer's sudden death. Rain never had the strongest voice or widest range, but something about her raw vulnerability perfectly complemented her lyrics, which almost always focused on themes of hurt and loss. Julie once heard a critic compare Rain's music to "the song of a bird with a broken wing," and that seems particularly apt now.

Julie promised Anson that she would give him time to find out where the investigation into the DNP-related deaths stood within his department. And, after speaking to Marcia's daughter, she hasn't reached out to any other of her family members or those of the other local victims. But she can't resist doing a bit of amateur online sleuthing.

The first website she searches for is Dr. Slim Pharmaceuticals, but the link is broken, and the site doesn't seem to exist. Julie moves on to searching other DNP deaths. She finds a compelling article in the *Telegraph*, describing the insidious spread of DNP through the UK. The piece is particularly poignant, delving into the background stories of some of the recent DNP-related fatalities in and around London, where there have been eleven documented deaths alone in the past four years. One woman, who survived DNP poisoning, described the ordeal as feeling like "being trapped inside a sauna with the door nailed shut." The article also describes British law enforcement's challenges in tracking down the anonymous online distributors of the poison. Even when successful, prosecuting the perpetrators had proven difficult. One dealer, who alone was responsible for distributing the pills that killed at least four young Brits, was only sentenced to three years in prison for manslaughter.

Next, Julie Googles "order DNP online." She's horrified to see the number of pages that pop up in response. DNP appears to be marketed under countless different brand names, and she begins to click randomly on some of the sites. Some appear amateurish while others look much more professional. They're littered with photos and testimonials that promote DNP as a panacea for weight loss and building muscle definition. The sellers all promise easy and discreet shipping. Many of the sites don't mention their product's toxicity. The ones that do carry warnings invariably bury them deep in their pages while swearing to the safety of their product when taken "correctly."

Julie's stomach turns as she realizes how susceptible someone with body image issues might be to this kind of advertising. But she can also relate. It's equivalent to someone having handed her the keys to a pharmacy when she was at the lowest point in her opioid addiction, over ten years before.

Her phone rings and she reaches for it, answering without checking the call display. "Hi."

"Hello, luv."

"Oh, Glen, hey," she says. "I'm not on call for Poison Control, am I?"

"Who knows? I'm sitting on my couch, nursing my third glass of cab sauv as we speak." He laughs. "Well, 'nursing' might be a tad of an understatement."

She chuckles. "Sounds like the perfect evening. What's up?"

"I'm anything but a gossip . . ."

Julie smiles at his self-contradictory words. "Go on."

"I have this dear friend who works at the city morgue. The poor fellow feels deeply indebted to me. And so he should be. I was the one to convince him to leave that dreadful, emotionally abusive boyfriend of his. He's been a new man ever since."

"OK . . ."

"Listen to me go on! A few glasses of the good stuff and I ramble on worse than my precious old ma. Maybe the wine explains all those soliloquies of hers over the dinner table."

"About your friend, Glen . . ."

"Yes, my friend. He tells me—very much on the QT, by the way!—that he was on yesterday when Rain herself was wheeled in," he says. "Such a tragic shame. Only twenty-three. The whole world in the poor dear's hand. And still, to me, there was always something so fragile about the girl. As if she could never—"

"Glen!" Julie cuts him off, too impatient to wait out another digression.

"Anyhoo, my friend, he saw Rain's initial tox screen."

Julie closes the lid of her laptop. "And?"

"Well, of course, it's not a complete panel, just the urine screen for the usual drugs of abuse."

"What did it show, Glen?"

"It's what it *didn't* show, luv!"

She grips her phone tighter. "And what was that?"

"Nothing. Nada. No recreational drugs whatsoever. Everyone is assuming Rain overdosed on heroin or fentanyl or one of the other usual suspects, but it's simply not the case, Julie. Must've been something else that did her in."

"What about her alcohol level?"

"Oh, I know nothing about the bloodwork, just the urine drug screen." Glen pauses. "Although my friend did mention one other curiosity."

"What kind of curiosity?"

"Of course, this absolutely has to stay between us." Glen's voice drops even lower. "He would be sacked for sure if word ever got out. Guaranteed."

"All of this stays confidential. Promise."

"My friend couldn't help but catch a glimpse of the princess herself when they were loading her into the drawer or what have you."

"What he did see, Glen?"

"To begin with, he said up close she was desperately thin. Not much more than a skeleton, really. But he also noticed that her skin was a bit . . . discolored."

"Discolored how?"

"He described it as yellowish. Not jaundiced, mind you. He's very familiar with that shade from all the alcoholics and liver patients who end up under his care. No, he said it was a lighter yellow. At first, he thought it might be cosmetic bronzer or something. But on closer inspection, he believes it was under her skin."

Julie's pulse pounds in her ears. Without realizing it, Glen has just revealed Rain's cause of death as clearly as an autopsy report.

"Does this ring any bells for you, Julie?" Glen asks.

"Maybe," she says vaguely. "Let me do a little reading up, and I'll get back to you."

"No rush, luv." He laughs joyfully. "I've still got more in the bottle and the whole night to myself. Stan's off at some silly poker game. Can you imagine that? Poker!"

The moment she hangs up, Julie explodes out of her chair. She sprints into the kitchen, startling Anson where he sits at the counter, typing on his laptop.

He frowns. "What's up with you?"

"I know what killed Rain!"

CHAPTER 18

"**A**m I going to like what have you have to report, Detective Chen?" the deputy chief rasps, as Anson sits down across the desk from her.

He screws up his face. "If I had to guess . . . ?"

"Oh, shit." She rubs her eyes aggressively. "Let's have it."

"I don't have anything official back in terms of a path report or toxicology—"

"Disclaimer duly noted, Detective. What killed Rain?"

"DNP. At least, I'm ninety-nine percent certain it did."

"What the hell is DNP?"

"An explosive, apparently."

The deputy chief listens, slack-jawed, as he tells her what he knows about the potentially poisonous diet pill. Then he shares the tip regarding Rain's negative drug screen and her skin's telltale yellowish tinge. He doesn't reveal his source, and she doesn't ask. "You're sure that diabetic injector thing didn't play a role in her death?"

"I'm not sure of anything yet, DC. But I'm told you can't really overdose on Ozempic."

"Must be convenient dating a toxicologist." She goes quiet for a moment. "We're not going to get a pass on this one, are we?"

Anson shakes his head. "If we include Rain, we have at least four recent deaths—in Vancouver alone—related to DNP. At a minimum, we're looking at conspiracy to traffic. And manslaughter."

She groans. "OK, I want you and Theo on this. Full-time."

"What about the Maddox and Grewal murders?"

"The streets will probably settle those scores sooner than we can."

"DC . . ."

"I'll put Lewis and Ocampo on them, Anson." She sighs. "When I inform the chief and the mayor, just imagine how their heads will spin!"

"Understood." Anson rises. "But we have to lock this down, DC. Leakproof. The fewer who know, the better."

"Ain't that God's honest truth."

On the way out of the VPD building, Anson calls Theo to update him. His partner has just arrived at the morgue, and Anson agrees to meet him there.

Anson can feel the temperature drop the moment he steps through the doors to the morgue at Vancouver General Hospital. Theo stands in front of a wall of square, stainless-steel refrigerator doors beside two men: Desmond Wilson and a gray-bearded man who Anson recognizes as Dr. Klaus Gruber, one of the city's forensic pathologists. The pair of them strike a glaring contrast. Gruber is as lanky as a pro basketball player, and his height is only accentuated by the chief coroner's diminutiveness.

"Dr. Gruber was just telling us that the bloodwork on Rain was all out of whack," Theo says.

"*Ja*," says Gruber in his crisp German accent. "She was experiencing acute kidney failure at the time of her death."

Anson frowns. "Did she have any history of kidney problems?"

"There's no record of kidney issues," Desmond pipes up. "Must have been new onset. Right, Klaus?"

"Thus the term *acute*." Gruber throws the coroner a sidelong glance. "Obviously, the autopsy will give us the definitive answer, but I believe her renal failure was caused by rhabdomyolysis."

Theo grimaces. "Rabdo what?"

"Rhab-do-my-o-ly-sis." Gruber sounds out each syllable. "It is a condition caused by the breakdown of significant muscle tissue. This results in the leakage of large quantities of the protein creatine kinase into the bloodstream. If the concentration is significant enough—as it was in the case of the deceased—it will plug the tubules in the kidneys and lead to acute kidney failure."

Theo shakes his head. "And what would cause muscle damage like that?"

"Could be one of several causes," Gruber says. "A crush injury of some kind. We also see it in people lying passed out too long on hard surfaces. It can even happen with exercise and overexertion."

"What about with drugs or medications?" Anson asks.

"Most definitely," Gruber says. "There is a long list of medications that could be responsible."

"But you don't have the toxicology results back yet, right?" Anson asks.

"Not the full panel, no," Gruber says.

Desmond flashes Anson a smug look. "The urine screen showed she had no recreational drugs on board," he says. "Definitely no opioids."

Gruber nods. "She had no acetaminophen or aspirin in her system, either. And her alcohol level was only twenty-four millimoles per liter."

Anson feels his phone vibrate in his pocket with the staccato pattern indicating a text from Julie, but he ignores it. Instead, he asks, "How drunk would that make her, do you figure?"

"She'd have been above the legal driving limit, for sure," Desmond answers for the pathologist. "But she still could've probably parked her car without ramming into a pole or anything."

Anson ignores Desmond. He doesn't know if it's the distasteful joke or the teller himself that he finds more offensive. "No signs of diabetes?" he asks the pathologist.

"No," Gruber says. "Her blood sugar was within the normal range."

"When will you get the complete toxicology results?" Theo asks.

"Those will take another twenty-four hours to forty-eight hours, at a minimum."

Anson resists the urge to ask about signs of DNP poisoning. He doesn't want to reveal his suspicions just yet. Especially not to Desmond. "Can we see the body?"

"Didn't you see it at the scene of death, Detective?" Desmond asks.

"I did," Anson says. "And now I'm asking to see it again."

"It is not a problem, Desmond," Dr. Gruber says as he turns to the square door behind him. "We are about to do the autopsy anyway." He pulls it open and slides out the long metallic tray where Rain lies, covered from the chest down in a sheet.

Under the bright morgue lights, Anson now notices the slight yellowish tinge to the skin around her eyes and in her cheeks that he hadn't picked up on in her more dimly lit bedroom.

"Would you like to observe the autopsy, detectives?" Gruber asks.

"No, we're good, thanks," Theo says. "One of the Forensic Ident techs will be attending. And they're a territorial bunch."

"You'll update us as soon as you have any results?" Anson adds.

"We always do," Desmond snaps.

"Thank you," Theo says with a friendly nod, despite the slight note of derision in his tone.

Anson spins away to stop himself from unloading on the obnoxious coroner. And the two detectives leave the hospital together.

Standing on the sidewalk under the gray drizzle, Theo says, "It's all consistent with that DNP, huh?"

"Yup."

"Word is going to get out. Probably sooner than later."

"And when it does, whoever sold her the crap will probably go to ground," Anson says. "Which means now is our best window to try to hunt down the source. I say we start with the other recent victims."

Theo scratches his chin. "But we have no idea if those other purchases are connected to Rain's. She's only been in Vancouver for what, three weeks? There's every chance she brought the DNP with her from Los Angeles."

"What do you suggest?"

"Why don't we talk to the rest of Rain's entourage? Before they leave town. See if they know anything about where or how she got the DNP."

Anson nods. "Maybe we speak to her therapist again, too? I got a slippery vibe from that one."

"Agreed."

Anson's phone sounds again with the ringtone specific for Julie. He pulls it out of his jacket. "Hi, what's up?"

"Did you see the text I sent?" Julie asks.

"No, I was just in the morgue."

"I think you might want to have a look, Anson."

He puts the phone on speaker mode, taps the screen a couple of times until he finds her text, and then clicks on the hyperlink she sent.

The headline reads: "Best Friend Says Diet Pill Killed Rain."

CHAPTER 19

"Just wanted you to know I'm thinking of you." The text ends with a heart emoji.

Just wanted you to know: fuck you! Cari wants to type but instead deletes Mattias's text without responding.

Annoyance trumps her hurt. Right now, she misses him more as a colleague than a lover. No matter which detectives the captain appoints to the new DNP task force, none can replace Mattias. After six years of partnership, the two of them developed a seamless rhythm to their work, naturally complementing each other. In interviews and interrogations, they played off each other wordlessly. Between her intuition and his attention to detail, they solved several complex homicides. As investigators, the whole of their partnership was stronger than the sum of their individual parts.

They used to discuss in bed—sometimes joking, other times with genuine unease—how their romance could one day jeopardize their stellar investigative record. But they managed to balance their affair and their work life for over a year without any of it blowing up, and Cari assumed things would only get easier once Mattias finally left his wife and they didn't have to hide their feelings.

Except, Mattias didn't leave his wife. Instead, he confessed everything to her and agreed to move to Sacramento to save their marriage. "For my son," he explained to Cari when he broke the news to her. Over the phone. But in the six months since Mattias quit Cari and the LAPD, neither his commitment to his marriage nor his devotion to his eight-year-old has stopped him from hounding Cari with emotionally manipulative texts like the most recent one. And she hates him more for that than for leaving her.

To distract herself from the painful memories, Cari leans back in her chair and clicks open her favorite news app. The headlines all focus on Rain's death. But Cari has no interest in reading about another young victim of a presumed overdose, famous or not. Right as her finger moves to close the app, two words catch her eye: *diet pills*. She immediately clicks open the article.

The story cites social media posts by Rain's best friend, a backup singer named Maleeka Khan, which have gone viral. "They were like may-contain-peanuts level sketch, but BFF said it was so worth the peril," Maleeka wrote in one post. "I begged boo not to go there. Only wish I'd found the pills and turfed them in time."

None of the articles specify the type of diet pill involved, but Cari's gut tells her it must be DNP. She Googles the contact number for the Vancouver Police Department and then dials it. Reaching the automated phone tree, she taps the number for the Homicide Unit. "VPD, Homicide," a woman answers in a stern voice.

"Hello, I'm Detective Garcia with the Los Angeles Police's Robbery and Homicide Division. I have information potentially related to the death of Rain Flynn."

"The LAPD. Is that right?" The receptionist's tone drips with skepticism.

Cari understands that the VPD must be inundated with calls from the media, the public, and random kooks since Rain's death. Undoubtedly, some of them would try to impersonate officials to gain privileged information. "I'm happy to provide my badge number as well as my extension where I can be reached directly through the LAPD switchboard."

After recording Cari's badge number, the woman asks, "How can I help you, Detective Garcia?"

"I was hoping to talk to the lead investigator in the Rain Flynn case. I have some important information to share."

"Those would be Detectives Chen and Kostas."

"Can I speak to one of them?"

"Please hold." A minute or two later, the receptionist returns to the line. "I couldn't reach either detective, but if you give me your number, I'll leave messages with them."

While waiting for a call back, Cari finishes reading the last article on Rain. She didn't realize that the singer was only twenty-three years old, the same age as Lucia was at the time of her death. And like Lucia, Rain also died, at least indirectly, from an eating disorder.

Cari's last conversation—more accurately, *altercation*—with her little sister floods to mind. At the time, Lucia had been living with Cari and her boyfriend, Vicente, in their two-bedroom apartment in West Hollywood. Lucia had sworn she would only be staying a week or two, but she was still there a month after making that promise. The ever-patient Vicente accepted Lucia's presence without complaint. Cari wasn't always so tolerant, but she was relieved to have her desperately thin sister under the same roof. She had never seen Lucia acting as erratically. And Cari hoped to convince her to go back into inpatient treatment for her eating disorder.

That morning had started off innocently enough. Over breakfast, the sisters reminisced about their dad's OCD tendencies, laughing about the time he had packed a survival kit and worn a money belt for a two-hour car trip to Disneyland. Lucia even ate some of the eggs Cari scrambled. But an hour later, when Cari unexpectedly returned to the apartment to grab the extra tampon she had forgotten to pack for work, she found Lucia sitting at the kitchen counter, a shocked look on her face. Then Cari spotted the dusting of powder across the countertop, which matched the fine white rim lining one of Lucia's nostrils.

"You didn't!" Cari snapped.

"It's not like that!" Lucia pleaded as she wiped frantically at her nose with a thumb and forefinger.

"*Blow?* In my home!"

"Just this once. I don't ever do it here. I . . . I was heading out. Going to a meeting—"

"I'm a cop, Luci! So is Vicente."

"I know, I know."

"Do you have any idea what would happen to us—to our careers—if the department found out? Coke? *In my home?*"

"I wouldn't let that—"

"What is wrong with you? Why do you have to be so toxic?"

Lucia's eyes teared up. "I don't mean to be."

"Yeah, you do," Cari growled. "Look at you. You're a disaster. It's bad enough that you're just skin and bones and doing blow to somehow make yourself even skinnier. But now you want to drag me down to rock bottom with you! Don't you?"

"Never." Lucia started moving toward her with arms extended. "I love you, Car. You're the best thing I've got."

Cari backed away. "No, no, no! No more of your bullshit. You're not ruining my life along with yours. Get the fuck out of here!"

Lucia dropped her arms to her side and stared plaintively at Cari for several seconds. Then she trudged off to the spare room to collect her things. Cari was so angry that she didn't even hang around while her sister packed.

She would never see Lucia again.

Cari's phone rings in her hand and "Vancouver, Canada" appears on the call display. "Detective Garcia," she answers.

"Hello, this is Detective Chen from VPD Homicide returning your call."

"Thanks for getting back to me, Detective Chen. I understand you're looking into the death of Rain Flynn. And I read a report that toxic diet pills might be involved."

"Too soon to say. We won't have toxicology results for a few more days."

"Of course. But it sounds to me as if it would all fit with DNP poisoning."

"DNP?" His tone switches from polite to curious. "You're familiar with it?"

"Matter of fact, I'm working a series of DNP-related deaths in LA. And since Rain lives—lived—here, I thought they could possibly be related."

"A series?"

"Yes, we just had our eighth confirmed death this year." Cari goes on to tell him about Owen Galloway and briefly summarizes what she knows of the other victims. "As I'm sure you're aware, DNP is easily available online. Scarily so. And we've found links between a few of the victims in terms of their supplier."

"What kind of links?"

"At least three of the LA victims ordered their DNP through the same website."

"Which site?"

"It goes by a number of aliases," Cari says. "Kind of straddles the dark web. I don't understand all the technical ins and outs. But the same supplier keeps popping up, each time with a new name and new site. They blitz social media with promotions, sell a bunch of product, shut the site down, and then start all over again with a new one. What's more, our computer crimes experts think the distributor might be based in Canada."

The other detective is quiet for a few seconds. "Can you tell me the names of the aliases this site uses?"

"Sure. They're moronic but easily memorable. Word plays on weight loss and muscle gain. A lot of Dr. whatever Pharmaceuticals. Like Dr. Beefcake Pharmaceuticals, Dr. Muscles Pharmaceuticals, Dr. Slim Pharmaceuticals—"

"Seriously? *Dr. Slim Pharmaceuticals?*"

CHAPTER 20

Theo sits in the passenger seat, mulling over what his partner just relayed to him. "Think about it, Anson," he finally says. "At least three of the victims in LA and one in Vancouver all ordered DNP through that same Dr. Fill-in-the-blank Pharmaceuticals website."

"Exactly." Anson glimpses himself in the rearview mirror and straightens his tie. "And like us, the LAPD hasn't yet tracked down where their other victims got their supply. It's possible they all ordered through that same site."

"Unlikely. You saw how many different sites are selling DNP online. Almost as bad as all those ones peddling Viagra."

"Viagra? You seeing a lot of those ads, Theo?" Anson glances over to him with a straight face. "You do realize those algorithms tailor their ads based on your search history?"

"Ha! Five kids later, last thing I need is Viagra." Theo grunts. "But let's say the majority of the victims here and in LA did order DNP through the same site."

"Along with God knows how many other cities across the planet."

"Think about it, Anson. Julie told you DNP has been circulating online for well over a decade. But Vancouver and LA have *only* seen spikes in DNP poisonings over the past year. What I'd love to know is when did Dr. X Pharmaceuticals first set up shop and start their advertising blitz?"

"It's the chicken or the egg thing, huh?" Anson says. "Did Dr. X Pharmaceuticals jump on a viral trend, or did they create it?"

"Exactly!"

"Would be a hell of a lot easier to break the cycle if they're the ones responsible for it."

"Especially if they're operating out of Canada," Theo says. "Then again, the cat might already be out of the bag."

"How so?"

"Once the news goes global that Rain did die from DNP, it might only encourage other vulnerable kids to dabble. Despite the risk."

"The joy of celebrity influencers," Anson grumbles.

They lapse into silence. Waiting at a red light, Anson views the cracks of blue between the cumulus clouds overhead. *This city could use a little sunshine.*

"Big move day this weekend, huh?" Theo says apropos of nothing.

"Not really. I've stored most of my furniture and given the rest away. It's just a couple of suitcases."

Theo slaps a palm to his forehead. "Oh, God."

"What?"

"First of all, fitting your wardrobe into a couple of suitcases is like fitting an elephant into a birdcage."

Anson rolls his eyes. "And second?"

"It's a big deal, buddy. This moving in together business."

"We practically live together now."

"Like practically pregnant, huh?"

"Julie and I aren't kids. We've each been down this road before."

Theo says nothing.

"OK, yeah," Anson says. "It didn't end well for either one of us. I'm aware. But we've talked about it a lot. We're OK with it."

"How about those dreams? You still getting them?"

"Why did I ever mention those?" Anson asks, although he knows exactly why. The pressure of bottling them up had been getting to him. He needed to vent to someone he trusted.

"Maybe it's because you recognize me for the sensitive and intuitive soul that I am?" Theo suggests.

"That, or because I'm trapped with you for hours a day with nothing else to talk about." Telling Theo about the dreams proved painful and draining for Anson. The prospect of revisiting the conversation now doesn't appeal.

"So, are you?" Theo asks. "Still dreaming of Nicole?"

"From time to time. It's natural, right?" But Anson has never had dreams like these before. Or experienced the anxiety, irrational as it might be, that something bad might happen to Julie if they do move in together. "Anyone would dream about a spouse they lost."

"Yeah, but why now specifically?" Theo asks. "All these years later? Is it because of the move?"

"Could be," Anson mumbles and turns into the driveway of the Sutton Place Hotel, relieved that their arrival will put an end to their conversation. He has yet to even open up to Julie about his dreams.

On the twentieth floor of the hotel, halfway down the hallway, Anson hears raised voices. The commotion only grows as they approach the suite at the end of the hall. Theo knocks at the door, and the yelling suddenly quiets.

A young woman opens it. Her thick black hair is tied in a tight bun, and her eyes are red under prominent fake eyelashes. Her flustered look gives way to a wry smile. "Oh, you must be the *poh-lease.*"

"Detectives Kostas and Chen," Theo says. "Are you Ms. Khan?"

"Maleeka." She opens the door wider. "*Entrez.*"

Anson follows Theo and Maleeka inside the one-bedroom suite. A middle-aged man with graying hair and stubbled cheeks bounds over from the other side of the room. Though he wears a simple black T-shirt with faded jeans, Anson notes that his Ferragamo shoes are worth over two thousand dollars.

The man extends his arm. "Braden Hollands," he says as he pumps each of the detectives' hands in turn. "I am—I was—Rain's manager."

"Hope we aren't interrupting," Anson says.

"Oh, that? No." Braden chuckles. "Just a slight disagreement over social media etiquette. Nothing Maleeka and I haven't been through before." He turns to her. "Right?"

"Not more than a million times," she says without meeting his eyes.

"Please, detectives." Braden motions to the sitting area.

Anson and Theo take the chairs across from Maleeka and Braden, who sit at the opposite ends of the couch.

"We wanted to ask you about those diet pills you said Rain was taking, Maleeka," Theo says.

She shakes her head dramatically. "So skeezy. Never should've happened."

"What did Rain tell you about them?" Theo asks. "Did she mention the name or where she got them from?"

"Nah," Maleeka says. "Just said they were different from everything else. And trust me, that *chica* tried *everything*!"

"Different how?"

"She said the pounds melted away no matter what she stuffed down her throat."

"How long had she been taking them?" Anson asks.

"No idea. Ray-Ray only fessed to me in the last couple weeks." Maleeka spins loops of hair around a finger. "I had to drag it out of her."

"And Rain said they were pills, right?" Theo asks. "Or capsules, at least."

Maleeka grimaces. "Like what else?"

"An injection?"

She shakes her head. "Straight-up caps."

"Did Dr. Markstrom know she was taking DNP?"

Maleeka snorts. "That scumbag didn't help my baby girl one speck. Just made her feel worse about herself. It kept his billing hours rolling, though. So parasitic!"

"But do you think Dr. Markstrom could have been giving her those pills?" Anson asks.

Maleeka shrugs. "Not a single clue."

"You sure Rain never mentioned how long she had been taking them?"

"Nope. But must've been months. She'd gotten so freakin' scrawny— even for Ray-Ray. Since at least September, I'd say."

"I was concerned, too," Braden pipes up. "We all were. Last few years, after the struggles, her weight had been good. Stable. But we all noticed the . . . change this fall."

Maleeka shoots Braden a look but doesn't comment.

"Did she tell you about the pills?" Anson asks him.

Braden lowers his gaze. "Rain knew better than to tell me. I would've gotten her straight back into treatment. The inpatient kind."

"Would you though?" Maleeka asks.

"Of course I would've."

Maleeka throws up her hands. "Who the fuck are you fooling, David Copperfield?"

"Don't, Maleeka," Braden says through gritted teeth.

"Cash aside, you didn't give a flying fuck about Rain!"

Braden glares at her. "And you did?"

"Damn right."

"Oh, pardon me. I didn't realize I was the one trying to launch a career for myself off her grave."

"As if! I loved Ray-Ray. And I sure as fuck didn't snap her heart in two."

"I loved her, too."

"Loved?" Maleeka huffs. "You would've stuffed those caps down her piehole with a shovel if you thought it would've made you a few more bucks."

CHAPTER 21

Cari leans against the wall behind Captain Taylor, wishing she could melt into it, as she faces the rows of reporters and cameramen. She has never enjoyed being the center of attention. And consequently, she dresses low-key, usually wearing little makeup and loose outfits in basic colors. But today it's unavoidable.

Cari is flanked on one side by Lieutenant Greene, who also looks like he'd rather be anywhere else, and on the other by Senator Galloway, who wears a dark suit that clearly signals "grieving mother." The captain stands in his tailored uniform at the lectern with his shoulders rigidly squared. He waits as a technician adjusts the bank of microphones in front of him.

Cari had only gotten the text from the captain thirty minutes earlier, requesting her immediate presence in the briefing room. She called him, but rather than explaining over the phone, he texted back, "No time to talk. Just need you to be there."

There was no discussion of a press conference. Or publicity of any kind. They haven't even chosen most of the task force members. And yet here the captain stands in front of a sea of media. Cari can already feel the sweat beading under her arms. She has a near phobia of public speaking.

"Thank you for coming today," the captain finally says in his most somber voice. "I am here to announce the formation of a task force to investigate the recent spate of deaths involving the weight loss and/or body building supplement dinitrophenol, better known as DNP. In the past twelve months, this poison has been responsible for eight deaths in LA County alone. The ages of the deceased range from eighteen to forty-nine and include those of both genders." He hurries to add, "I mean, of course, in the sense that five of the victims identified as female, and three as male."

The captain goes on to describe the lethal nature of the chemical and its pervasive online presence, and then he says, "We here at the LAPD consider all of these deaths to be homicides."

He pauses to survey the room with a long sweep of his head. In case any of the reporters doubt his righteous indignation, Cari thinks.

"The goal of the task force will be twofold," he continues. "One, to bring the distributors and all perpetrators involved to justice. And two, to shut down any organized criminal elements that continue to endanger Los Angelinos through the reckless sale of DNP. Before we take questions . . ." The captain extends an arm behind him, and for a horrified moment, Cari thinks he might summon her to the lectern. "I would like to invite Senator Galloway to make a statement."

The captain steps aside and the senator assumes her spot in front of the microphones. "It's not easy for me to share my family's—or my own—grief with all of you. But as a public servant and the mother of one of the victims, I see it as my duty to speak up for all the victims of this . . ." Her voice trails off.

Though Cari can only see the back of the senator's head, she senses the pain in her words. The senator has come across as so cool that, at times, Cari forgets the woman has lost her only son. And she regrets her earlier cynical thought about the senator's appearance.

"As the captain has already stated," the senator continues, "DNP is marketed by online predators who misrepresent it as an easy, effective, and harmless supplement, knowing all the while that it is highly lethal and was never intended for human consumption. These criminals prey on the most susceptible—those with eating disorders, body image issues, or a hyper-focus on bodybuilding."

The senator brings a hand to her chest. "My son Owen was an elite distance runner who was desperate for an extra edge while competing for the best collegiate track programs. Since his . . . passing, I stay awake at night wondering if I missed the signs. Any sign. If only I'd noticed the weight loss or . . ."

Cari is surprised to hear the senator admit to her son's willful consumption of DNP, but assumes she can no longer overlook all the evidence and has instead focused on rationalizing his usage.

The senator lets her hand fall to her side. "I've come today to raise awareness. To sound the warning. To do anything I can to ensure no other loved ones have to endure what we—the families of those eight victims—have and will continue to endure." She motions directly to the cameras. "If you think someone you care about might be victimized by these online parasites, please warn them how deadly DNP is. Tell them how many healthy young people have died from using the pills exactly as they were directed to. And how many families have been needlessly ripped apart by grief."

Cari tries not to think of her sister, but it's no use. She wishes she, too, had picked up on the critical warning signs and hadn't thrown Lucia out at a time when she was so vulnerable.

"Also, if anyone has any information at all about these online predators, we are asking you to please come forward and contact the LAPD," the senator continues. "The site responsible for my son's death went by the name—or at least it did at the time he ordered the poison—of Dr. Muscles Pharmaceuticals."

No, no, no! Cari wants to scream. *What are you doing?*

"But it also has gone by several other aliases, including Dr. Slim Pharmaceuticals, Dr. Beefcake Pharmaceuticals, and Dr. Chiseled Pharmaceuticals."

Cari bites her lip so hard she almost breaks the skin as she fights the impulse to yank the senator away from the microphones. Anger wipes away her empathy. The last thing the LAPD needed was to publicize the names of the websites while their sting operation was underway.

"Thank you," the senator says as she steps away from the microphone, the damage done.

The captain returns to his original spot. "We will now take questions from the—"

Before he can even finish the sentence, hands spring up and several reporters call out at once. The captain waits until the din quiets, and then points to a bearded reporter up front. "Your question?"

"This DNP," he says. "It's the same stuff that killed Rain, right?"

The captain shakes his head. "To the best of my knowledge, the authorities in Vancouver have not released a cause of her death yet."

"But Rain was from LA," a female reporter yells out. "Stands to reason that she died from the same poison."

"I can't speculate on a death in another jurisdiction—"

"But surely you'll investigate to see if Rain's death is linked to these victims?"

Cari feels her watch buzz twice. She glances at it. A text from Zach on the screen reads: "Dr. Chiseled Pharmaceuticals just fell off the web."

Fuck! Their best lead wiped out by an unnecessary press conference.

The bitter irony is that the media seems only interested in Rain, who died in another country, and not in any of the local victims, even the senator's son. The reporters fire question after question about the singer, despite the captain's insistence that the LAPD doesn't have any details to share about her death.

Cari is so consumed by the senseless setback in her investigation that she barely notices the captain is even talking about her until she hears him say, "We will be sending our lead investigator, Detective Garcia, to Vancouver to liaise with their local law enforcement and determine if there are any possible connections."

CHAPTER 22

Julie loves seeing her good friend Goran, but this morning she was hoping to have the ER doctors' office to herself to catch up on charting and correspondence. Her shift doesn't start until seven a.m., but she has come in an hour early—as she often does before the morning shifts—to do her paperwork.

Goran's shift ended almost three hours earlier, but as usual, the veteran ER doctor has lingered behind to leisurely finish his own charting, grab a coffee, and, likely, to socialize.

"Me?" Goran says, even though Julie didn't ask him anything. "I like my singers with a bit more fortissimo behind their voice than this Snow woman."

"It's Rain, Gor. And definitely too soon."

He waves away her concern. "Now if you insist on a mononymous singer"—Goran, who has a gift for languages and speaks five of them, uses an obscure English word that Julie has to decipher in her head to mean "having only one name"—"I offer you Severina as Exhibit B. Croatia's own Madonna. Only more talented. Truly, the voice of an angel. If Severina sang in English, you wouldn't hear anyone else on the radio." He shrugs. "Although, if you put a gun to my temple, I will admit 'Can't Go Back' is danceable enough."

Julie laughs, surprised to hear that her old friend knows any of Rain's music. She suspects that his younger wife, Maria, must have introduced him. "Are you getting to a point, Gor?"

"You really think Rain died from the same poison as my bodybuilder, Nicholas?"

"I do."

"How many young lives have we already lost to fentanyl? Now this." He sighs. "What do you think is going to happen when all those impressionable teens who worshipped Rain hear about DNP?"

Julie has been worrying about the same thing. But before she can respond, the office door opens and their colleague Manoj Sharma pops his head into the office. "Oh, awesome, you're already here, Julie," he says.

"What's up, Manoj?" she asks.

"Realize you're not starting until seven, but the paramedics just called. They're three minutes out with a *status epilepticus*. And I'm just about to reduce a dislocated hip . . ."

"Happy to take it." Julie hops to her feet. "Go fix that hip."

"Thanks!" Manoj says and then disappears from the doorway.

"You need any help, Julija?" Goran asks as she heads for the door.

"Thanks, Gor, but no. Go home to Maria! And listen to some Severa to cheer yourself up."

"*Severina*," he stresses. "I'll message you a few YouTube links. Truly, euphonious. Like a cry from heaven."

Julie slips out the door and heads to the resuscitation room just as the two paramedics hurtle a gurney, wheels creaking as they round the corner, into the room. She breaks into a jog to catch up with them.

Inside the room, the rest of the team is already gowned, masked, and gloved. A petite woman lies on the stretcher, her limbs jerking in rhythmic contractions while her whole face twitches with spasms. Despite her size, the paramedics struggle to lift her by her thrashing shoulders and legs to transfer her onto the hospital bed.

Julie's stomach flutters in anticipation, but she forces herself not to jump to conclusions. "What have you got, Tom?" she asks the paunchy, balding paramedic as she dons her own protective equipment.

"Cecilia Hunter," Tom says. "Forty years old. Found seizing in bed this morning by her husband at oh-six-ten. Miraculously, we managed to get an IV in en route. We've given her repeated doses of Valium, but it's not touching the seizure."

"How long has she been in status?" Julie asks as the nurses swarm the patient from either side, attaching her to monitors and hooking her IV line to an overhead bag.

"Husband wasn't sure," Tom says. "We've been with her for over thirty minutes. Extrication from that mansion was a bitch. Had to get the stretcher down a circular stairway. I'd estimate she's been seizing an hour, at least."

Way too long, Julie thinks. "And her vital signs?"

"Heart rate is pretty fast, but blood pressure has held stable. She's burning up, though, Dr. Rees. I'm guessing at least forty degrees."

"Forty-one point six," the bedside nurse calls, confirming Julie's initial hunch.

"I'm thinking infection," Tom says. "Maybe meningitis?"

"Don't think so," Julie says, as Cecilia continues to buck on the stretcher. "Any pill bottles on scene?"

"We didn't have time to look," the other paramedic says.

"More Valium, Julie?" Ian, the redheaded nurse, asks from across the stretcher.

"Let's switch to midazolam," Julie says. "Big doses. Five milligrams at a time. Load her with dantrolene, too. And maximum cooling. Ice packs, fans, cold saline. Anything to get the temperature down and to stop this seizure!"

She knows all too well that a seizure lasting longer than thirty minutes can cause irreversible brain damage, and the patient has already been convulsing for at least twice that long. "Prepare for intubation," she tells Ian. "The usual drugs."

As Julie readies her equipment at the head of the bed, she marvels at the efficiency of her team. In less than two minutes, the patient receives all the intravenous medications she ordered, and ice packs are applied to her groin, neck, and armpits. In another thirty seconds, Cecilia finally stills on the bed.

But Julie realizes that the patient is only motionless because she has been medically paralyzed. The electrical storm in the brain that the seizure represents continues unabated inside her skull. And by paralyzing Cecilia, Julie has introduced a new but necessary risk: the patient is no longer breathing on her own.

Julie grabs the laryngoscope and slides the blade over Cecilia's tongue. She pulls back the handle and the vocal cords pop into full view. With her other hand, Julie easily snakes the endotracheal tube into the windpipe. She hands the closer end to the respiratory technologist, who connects it to the ventilator piping and flashes Julie a thumbs-up sign to indicate the tube is well placed.

"Let's start a continuous drip of midazolam at ten milligrams per hour, Ian," Julie instructs.

Julie orders other medications and asks the charge nurse to have a canister of inhaled anesthetic—often, the last line of defense against an unstoppable seizure—sent down from the operating room. She completes a thorough physical exam, which doesn't tell her much except that the patient appears otherwise healthy and has the lean physique of a ballerina.

Another masked and gowned person steps up to the stretcher. "I'm the CT tech," she says gruffly. "OK to take the patient for imaging now?"

"Please," Julie says, stepping out of the way. And within moments, Cecilia is wheeled out of the room.

While Julie waits for the patient to return from the CT scanner, she begins to dictate her resuscitation note into the electronic chart. She is halfway through her dictation when a middle-aged man bursts through the doorway with a security guard hot on his heels. "Where is my wife?" he demands.

"You can't be in—" the security guard starts, but Julie waves him off.

"I'm Dr. Rees," Julie says to the man. "Cecilia has gone for a CT scan."

"Lloyd Hunter." He bobs from foot to foot. "How is she?"

"Your wife's in critical condition, Mr. Hunter. We've stopped the seizures but only by medically paralyzing her and placing her on a ventilator."

His eyes go bigger. "You *paralyzed* her?"

"Only temporarily," Julie says to soothe him. "At this point, Mr. Hunter, we're more concerned about her raging fever."

"Why would she have a fever? She wasn't sick until this morning."

"I believe Cecilia is suffering from DNP poisoning."

"*DNP?* The stuff they're saying killed Rain? You can't be serious!"

"Do you know if your wife was taking any kind of weight loss supplement or diet pills?"

"No! Nothing like that. Cecilia is all about natural health. DNP?" He shakes his head as though willing away the possibility. "Can't be."

"We've been seeing it in . . . unexpected patients of late."

Lloyd reaches out and grasps her shoulder, tight enough that Julie has to resist the urge to pry his hand free. "Is she going to be all right, Dr. Rees?"

The memory of Marcia flashes to mind. Julie is determined not to mislead another patient or her family. "I don't know, Mr. Hunter."

He digs his fingers into her shoulders. "Why not?"

"The CT is back," Ian whispers from over her other shoulder.

"Excuse me, Mr. Hunter." Julie gently wriggles free of Lloyd's grip.

She steps over to the nearest terminal and quickly pulls up Cecilia's CT scan on the screen.

Julie's heart sinks as she scrolls through the images, or cuts, on the screen. Cecilia's brain is grossly swollen. The normally clear demarcation that separates the gray brain matter from the white is obliterated.

Cecilia is already brain dead.

CHAPTER 23

"**S**he's in a coma," Lloyd mutters from where he leans, slumped against the seat of a spin bike, flanked by Adèle and Gerard. "She's going to die."

"Don't say that, Lloyd!" Adèle rubs his arm. "You have to believe. For Cecilia's sake, too."

"There's nothing to believe," Lloyd says blankly. "She's brain dead."

Adèle's face falls, and she shoots a hand to her mouth.

"They're only keeping her alive now to be an organ donor," Lloyd continues. "She would've wanted that. Cecilia hated to waste."

Hated to waste? Gerard had once seen her dump a two-thousand-dollar bottle of champagne on a hostess's T-shirt. "She was—is—" He doesn't even know what tense to use. "An incredible spirit. So full of life and passion. I can't believe we won't get to say goodbye." *Or ask her just how much of our special supplement she drank.*

"Can't we?" Adèle asks in a whisper.

"Can't we what, babe?" Gerard asks.

"Say goodbye."

Lloyd shakes his head. "There's no point. She's got no brain function left. She's not really there anymore."

Adèle launches herself forward, almost toppling Lloyd over as she wraps him in a tight hug. "I'm so sorry, Lloyd. I know how much you loved her. And she adored you."

"Thanks," he mumbles, motionless in her arms.

"And we're here for you, my friend," Gerard says, patting his shoulder. "Always. If there's anything we can do or help with arrangements . . ."

"I've got it covered," Lloyd says as he pulls free of Adèle's embrace.

"Do you know what her . . . wishes would have been?" Adèle asks.

"Cremation," he says. "And a big memorial service. No one loved a party more than Cecilia."

She really did. *Especially a depraved one.* "They're certain it was DNP, Lloyd?" Gerard asks. "Just like with Rain?"

He nods. "The ER doctor is also some kind of poison expert. She had no doubt."

"But how?" Adèle asks. "Where would Cecilia get it?"

"Damned if I know," Lloyd mutters. "It makes no sense. Never known anyone—not even you two—to treat their body as such a temple. A poisonous weight loss pill? Why would she need it?" He looks from Adèle to Gerard and back. "From the day I met Cecilia, she was always so slim and fit. It makes no sense."

"None at all." Gerard shakes his head. "Are the police looking into it?"

"No idea." Lloyd pushes himself away from the bike. "I've got to get back to the hospital. They'll be doing the . . . donor surgery soon. And then I guess they'll pull the plug." He swallows. "I should be there for that."

"Oh, Lloyd," Adèle breathes.

"I can't imagine what you're going through, my friend," Gerard says, as an idea begins to form. "Tell you what. Why don't Adèle and I go ahead to your place?" He glances over to her. "We'll cook dinner tonight."

"We absolutely will!" Adèle says, catching on. "We don't want you to be alone."

Lloyd views them glumly. "That's sweet of you both. But not necessary. My sister is coming over with dinner. There was no love lost between the two of them, but Cecilia respected Alice. And vice versa."

"We could cook for four," Gerard suggests. "Misery loves company."

Lloyd only shakes his head as he turns and trudges out of the room.

As soon as he's gone, Adèle turns frantically to Gerard. "What is it? Why is it so urgent for us to get into his house?"

Gerard hasn't told Adèle about his last conversation with Cecilia. Or the bottles he gave her. At the time, it seemed unnecessary. "Cecilia came to see me a couple days ago," he admits. "At first, I thought it was her usual games and flirty bullshit. But then she started talking about our supplement and how it wasn't working on Lloyd. She asked for—kind of demanded—a more potent supply. For *him*."

"Demanded?"

"Maybe that's not the right word. But it kind of felt like she was . . . blackmailing me."

"Oh, *merde*!" Adèle's eye dart around the room. "*Chéri*, you didn't . . ."

"Nothing much. I just doubled the strength."

"And Cecilia drank it herself instead of giving it to Lloyd?"

"I . . . I have no idea. Even at double strength, it should have been safe for—"

"But she was tiny!" she cries. "Less than half what Lloyd weighs."

"We've been so careful, babe. Diluting it down as much as we do. That's why we haven't had any incidents."

"Until now!"

"There's no way Cecilia could have drunk enough to reach the toxic level."

"But she's dead!" Adèle slaps her hand back to her mouth. "What have you done, Gerard?"

"This is not on me! I didn't go to her and make all these veiled threats and shit. She came to me!"

"What are we going to do now?"

"Only one thing to do. Get those fucking bottles back!"

CHAPTER 24

Anson has to kneel on the suitcase just to close the zipper. The "couple of suitcases" he told Theo he'd be bringing to Julie's have expanded into four, along with five bulky boxes. But that's not what is gnawing at him.

The nightmare recurred last night. Nicole was pleading for help, her face twisted with pain and fear as she repeatedly cried out his name. But Anson couldn't lift a finger or say a word to comfort her, rendering him a powerless and mute spectator to her suffering. The dream lasted longer than the previous ones, and when he finally did wake, he was in a sweat. He stayed awake the rest of the night, afraid of falling back to sleep.

The phone rings, and the words "Vancouver Hospital" flash across the call display. "Detective Chen," he answers.

"Good afternoon, Detective. Klaus Gruber calling."

"Hi, Dr. Gruber."

"Sorry to interrupt your weekend, but has Desmond informed you of our findings?"

That self-important, half-pint bureaucrat? Of course not. "No, I haven't heard from him."

"We have the final results of the autopsy and the toxicology screen on Ms. Flynn."

"Does it confirm that Rain died from DNP poisoning?" Anson asks.

"No question. Her blood level was at least ten milligrams per kilogram. She must have swallowed at least three or four capsules of DNP, possibly more, if they were indeed one-hundred-milligram capsules. Did you ever find the bottle, Detective?"

"No," Anson says, and it still bothers him that they found her other pills but not the DNP.

"The autopsy also confirmed that she was suffering from subacute DNP poisoning."

"Subacute? What's the difference, Dr. Gruber?"

"The skin discoloration and the structural changes we saw in her heart tell us that she had been taking DNP—most likely at a toxic dosage based on her weight—for several weeks, probably months."

Then what happened to the damn bottle? "Did anything else show up on the toxicology screen, Doctor?"

"The blood alcohol level, which we've discussed before. And of course, she had therapeutic levels of her two known prescription medications: Wellbutrin and Vyvanse. Neither contributed to her death."

"How about that diabetic medication?"

"Ozempic? No. That was not detectable in her blood."

Anson thanks Dr. Gruber and, as soon as he disconnects, calls Theo.

"Who do you think took the bottle of DNP from the scene?" Theo asks, reaching the same conclusion as Anson had.

"Anyone at the party, I suppose," Anson says. "But my bet is on the manager, the traveling therapist, or the BFF. Maybe all three? None of them have been on the level with us so far."

"Agreed. A lot of tension between those three. Although Maleeka is the one who went public about DNP."

"But it would've come out eventually," Anson points out. "Maybe she was just getting herself out in front of the story?"

"Possibly. Would help if we could read Rain's texts. I've got a call into Babar in Computer Crimes."

"Oh, he's gonna be grumpy."

"No worse than usual," Theo says. "The deputy chief already lit a fire under him. He's promised to get back to me soon."

"Maybe we go talk to the entourage again? Play them off against each other?"

"Worth a shot."

"Tomorrow morning?" Anson suggests.

"Bright and early," Theo says. "Hey, how did the move go? Was the fleet of trucks able to cart your whole wardrobe over?"

"No fleet. Just my Jeep Cherokee." Anson pauses. "And I'm about to head over there right now."

"On your tenth or fifteenth round trip?"

"My first. See you in the morning."

Anson drags all the suitcases and boxes out to the elevator and down to the garage. He manages to cram them in the back of the SUV, though he struggles to get the rear door to shut.

The drive to Julie's feels different from previous trips. The move was his idea. But Anson is edgy and far more unsettled than he anticipated. If not for his nightmares and residual anxiety, he would be far more excited. The weather isn't helping his mood, either. It's barely five o'clock and already dark outside. One of those cold and dreary late fall days when even a lifelong Vancouverite like him questions why people would pay such astronomical rents and mortgages to live in such a gloomy city.

"Welcome home," Julie says, greeting him at the door. She's barefoot. Her hair is tied up, and she wears nothing but a pale pink bathrobe. A playful look dances in her eyes. She rotates a bottle of Veuve Clicquot by its neck in a bell-ringing motion, while two champagne flutes dangle between the fingers of her other hand.

"Wow." Anson drops the only suitcase he brought up from the car and pulls her into a hug, kissing her responsive lips. The feel of the soft fabric against his chest and the scent of her citrus perfume helps to dispel much of his angst. "Is this your usual Sunday afternoon getup?"

"Wanted to make a decent impression on your first day in your new home."

"Mission accomplished," he says, as he guides her by the waist to the bedroom.

He eases the bottle out of her hand and rests it beside the two glasses on the nightstand. She slides the robe off her shoulders and then, naked, falls backward on the bed. He hurries to strip out of his own clothes. Just as he steps free of his pants, she pulls him down onto the bed on top of her.

Their sex is hungry and urgent. Anson senses Julie needs the release as much as he does. Afterwards, still breathing heavily, he reaches across her for the bottle. He strips off the covering wire and lets the cork fly across the room. He fills the two flutes and raises his glass to toast her. "To our new daily ritual."

Julie taps her glass to his and then kisses him softly on the cheek. "Why not? Has to be some upside to getting a roommate."

Anson takes a sip of the champagne, enjoying the hint of honey and apple. Julie eyes him silently. Staring into those pools of green, he realizes he can't put if off any longer. He lowers his glass and reaches for her hand. "Julie . . ."

"What's with the serious face?"

"I've been having these dreams."

She tilts her head slightly. "What sort of dreams?"

"They're more like nightmares."

"About Nicole?"

"How'd you know?"

"You muttered her name a few nights ago." Julie puts down her glass. "Tell me about them."

"They're super vague. I don't even know where we are most of the time. But it's always the same. Nicole is calling out to me for help." He looks down. "And I can't do anything. I don't even know how."

Julie squeezes his hand. "Anson . . ."

"Yeah, yeah. I get it. It wouldn't take a PhD in psychology to interpret them, huh?"

"You still feel guilty," she says quietly.

"Impossible not to."

"Stop."

But Anson has never shed the sense of responsibility for the freak moped accident that killed his wife. It was his idea to rent the bikes on their holiday. The guilt has simmered under the surface for years, but the step of moving in with someone new has blasted it to front of mind. Along with the irrational fear of history repeating itself.

"Does it feel like you're cheating on Nicole by moving in with me?" Julie asks.

"No, nothing like that." He brings her hand to his mouth and kisses it. "I'm just a little scared. I don't want to screw this up." But he's too embarrassed to mention the other anxiety: *What if something were to happen to you because of me?*

"I'm scared, too, Anson. My track record isn't exactly perfect, either." She grabs his face in her hands and pulls it to hers. "Trust me. I won't let you screw this up."

He kisses her. "OK."

Holding hands, they finish their glasses in comfortable silence. As he reaches to refill them, she says, "Anson, I wasn't going to bring work home today of all days . . ."

"But?"

"I lost a patient in the ER. Another DNP poisoning. I thought you should know."

Anson puts down the bottle. "Who?"

"A forty-year-old woman."

"With an eating disorder?"

"Not according to the husband. He swore his wife was a health nut. That she wouldn't have touched anything like DNP."

"And he has no idea where she got it from?"

"None."

He puts his glass on the nightstand. "She would be the fifth DNP death in Vancouver, Julie. In the past three months alone."

"Do you think all the victims got their DNP from the same source?"

"Not sure yet. But God, I hope so." He sighs. "It's our best chance at stopping—at least slowing—this deadly train. After Rain . . . maybe our only chance."

"I have the husband's number. Why don't I speak to him again when he's calmer? Or maybe I could talk to one of her friends—"

"No, Julie. This is an active investigation now. I'll speak to him."

"OK. Understood."

But Anson doesn't fully trust her conciliatory tone or expression.

CHAPTER 25

"I'm tempted to call him, Benny," Cari says from the passenger seat of her best friend's car.

Benny's head swivels toward her. "Why in God's name would you do that?"

"I could use his help," Cari says with a nonchalance she doesn't feel.

"His help? Right!" Benny snorts as he turns his gaze back to the dense morning traffic ahead, clogging the 405.

"I could, Benny. This case keeps getting more and more complicated."

"Sure. It'd just be a purely professional outreach to a former colleague."

Cari isn't fooling her best friend any more than she is herself. "Maybe not purely." She looks down at her hands resting on her lap. "Mattias would get it."

"Get what?"

"How triggering this is for me."

Benny goes quiet for a moment. "Don't."

"It's just a phone call."

"Don't let him back in, Cari." Benny's tone softens. "You *are* triggered by this case. How could you not be after Lucia? And you're also lonely and vulnerable right now."

"Could you make me sound any more pathetic?"

"You're never pathetic, hon. Or weak. You're just confused. And he'll prey on that if you let him."

She reaches over and squeezes Benny's arm, grateful for his protectiveness. "Mattias wants to come to LA to see me."

"He wants a long-distance affair now, does he?"

"He's not as bad as you make him out to be, Benjamin."

"What do *you* want, Caridad?"

"I want things to be what they were."

"What they were was an illusion."

The truth behind his words hurts more than Cari lets on. "I guess so, maybe."

Benny pats her thigh and laughs. "Listen to me, high on my pulpit. I'm one to talk!" He pauses. "Lawrence just moved back home."

"Not so easy to shake your soulmate, is it?" Cari smiles. "Even if he is as big a drama queen as you are."

Benny chuckles. "I stand corrected. You and I are equally pathetic."

They pass a sign for LAX, and Benny takes the off-ramp. "I'll tell you what I don't want," she says.

He glances at her with a raised eyebrow.

"To be jetting off to another country in the middle of an active investigation. Just because my captain blurts something on a whim at a press conference."

"But the cases in LA and Vancouver are linked, aren't they? Through Rain and all?"

"Looks like," Cari says. "But we do have phones and other communication devices. I could liaise with the Vancouver detectives without flying all the way up there. This is nothing more than a publicity stunt."

Benny thumbs at the window. "Haven't you noticed, hon? We live in the cradle of the publicity stunt."

He pulls up to the curb at the departure zone of the United terminal. After Cari unloads her carry-on luggage, he wraps her in a tight hug. "If you have the overwhelming urge to text someone, try yours truly," he says as he releases her.

"I'll think about it." She blows him a kiss as she turns for the door.

Inside the terminal, Cari clears the security checkpoint and walks to her gate. The boarding process is already well underway, and her phone rings while she's standing in line. She recognizes Zach's number on the call display and answers. "Hi," she says. "I don't have long. Just about to board a flight."

"It's about our online order," Zach says.

Cari steps out of the line. "I thought you said Dr. Chiseled Pharmaceuticals shut down their website during that gong show of a press conference."

"Oh, they did," he says. "But not before accepting our money."

Cari's breath catches. "Where are they, Zach?"

"It's a complex algorithm, Detective. The money moves faster than you can follow it."

"You can't pinpoint where they're based?"

"Not yet, no. But they did leave a few bread crumbs." It's clear to her that Zach is enjoying himself. "And I don't think they're based out of Canada, after all."

"No?"

"It looks like our payment was routed locally before being moved to Eastern Europe and then onto cryptocurrency."

"Locally? As in LA?"

"Yup."

Then why the fuck am I flying to Canada?

"Most promisingly, I have the name of their Bitcoin exchange now," Zach says with obvious satisfaction.

"What does that mean?"

"Banks and Bitcoin exchanges can trace transactions backwards, through the blockchain, to see which online wallets the funds came from."

"But don't they just keep shutting those websites down?"

"The websites are shells. Online pop-up stores to sell the products. But they have to keep the money somewhere more permanent."

"You're saying that if we find the wallet, we find them?"

"That's the general idea."

The rest of the line has cleared, and a flight attendant beckons Cari toward the gate with an impatient wave. "I got to go, Zach. Good work! Keep me posted."

Cari boards the plane and, within minutes of taking off, falls asleep, as she does on most flights. She's awakened by the jerk of the wheels striking the runway.

She fires off a text to Detective Chen, notifying him that she has landed. He texts back almost immediately, and they arrange to meet at her hotel.

Cari has never been to Vancouver, but riding in the backseat of the cab, she's too preoccupied with responding to the emails and texts that have accumulated during her flight to pay much attention to her surroundings. That changes as soon as they drive onto what, according to her driver, is the Burrard Bridge. She lowers her phone and drinks in the stunning scenery.

Cari has always found sanctuary in Southern California's rolling coastline and endless ocean vistas, but she has never seen a city like Vancouver, where snowcapped mountains loom so close to the ocean and downtown buildings that they appear to be standing in the water and guarding over the inlet as it opens out into the Pacific.

Cari is still thinking about the city's lush natural beauty when the driver drops her off in front of the Wall Centre Hotel. Inside the lobby, she heads for the two men standing near the check-in desk, assuming they must be the local detectives. The older one, talking on his phone, wears a loose, beige raincoat in a style she hasn't seen in at least a decade. The younger one has on a form-fitting navy coat and polished oxfords. His good looks and style remind her of an Asian movie star whose name just won't come to her.

"Hi. Theo Kostas," the first detective says, still cradling the phone between his head and neck.

"I'm Anson," the other one says and meets her handshake. "Welcome to Vancouver, Detective Garcia."

"Cari, please."

"Don't mind this one, Cari." Anson jerks a thumb at Theo. "Social graces have never been his strong suit."

Theo looks skyward as he continues to speak into the phone.

"Thanks again for letting me tag along on your investigation," she says. "I honestly thought we could've done this remotely, but my captain thought otherwise."

Anson shrugs. "Captains think better than us lowly detectives, don't they?"

"They certainly think they do."

"Your timing is good, though," he says. "We're just heading out to see Rain's best friend again. We're fairly certain someone in Rain's entourage must have snatched her supply of DNP before the crime techs arrived on scene."

Theo pulls the phone from his ear and tucks it into his jacket. He shoots Cari an apologetic smile. "Sorry about that."

She holds up a hand in understanding.

"What did Babar have to say?" Anson asks.

"Babar's one of our computer crimes techs," Theo explains. "He says that, unlike with the other victims, there's zero electronic record of Rain having ordered DNP from one of those Dr. Pharmaceuticals sites. Or any other site."

"One of her peeps must've gotten the DNP for her," Anson says.

"Speaking of computer crimes, I just heard from my guy in the LAPD." Cari goes on to update them on what Zach told her right before her flight departed.

"He now thinks the people behind Dr. Pharmaceuticals are based in LA?" Theo asks.

"He does."

"Did he say how long it will take to follow the money—or the crypto—back to its source?" Anson asks.

Cari shakes her head. "He's not even certain he can follow it."

"Meanwhile, we might as well follow a lower tech trail," Anson says.

"Agreed." Theo gestures to the bell desk. "Why don't you drop off your bag, Cari? And then come with us to interview Maleeka?"

"She's the one who posted about Rain's DNP use, right?" Cari asks.

"Yup," Theo says. "Rain's self-declared best friend."

"If nothing else," Anson says, "a conversation with her is an immersive experience in Gen Z speak."

Cari drops her bag off at the bell desk and leaves the hotel with the other detectives. Rather than drive, they head north on foot down a short hill to another hotel on the opposite side of the street and enter a lobby that is fancier than the one they just left.

Up on the twentieth floor, Theo knocks at a door, and a young woman in a baggy sweatshirt answers. Her black hair is cropped short, and she wears round, wire-rimmed glasses over a makeup-free face. "Yes?" she says blankly.

"We're looking for Maleeka Khan," Theo says.

"And you are?" the woman asks, without moving from the door.

"They're the *poh-lease*," says another young woman, who appears behind the first. Sporting a long mane of black hair, she wears thick mascara and her eyes are circled with well-applied kohl. "And they're thirsty for my time."

While the two women are a total contrast in terms of dress and demeanor, Cari recognizes the strong resemblance in their facial bone structure.

The first woman opens the door wider, and the other one waves them inside.

"Officers, meet my big sib, Shawna," Maleeka says. "She's the brains of the Khan fam. Got, like, a PhD from Harvard."

"Wrong coast, Mal. I went to Stanford. And it's only a bachelor's degree." Shawna motions to the pile of suitcases in the main room behind her. "Besides, I'm only here as the mover."

Maleeka grins. "Big sib to the rescue."

"Again," Shawna says, her tone as flat as her expression.

"Ray-ray's shoot was supposed to go the full three months," Maleeka explains to the others with a shrug. "Thought I was gonna be logging some serious time in this hood. Didn't exactly pack light. Now I have to head back to La-La Land tomorrow."

Theo nods to Cari. "This is Detective Garcia," he says without mentioning that she works for the LAPD. "We've got a couple follow-up questions from the last time we spoke."

Maleeka turns to Shawna with an amused look. "'Follow-up questions.' They always use that line in those crime shows when they're trying to trip up the perp."

"Stop being an idiot!" Shawna snaps.

"Ooh, someone's salty," Maleeka says and turns back to the detectives. "What questions?"

"We found all Rain's pills and supplements in her bathroom," Theo says. "Except we couldn't find any capsules of DNP. Or the bottle."

Maleeka frowns. "And?"

"They're asking if you hid them, Mal," Shawna says.

"Naw," Maleeka says, unfazed. "Let's not forget who blew the whistle on Ray-Ray's DNP habit."

"Someone at that party got rid of the bottle after Rain died," Anson says.

Maleeka shrugs. "A lot of peeps at that bash, Officer. Weren't there, Shawn?"

"Not that many when I was there," Shawna says. "Then again, I took off by about nine. I'd had my fill of those posers."

"Big sib isn't much of a party girl. Period."

"With that crowd? Who would be?"

The relationship between the seemingly polar opposite sisters intrigues Cari, but she stays quiet, appreciating that it's not her place to insert herself into the questioning.

"You still have no idea where Rain got her DNP?" Theo asks.

Maleeka scoffs. "Haven't heard much from Ray-Ray since the night of the party."

"How come you weren't staying there, Maleeka?" Anson asks.

"Where?"

"In the penthouse. Where Rain died."

"Rain didn't like to share her pad. Even with me."

"But wasn't Dr. Markstrom staying in another condo just a few floors down?"

Maleeka shrugs. "That part of town is snooze-ville. I way prefer it here. Closer to the action."

"Speaking of," Shawna interjects. "Have you looked into that therapist yet?"

Theo tilts his head. "You know Dr. Markstrom, too?"

"I met him once or twice through Maleeka. Rain had so many

hangers-on," Shawna says without a trace of irony, even though she's standing inches away from her sister, who epitomizes the description. "But pompous as he is, that Dr. Markstrom seemed like the biggest one of the bunch to me."

"You think he would've given Rain DNP?" Theo asks.

Shawna looks over to her sister. "Tell him, Mal."

Maleeka grimaces. "Tell him what?"

"What Rain told you. About the diabetes medication."

"Oh, yeah." Maleeka turns back to the detectives. "Ray-Ray was wigging out last spring about her weight gain. As usual, it was all in her head. Probably like four or five ounces of water weight—"

"Maleeka . . ." Shawna prompts.

"Ray-Ray told me that Dr. Evil got her on some med that would MacGyver her appetite away."

"A shot?" Anson asks.

"Yeah." Maleeka makes a face. "She had to inject it right into her abs."

"Rain told you that Dr. Markstrom was the one who gave her that medication?"

"She surely did."

"Rain basically told me the same," Shawna says. "That Dr. Markstrom was the one who helped her control her weight."

"Are you sure she didn't mean through counseling?" Anson asks.

Shawna eyes him for a moment and then breaks into a nasal laugh. "Rain wasn't talking about counseling."

CHAPTER 26

The young, chatty Irishman at the front desk informs the detectives that Dr. Markstrom checked out the day before. "He must be back in LA," Cari says, as they head out of the hotel and start back up the hill. "I'll go see him as soon as I get home."

"Not sure it'll help," Theo says. "Markstrom denied knowing anything about that diabetic drug. Doubt he'll change his story now. Not without proof."

"And the Ozempic injector we found had no prescription label on it," Anson points out.

"We do have the name of the psychiatrist who prescribed Rain the other two medications, right?" Cari says.

"Yeah, but unlikely a psychiatrist would be prescribing a diabetic medication."

"True," Cari says. "I'll see if someone in my office can pull up Rain's electronic prescription records. Find out who prescribed it for her."

"Do you have sufficient grounds?" Theo asks.

"I'm sure I can find something," Cari says.

With round cheeks and silken complexion, Cari appears younger than Anson expected. He wasn't excited at the prospect of a detective from another country shadowing their investigation, but he has already warmed to her. She strikes him as not only sharp but also practical, which are his favorite attributes in a cop.

"Can you believe it?" Theo gestures to the two media vans that are camped out in front of the hotel, days after Rain's death. "They're even staking out Maleeka's hotel. I've never seen this much media interest in anything, let alone an active investigation."

"Not surprised," Cari says. "Between the sudden death of a mega-celebrity and the task force we set up in LA, DNP is the *only* trending hashtag these days."

"Not to mention Desmond's press conference," Anson says.

"Who's Desmond?" Cari asks.

"A self-important garden gnome who's addicted to media attention."

"He's Vancouver's chief coroner," Theo explains. "Desmond threw an impromptu press conference. Not only did he confirm that Rain's autopsy showed she died of DNP, but he also publicized the news of the city's latest DNP death."

"Without consulting anyone in the VPD," Anson adds. "The deputy chief blew a gasket."

"I don't blame him," Cari says.

"*Her*," Anson says with a mischievous grin.

"Oops. Guess it's back to remedial gender equity training for me."

Theo chuckles. "About those prescription records, Cari. Even if you could access them, that diabetic medication would've been prescribed by a medical doctor. And Markstrom isn't one."

"True," she says. "But if we can track down the prescribing MD, then we can work backwards from him or her to see if it's connected to Markstrom."

"I bet you the prescription wasn't even in Rain's name," Anson says. "Ten to one says someone else gave her Ozempic. Possibly the same person who gave her those DNP capsules."

"Why don't we check Markstrom's prescription records?" Theo suggests. "See if that injector came from his own medicine cabinet."

"That'll be trickier to access," Cari says. "Legally, anyway."

"Let's speak to Rain's manager again," Anson says as they reach the entrance to Cari's hotel. "See if he corroborates Maleeka and her sister's story about Markstrom."

"I'll check if he's still in town as soon as I get back to the office." Theo moves away from the other two. "I gotta go there now to update the Gang Squad on the PG and Maddox hits."

Anson looks over to Cari. "I'm heading to go see the husband of that latest DNP victim," he says. "You want to ride along?"

"I'd love to."

As they drive back over the Burrard Bridge, Cari stares out at the mountains, shaking her head in awe. "I can't get over these views."

"Yeah, well, you're lucky. Catching a blue-sky day in November in Vancouver is rare. Like almost lottery-winning rare."

Cari thumbs behind her. "What's that over there?"

"That neighborhood by the water's edge is called the West End. It's kind of misleading because Vancouver's a peninsula and extends farther west on the south side of the bridge. Out toward the University of British Columbia." They slow to a stop at a red light on the far side of the bridge. "The greenery beyond the West End, that's Stanley Park. Our equivalent of Central Park. You got to check it out before you go home. Walk or run the five-mile seawall around it. Especially on a day like today. You will not be disappointed."

"Sold."

"So what's your partner up to while you're doing all this international reconnaissance?" he asks.

"Long story, but I'm kind of between partners right now."

"You want Theo?"

Cari laughs. "I would take him in a heartbeat. But the transfer paperwork would be a bitch."

"Don't tell him this, but I'd actually hate to lose him."

"Good partners are hard to find," she sighs. Her tone piques his curiosity, but he keeps it to himself.

They soon reach a residential neighborhood with wide, tree-lined streets and a mix of old and new houses, most of which are perched on huge lots with manicured lawns and sprawling gardens. "This is Shaughnessy," Anson explains. "Railroad executives built their mansions here during the city's infancy, at the turn of the last century. The same elites 'employed' my ancestors who came over from China—if you can call slave wages and deadly hazardous working conditions employment—to build their railways. Some of the original houses are still standing. And today, just like back then, you don't wind up living in Shaughnessy without a bunch of zeroes at the end of your bank accounts."

"Looks like," she says with an appreciative nod.

"And here's where the one-percenters of Shaughnessy reside." Anson turns onto a wide boulevard that ends in a cul-de-sac, with a park in its center, known as the Crescent. He pulls into a long driveway that leads to an older green, Craftsman-style mansion and parks the car.

A middle-aged man in a black tracksuit meets them at the door. His face is unshaven, and his eyes are slightly bloodshot. After introductions, Lloyd Hunter offers a weak smile. "Thanks for coming, detectives," he says, as if he invited them over, rather than vice versa. "Please, come in."

They walk into a spotless, high-ceilinged foyer finished in wood. The floors and wainscoting look to be original or, at least, impeccable reproductions. The spiral staircase winding upward is railed in more dark, heavy wood. Lloyd leads them into the dining room and over to a lacquered white oval table that stands in stark contrast to the rest of the decor. He motions to the chairs on either side of him as he sits down at the end of the table.

"I'm sorry for your loss, Mr. Hunter," Cari says.

"Thank you. It was so . . ." Lloyd doesn't finish.

"Can't imagine how difficult this is for you," Anson says, though he knows what it's like to lose a spouse unexpectedly. And how, despite what everyone promises, it doesn't always get easier. "We heard you were home the morning it happened."

"I was, yes."

"Was your wife in bed when the seizure began, Mr. Hunter?"

"Yes."

"And you woke up to find her that way?"

"No, no. Cecilia was still asleep when I got up. I'm usually up by five. To be ready when the markets open back east." Lloyd indicates the upper level with a sweep of his hand. "I was working in my home office."

"You heard something?"

"There was this flapping noise." His chin falls to his chest. "I . . . I ignored it at first. I was on a phone call. And it didn't sound serious to me."

"But you decided to check it out anyway?"

"When it didn't stop. Sure. And . . ." Lloyd swallows. "Cecilia was under the covers, but her head was jerking up and down. And she was bucking so hard it looked like she was . . . trying to levitate or something."

"What did you do?"

"When I was a kid, my cousin used to get seizures. I was always taught to turn him on his side, so he wouldn't choke. That's the first thing I did with Cecilia. And I wedged a couple pillows behind her back. Then I called 911." Lloyd's voice cracks. "It took forever for the ambulance to get here. My cousin's seizures, they used to last a minute or two. At most. I kept expecting Cecilia to stop and go still like he used to." He pauses, clearly trying to get his voice under control. "But she never did."

"That must've been terrifying," Cari says.

Lloyd nods slightly.

"Just to clarify, Mr. Hunter," Anson says. "You had no idea your wife was taking DNP?"

"God, no," he says. "And afterwards . . . I went through her stuff. The bathroom, her closet. I checked everywhere. I didn't find so much as a single pill, let alone a bottle. Besides . . ."

The detectives stare at Lloyd, waiting for him to expand.

"Cecilia, she was so health conscious," he finally says. "When she went for groceries, she wouldn't put anything into the cart without checking every ingredient first. Nothing but organic, preservative-free food."

"Was Mrs. Hunter actively trying to lose weight?" Cari asks. "Dieting?"

"No," Lloyd says. "She was super-fit from the day I met her. Over ten years ago."

"And she never took anything to help keep her in shape?"

"Not Cecilia. No. She didn't need to."

"How about bodybuilding?" Cari asks. "Or training for fitness competitions?"

"Nothing like that. None of it makes any sense," Lloyd mutters. "We own a wellness center, for Christ's sake! Three of them, as a matter of fact."

Anson cocks his head. "A wellness center?"

"Mind Over Body Wellness Center. With locations in LA and Vancouver. Another about to open in San Fran, in a month or two."

Anson shares a quick glance with Cari, but neither comment.

"I mean, to be accurate, we co-own them," Lloyd continues. "But they've been doing phenomenally well. A holistic approach to well-being. The clients love it."

"A holistic approach?" Cari asks. "What does that involve?"

"You know . . . mental, spiritual, and physical health. We provide it all. From meditation, yoga, and TED Talk–level inspirational lectures to outdoor excursions. Our slogan is: 'Change your mind and your body will follow.'"

The whole spiel sounds rehearsed to Anson. "Would that also include fitness and nutrition?" he asks.

"Of course," Lloyd says. "That's a big part of it, too. But it's way more than just a gym or anything."

"And Mrs. Hunter was involved in running these centers?"

"We were always more on the financial side. But we definitely contributed to the big-picture vision. Especially Cecilia. She was the one who brought in the massage therapists and the float spas for sensory deprivation."

"Who are your other partners?"

"Gerard Martin." Lloyd rubs his palm with his thumb. "I mean, to give credit where credit is due, the centers were Gerard's brainchild."

Anson makes a mental note of the name. "Is he based in Vancouver or LA?"

"Both." Lloyd frowns. "But he spends more time here now."

"And what's Mr. Martin's background?" Anson asks.

"Fitness training. What's that called, technically? Kinesiology?" Lloyd shrugs. "Matter of fact, Gerard used to be our favorite spin instructor a few years back."

CHAPTER 27

Lloyd opens the door, and Adèle extends the clay casserole dish she holds in both hands toward him. The steam rises from under the loose silver foil and, along with it, the scent of melted cheese. "Veggie lasagna," she says. "My mom's recipe. Not exactly low-cal, but the Gruyère makes the indulgence so worth it!"

The Gruyère was Adèle's only actual contribution to the dish. Gerard had brought the frozen lasagna home from the gourmet store around the corner. She carefully transferred it to a casserole dish and grated some Gruyère on top before baking it. It was as much cooking as Gerard had ever seen her tackle.

"Thank you," Lloyd says, showing little interest as he accepts it from her. "Come in."

Gerard and Adèle follow him through the foyer and into the living room to the low, white leather sectional and the coffee table that is meant to resemble a slab of granite.

Adèle rests a hand on his slumping shoulder. "How are you holding up, Lloyd?"

"Saying goodbye at the hospital . . ." He clears his throat. "Was one of the hardest things I've done."

"Can't even . . ." Gerard murmurs.

"Let me just put the lasagna in the warmer. Have a seat, please." Lloyd turns for the kitchen. "You want something to drink?"

"Are you having anything?" Gerard asks.

"A little red wouldn't hurt," Adèle says, before Lloyd can even answer.

"Good call," Lloyd says without turning back. "I've got just the right pinot noir to help us remember her."

As soon as he's gone, Gerard looks over to Adèle, who nods her understanding.

"Mind if I use the washroom, Lloyd?" she calls out to him.

"Of course," he responds from the kitchen. "You know where it is."

Gerard watches with admiration as Adèle grabs her oversized handbag and glides out of the living room, moving as silently as the ballerina she always wanted to be. Rather than head down the hallway to the powder room, she disappears up the spiral staircase. Asking Lloyd to open a bottle of wine was a small stroke of genius. It will buy more time for her search.

Gerard rises and joins Lloyd in the expansive kitchen with its marble countertops, long central island, and state-of-the-art stainless steel appliances. Lloyd pulls down three stemless glasses from a cupboard and digs a wine opener out of a drawer.

"Is there anything we can do to help, Lloyd?" Gerard asks.

"Your moral support is help enough."

"I know it's a cliché, but we really do mean it. Anything . . . anything at all . . . you just tell us."

Lloyd uncorks the bottle. "I'm good, Ger."

"It's a given that Adèle and I will take care of the Bay Area opening—"

"I aim to be there, too."

We don't want you there! "You don't have to, Lloyd. Not after what's happened."

"What else am I supposed to do?" he asks plaintively. "Sit around all day and mope? Anything that distracts me from the memories is a good thing. Trust me."

"You sure?"

Lloyd pours out three generous glasses and passes one to Gerard. "Absolutely."

"OK. Thanks." Gerard brings the glass to his lips, though he has little interest in wine tonight.

"Oh, by the way," Lloyd says. "I think you're going to be hearing from a couple of detectives."

Gerard almost chokes on the wine. "Oh?" He lowers his glass to the counter. "What about?"

"They came by earlier. Detectives Chen and . . . Lopez? No, um . . . Garcia. They're the same ones looking into Rain's death."

"Rain's death?"

"It's the DNP. They think it could all be connected."

"Rain and Cecilia?" Gerard spins the wineglass on its base. "Doesn't seem likely."

"Yeah, well, they kept asking me about Cecilia. They're trying to figure out where she got DNP. They asked me if she was dieting or taking any kind of supplements or what-have-you."

"Cecilia? Of all people?"

"That's what I told them! The detectives were respectful and all, but it's almost like they didn't believe me. Like they thought I was withholding something."

Gerard can feel the pulse pounding in his temple, but he offers the most casual shrug he can muster. "Wonder if you—or they—will ever find out? I still can't believe it. Matter of fact, I don't believe it. Some toxic diet pill? *Cecilia?*"

"Hard to fathom, isn't it?"

Gerard lets the conversation lapse for a while and then asks, "What makes you think the detectives are going to come see me?"

"I told them how Cecilia and I are—were—silent partners in Mind Over Body," Lloyd says. "They were very curious. They took down your name."

Fuck! "Happy to talk to them. Not sure how much help I can be." Gerard forces a smile. "But whatever it takes. Poor Cecilia."

Lloyd lifts the other two glasses and waves one toward the living room. "Shall we?"

"Of course," Gerard mumbles, totally distracted by the thought of the police poking around in his business.

Just as they step into the living room, Adèle strides in from the other side. She points to the extra glass in Lloyd's hands. "Aren't you a sight for sore eyes!"

After they're seated on the sectional, Gerard meets her gaze. The subtle shake of her head tells him all he needs to know. She couldn't find the bottles to switch out.

Could today get any worse?

CHAPTER 28

Julie hasn't had a full day off work from both the ER and Poison Control in over a week. Not until today. She has already capitalized on her free time with a hot yoga class, a rare shopping spree, and lunch with her mom. And now, while leisurely preparing dinner, she samples the pesto again, pleased with the result. The flavor is dependent on finding the precisely aged block of Reggiano Parmesan and toasting the pine nuts to the perfect crispness before blending them in with basil, garlic, and olive oil, exactly as her high school boyfriend's mother, Mrs. Abruzzese, had taught her.

But despite her unhurried day—or maybe because of it—her thoughts keep drifting back to the previous night and how restless Anson was. He flipped and flopped the night away, waking her repeatedly with inadvertent knees and elbows to her back. At one point, she heard him mumble Nicole's name again. But when they got up in the morning, Anson didn't mention anything about his dreams. Even when she specifically asked him.

Julie has never felt insecure in their relationship, but Anson's recent evasiveness is unlike him. It's making her uneasy. *Did we move in together too soon?* she wonders. *Does he regret it?*

Her phone buzzes three times in rapid succession, signaling that someone is at the intercom. She opens the door remotely, and two minutes later, Goran bounds into her condo with a bottle of wine tucked under each arm.

He holds the wines out to her and raises the first one. "A Californian Cabernet Sauvignon. Out of respect for the guest of honor." Then he lifts up the second. "But I draw the line at Chardonnay. That simply must be French."

Julie kisses him on the cheek, inhaling the distinctive woody scent of his cologne. "I'm sorry Maria couldn't join us," she says.

"She is, too, Julija. But she had this reunion with her family in the Philippines booked for months. They only speak Tagalog. Or maybe that's what she says to keep me away. Regardless, I'm not invited."

"Maria's in Manila?"

"No, no. It's one of those Zoom deals. Better than nothing, I suppose. But the whole business is highly overrated," he grumbles. "The socializing equivalent of being on *Hollywood Squares*."

"*Hollywood Squares*?" She shakes her head.

"A classic TV game show! Paul Lynde. Are you kidding me, Julija? Millennials . . ." He rolls his eyes. "I don't know why I even bother."

Julie pulls him by the arm into the kitchen. Goran stands the bottle of red on the counter and puts the white in the fridge. "Where is everyone?" he asks.

"They'll be here soon. What can I get you to drink?"

"Eh, I'll wait." He waves a hand. "So?"

Julie reads the question in his expectant eyes. "It's only been one night, Gor."

"I remember the day Maria moved in. It was more nerve-wracking than I anticipated. Not sure why I didn't expect it. After all, Lada and I lived together for thirty-two years." Goran juts out his lower lip. "Moving in with someone new . . . that, as my son would say, is a BFD."

"BFD?"

"Big freaking deal." He winks. "In its more polite variation."

Julie appreciates the way her friend always picks up on her anxieties and tries to find ways to reassure her. Her dad died when she was only nine, and Goran is the closest thing to a father figure she has in her life.

She's sorely tempted to tell him about Anson's dreams but realizes it's not the time or place. "BFD sums it up pretty good," she says.

The door opens again, and they both turn at the sound of the chatter coming from the hallway. Anson walks into the kitchen beside a dark-haired woman in a gray pantsuit. He smiles at Julie and then nods to Goran. "Julie, Goran, meet Detective Cari Garcia from LA."

"Good to meet you both," Cari says with a soft Californian drawl.

"Who knew detectives could be so striking?" Goran says, voicing exactly what Julie is thinking. With fluid amber eyes, plump lips, and a flawless olive complexion to complement her thick hair and curvy figure, Cari is stunning.

"What can we get you to drink, Cari?" Julie asks.

"Whatever you've got going is fine."

"Careful what you ask for, Detective," Goran says. "Otherwise, I will pour you a rakija. And you won't ever let anything else touch your lips."

"Only because you won't be able to swallow anything after that Croatian paint thinner," Anson jokes.

Goran looks skyward. "To think I once respected you. Sort of."

"Red or white?" Julie asks Cari, ignoring the two men.

"White, please," Cari says.

Anson fills her glass and then pours red for Goran and Julie, without needing to ask, as well as himself. They gather around the hors d'oeuvres plates on the counter.

"How long are you in Vancouver for, Cari?" Julie asks.

"I'm going back the day after tomorrow," Cari says.

"So?" Goran motions to her with his wineglass. "How does Canadian policing compare with American?"

"I can't speak for entire countries. But from what I've seen so far, it's quite similar. Like with medicine, I'm guessing. Policing is policing, wherever you go."

Goran exhales again. "Not so sure you would feel the same if you had seen the kind of policing I saw behind the Iron Curtain. Or, for that matter, the medicine."

"We know, Gor, we know," Anson groans. "In your day, you had to get up an hour before you went to bed to sweep out the lake."

Julie doesn't get the reference, but Goran roars with laughter. "Monty Python! I love it! The bards of their time."

Thanks largely to Goran's contribution, they finish most of the appetizers, and then Julie shepherds everyone over to the dining table. The conversation flows freely and easily over dinner, and they finish another bottle of wine. Soon Cari and Anson begin swapping detective stories and bitching about mutual work frustrations.

"This one time," Anson says, waving his fork, "these two gangbangers get into it at a restaurant—a local gang haunt—over a particular table they both want. Guns are pulled. One shoots the other in the head. In front of twelve eyewitnesses! But the prosecutor couldn't press charges because no one was willing to testify."

"It's infuriating!" Cari cries. "We run into that all the time in RHD. We almost always know who pulled the trigger. And who ordered it."

"Yet the public thinks we don't know our asses from our elbows," Anson says.

"Thanks to the press," Cari says with a dismissive shake of her head. "And social media."

"Not to mention those cheesy cop shows."

"Exactly! Everything's wrapped up in a few hours. Due process isn't even a thing!"

Anson views her conspiratorially. "Wouldn't it feel good to just once post the names of the actual killers with the hashtag #Ididmypart?"

"In all caps!" Cari says, bursting into laughter.

Goran turns to Julie as he wiggles a finger between Anson and Cari. "Aren't they two peas in a pod?"

"Aren't they though?" Julie says, as she rises from table to start clearing the dishes.

Anson hops to his feet. "Julie, no," he says. "Let me. Please. You did all the work tonight."

Julie sinks back into her chair.

As Anson disappears into the kitchen with his arms full of dishes, Cari says, "That was so delicious, Julie. Thank you."

"The chicken turned out OK," Julie says. "But sorry about the salad. I overdid the pomegranate dressing. It was drenched."

"You're kidding, right? It was perfect."

"Eh," Goran tilts his head from side to side. "It was a little soupy."

Cari smiles. "Guess I'm less discerning."

"Or less rude," Julie says.

Cari laughs. "Anson told me both of you have experience in treating DNP poisoning?"

Goran shakes his head. "*Treating* implies some degree of success."

Julie nods. "It's a very helpless feeling to lose a patient to DNP."

"Different from other causes?" Cari asks.

"In our job, it's rare to see a patient who comes in awake and talking to you one minute, and dead the next. At least, not without us being able to do something to intervene."

"DNP is that poisonous?"

"You have no idea," Goran groans. "And the victims!"

"What about them?" Cari asks.

"It's always the same in these situations," Goran laments. "These predators—the ones who are selling this poison—this *explosive!*—they prey on the most vulnerable. The wounded elks of our society. It's no different from the drug dealers and traffickers on the street."

"It's beyond exploitative." Julie waves her glass. "These victims all have overwhelming body image issues."

"Which is mostly in their heads," Goran points out. "A delusion. Body dysmorphia is the psychiatric term."

Julie shakes her head. "Doesn't matter. To them it's the most real thing in the world. They would do anything or *take* anything to change the way they look to themselves."

"No matter how dangerous."

Anson returns to the table and takes his seat. "What did I miss?" he asks.

Ignoring him, Julie turns to Goran. "You were right to compare DNP to street drugs. Back when I was hooked on fentanyl—"

"Hooked, Julie?" Cari's forehead creases. "You?"

"I've been sober for the past ten years now. But yes, I'm an addict."

"Oh." Cari's look of surprise gives way to something that might be admiration. "Must take a lot of strength to overcome that."

"It was a brief spell," Goran says protectively. "And she was heavily influenced by her then fiancé."

"Brief but intense," Julie says. "And it was very much my choice, Gor. I understood I was risking my life every time I used. But I was in way too deep to let that stop me. It's got to be similar with DNP. Especially for those with an eating disorder."

"I know exactly how self-destructive eating disorders can be." Cari's voice is calm, but her eyes are now burning. "Trust me."

No one else says anything as they wait for her to expand. But after a moment, Cari clears her throat and then says, "I've been talking to families in LA. I've heard some tragic stories."

Sensing her guest's discomfort, Julie changes the subject. "I understand there are a lot of parallels between the recent deaths in LA and Vancouver."

"The overlaps are kind of uncanny," Cari says.

"That's a good word for it," Anson agrees. "Wish we could share more of the specifics."

"You can't?" Goran raises an eyebrow. "Wasn't Julija the one who alerted you to this DNP scourge in the first place?"

Julie pats Goran's arm. "They're in the same boat as we are. Client confidentiality and all."

He only snorts.

Anson caresses Julie's knee under the table. "You make a good point, Gor," he says. "Julie dragged me into this investigation, practically kicking and screaming. But it's an active investigation and a lot of the details are highly privileged."

Julie clutches Anson's hand, but she can't ward off the hurt. Despite her curiosity and the temptation, she kept her word to not pry further into the investigation. She wasn't expecting Anson to share the most privileged information, only to provide a general sense of its direction. But he seems determined to keep her in the dark. Between that exclusion, his intimate rapport with his new colleague, and the downplaying of his dreams about Nicole, Julie feels left out of his life right when they've taken a huge step toward building one together.

CHAPTER 29

Cari can't stifle her yawn as she sits across the table from the other two detectives inside the coffee shop. Theo glances from her to Anson, who had yawned only a minute or two earlier. "Am I the only one who got a decent night's sleep?" he asks.

"I had a bit more wine than I'm used to," Cari says, as she reaches for her coffee. "Plus, I've got jet lag as an excuse. Or do you have to change time zones for that to count?"

Anson shrugs unapologetically at Theo. "You and Eleni should've come."

"And leave all five boys alone in the house? There aren't enough firemen in this city to handle that potential blaze." Theo chuckles. "Plus, I was doing some actual police work."

"What a pleasant change for you," Anson says. "What kind of work?"

"For starters, I confirmed that both Dr. Markstrom and Braden Hollands have returned to LA."

"Oh, perfect."

"I'll be going back tomorrow, myself," Cari says. "I'll go see them both."

"That will help, thanks," Theo says.

"I wonder," Anson says with a doleful shake of his head. "It'll be tough enough to figure out if Markstrom gave Rain the DNP. But proving it?"

"One step at a time, Eeyore."

Cari enjoys the yin and yang of the other two detectives' personalities. Their rapport reminds her of what her partnership used to be like with Mattias before they complicated it with sex and love. And she even recognizes a similarity to their respective approaches: Theo is more detail oriented like Mattias, while Anson is more intuitive like she is.

"Also, Babar forwarded me something interesting," Theo continues.

"What's that?" Cari asks.

He pulls his phone out of his pocket and lays it on the table. A crack snakes up all the way from the bottom corner to the far one. Anson frowns at him. "You still haven't heard of screen protectors?"

Ignoring the comment, Theo says, "I didn't quite follow all the technical explanation, but Babar dug up a video promo for Dr. Slim Pharmaceuticals."

"I thought that site was dead," Cari says.

Anson nods. "Haven't all the Dr. X Pharmaceuticals gone dark?"

"They have, yes," Theo says. "It's a bit confusing, and I wasn't about to ask Babar to explain it twice—trust me. But it has something to do with screen recording or capture. In other words, some user recorded the original TikTok video and then uploaded it to his or her own page."

Cari points to the screen. "Can we?"

Theo taps a button. The electronic beat of a typical TikTok soundtrack plays even before a young woman appears in the narrow frame that fills only the center of the screen. With long hair and minimal makeup, she looks to be twentyish and has a cute though not particularly memorable face. In gray yoga pants and a matching bra top, she has the lean, sculpted physique of a beach volleyball player.

The woman is standing slightly off-center in the frame. And the camera is set low enough that she has to look down to gaze into the lens. The whole clip feels amateurish which, Cari suspects, is by design.

"Nope, nope, nope." The young woman wags her finger at the camera. "Wasn't always like what you see here before you. This used to be me." She snaps her fingers, and a still photo fills the screen. In it, she is wearing a similar outfit but her body is different. Her face is rounder, her arms thicker. Instead of muscles, the soft curves of her belly are visible with a fold of skin hanging over her waistband. "That's right. I was thirty-eight pounds heavier way back then." She pauses, and then adds with a giggle, "Eight weeks ago!

"I tried every diet known to man or beast—keto, Mediterranean, South Beach, vegan, you name it . . . I used to work out till I threw up. I starved myself. Nothing made a dent. Nada." As she continues to speak, time-lapse photos appear on the screen and her body slims from one image to the next. "Then I found Dr. Slim Pharmaceuticals. And . . ."

Her fit and animated form appears back on the screen. "One pill a day," she says. "Cheap, safe, and sooooo effective. Eat what you want. Do what you want. And it all still melts away!"

She leans in closer toward the screen as the music grows louder. "Eight weeks, people! Dr. Slim Pharmaceuticals changed my whole life." She runs a hand across the ripples of her abs and then offers an exaggerated shrug. "Might change yours, too."

"Brutal," Anson grumbles, as the screen goes dark. "Feeding off the insecurities of people like that. Mainly teenagers, I bet, too."

"It's the exact kind of guerilla marketing campaign we heard about!" Cari says. "Dr. X bombards TikTok and Instagram with these made-to-look-organic posts until they drive enough buyers to their latest pop-up website."

"Yup. Then they close up shop and move on to a new website. Rinse and repeat." Theo sweeps the phone off the table and stuffs it back into his pocket. "Interestingly, Babar believes the 'pre' images in the video are fake."

"As in photoshopped?" Anson asks.

Theo nods. "He thinks they're simulated to make the actor appear as if she used to be a lot heavier, when she never was."

"Can he track down the girl in the video?" Cari asks.

"Babar has been running the images through some facial recognition software. Nothing so far, though."

"Can you forward me the link?" she asks. "I'll get my computer guy at the LAPD to do the same."

"Will do."

Anson takes a long sip of coffee. "Aside from locating the actor, maybe, is there anything in the video that gets us closer to whoever's behind Dr. X Pharmaceuticals?"

Theo only shrugs.

Anson pushes himself up from the table. "Let's go see that guy at the wellness center."

Following him out of the café, Cari thinks about what her sister would have made of such manipulative online advertising. Lucia was always so impressionable, and Cari couldn't see her being able to resist that kind of outreach.

They drive less than a mile to a trendy commercial neighborhood lined with low-rise brick buildings and restored old factories. Anson pulls into a vacant parking spot on Mainland Street. As they enter the building, Cari almost misses the modest "Mind Over Body Wellness Center" placard posted above the large wooden door. Inside, the reception area smells vaguely of cinnamon and reminds her of the lobby of some five-star boutique hotel in Beverly Hills, down to the marble floors and splashy abstract acrylics on the walls.

The buff young man behind the desk wears a form-fitting, navy polo shirt with the "Mind Over Body" logo across the left breast. He has light blue eyes and, despite his brawn, delicate facial features. If Cari were in LA, she would've automatically assumed he was an aspiring actor.

"Welcome! I'm Colby," he says. "How can I be of service?"

"We're with VPD," Theo says, flipping open his badge. "We'd like to speak to Gerard Martin."

"Absolutely!" Colby says, unfazed. "Let me find him for you."

After a quick call, Colby hops to his feet and leads the detectives down a short hallway and into an office in the back. The man inside rises from his desk to meet them. In a matching navy shirt to Colby's, his chest is as well defined, but he looks to be twenty years older. And his stubbled, smiling face is far more rugged.

Theo makes a round of introductions, again neglecting to mention that Cari works for the LAPD, and then says, "We understand you're a business partner of Lloyd and Cecilia Hunter, Mr. Martin?"

"Gerard, please. And yes. They were our partners from the outset."

Theo tilts his head. "Our?"

"My girlfriend, Adèle, and me. We started the business together. The Hunters, they were our financial backers."

"Is Adèle here now?" Anson asks.

He shakes his head. "She'll be back later this afternoon."

"Were you close with Cecilia?" Theo asks.

Gerard rubs his chin as he considers the question. "We didn't socialize too much, but I always liked her. A lot. She had such incredible energy. And so fun. But no, I wouldn't necessarily say we were close. To be honest, Cecilia could be a handful."

"How so?"

"She loved to stir things up."

"Can you be a bit more specific?" Anson asks.

"Cecilia came from this posh English family. But she had a real rebellious streak to her. And her sense of humor had a real edge. She loved to push boundaries. And people." He pauses. "Occasionally, she went too far. It could get . . . uncomfortable."

"She made you uncomfortable?"

"No, not me," Gerard says. "I've outgrown social discomfort. But she loved to shock people. She'd say anything to get a rise. It could be challenging at times, especially for those who didn't know or, at least, understand her. And for Lloyd, too. But he never complained."

"Did Mrs. Hunter ever tell you she was taking DNP?" Theo asks.

"No."

"Her husband told us she was health-conscious to the point of almost fanatical," Theo says.

"Poor Lloyd." Gerard sighs. "He worshipped the ground Cecilia walked on. But it's true. Cecilia really took the old cliché to heart about her body being a temple."

"Doesn't sound like someone who would have knowingly taken a poison like DNP," Anson says.

"I . . ." He hesitates. "Probably not, no."

"What is it, Gerard?"

"Botox is a poison, too, right?" He clicks his tongue. "And Cecilia had no problem taking plenty of that."

"Not exactly the same, is it?" Cari points out.

"No. But Cecilia, she was consumed with her appearance. And it only got worse after she turned forty. The rigorous diet, the intense fitness regimes, even her sleep . . . it all boiled down to staying super-fit and looking youthful. She talked about it constantly. It was the main reason we didn't see eye-to-eye on our vision for the business. For Cecilia, Mind Over Body was *all* about the body."

"So it wouldn't surprise you if Cecilia experimented with DNP?" Theo asks.

"I have no idea." Gerard pauses, looking lost in thought. "But it was weird. She came here. To this office. A day or two after Rain died." He rubs the hardwood floor with the toe of his shoe. "She was shaken by the news. More than I would've expected. Especially considering she wasn't a fan of Rain's music."

"Shaken how?"

"Cecilia couldn't believe a diet pill could kill a healthy young woman." Gerard holds up his palms. "And look, maybe I'm reading into all of this with the benefit of hindsight. But she seemed kind of scared. And I can't remember another time I would've ever said that about Cecilia."

"Did you ask her why?"

"Never occurred to me. And I was late for a conference call with the lawyers in San Francisco. Must admit, I sort of rushed her out."

"She never told you she was taking any kind of supplements?" Theo asks.

"No."

"Had you heard about DNP before all of this?" Anson asks.

"Only after the news about Rain."

There's a brief lull in the conversation that Cari breaks by asking, "You run another wellness center in LA, don't you?"

"We do, yes."

"I'm a detective with the LAPD."

"OK . . ."

"Not sure you've heard," Cari says. "But we also have a spate of DNP-related deaths in Los Angeles. Matter of fact, we just set up a task force to deal with them."

Gerard exhales. "Everyone wants a quick fix."

"A quick fix?"

"I mean with the diet pills," he says. "But I don't see what a task force in LA has to do with what happened to Cecilia in Vancouver."

"Maybe nothing," Anson answers for Cari. "It's just that it's a bit of a coincidence that you're running centers in the same two cities with the biggest clusters of DNP deaths."

Gerard's forehead creases. "And you're surprised?"

"You're not?"

"Not really, no. Vancouver and LA are the epicenters for health and wellness on the West Coast. Arguably, anywhere."

"And how's that relevant?"

"Don't you get it, Detective? Pretty much every fitness, anti-aging, or weight loss craze—no matter how out there, or dangerous—takes off in LA and in Vancouver before anywhere else. From spin to Pilates and a shitload of forgettable fads in between. You name it." He chuckles. "Did you know that one out of every five hundred people in Beverly Hills is a cosmetic surgeon?"

Anson stares at Gerard for several seconds. The sound of weights clinking in the nearby gym fills the void. "But your partner didn't die from complications of cosmetic surgery," he finally says.

"She did not." Gerard gestures to the office door. "She also didn't die from yoga, massage, spin, meditation, or anything else we offer in this center."

"But apparently she did die striving for what you promise." Anson nods to the placard above the desk reading: CHANGE YOUR MIND AND YOUR BODY WILL FOLLOW.

"Our method puts the mind *before* the body."

Cari can't stop herself from asking, "Rain didn't happen to be a client of yours, too, did she?"

CHAPTER 30

"Where the fuck have you been?" Gerard growls.

Adèle stands in the office's doorway in her damp raincoat. "And good morning to you, too, *chéri.*"

"You mean afternoon, don't you?" He waves angrily toward the wall clock that reads 12:35. "You have no idea what I've been through this morning!"

She sidles over and swallows him in a hug, caressing the back of his neck. "Tell me, *chéri.*"

The scent of her hair and the pressure of her hip against his groin do nothing for him. *You're not going to fuck your way out of this one. Not today.* He wriggles out of her embrace and pushes her away by her shoulders. "The cops came. Detectives. Three of them!"

Adèle's eyes go wide. "*Three?*"

"Two from Vancouver, and one from LA."

"What's going on, Gerard?"

"They're investigating Cecilia's death. Lloyd, of course, told them about Mind Over Body."

"And they think we . . . ?"

"They're sniffing around. That much is clear."

"But, obviously, they don't know anything." Her voice cracks. "They can't, right?"

"They know too much already. And they're trying to link the DNP deaths in Vancouver and LA together." He experiences the same tightness around his throat as he did during the detectives' interrogation. "To us, maybe."

"No!"

"For fuck's sake, Adèle. They wanted to know if Rain was our client!"

"*Mon dieu*," she mumbles. But then her expression relaxes, and the familiar self-assurance returns to her gaze. "Maybe it's good they're looking in the wrong place?"

"But for how long?" he asks. "When they go back to see Lloyd—and trust me, they will—what if he tells them about our supplement?"

"He won't."

"How do you know?"

She runs a finger along her lower lip. "'Cause I'll convince him not to."

"That's not going to work. His wife just died, Adèle! He's grieving."

"What do you suggest, then?"

"For starters, that we get him to return those bottles to us. They can't do shit without them."

Adèle considers it for a moment. "Wouldn't it be even better if the police did find those bottles?"

Gerard grimaces. "What are you talking about?"

"What if they analyze a sample?"

"You know exactly what would happen!"

"Yes, but what if this sample contains nothing but harmless electrolytes and green tea extract?"

Gerard absorbs the suggestion. "Maybe, yeah." The constriction across his neck loosens. "But how?"

"I'll help Lloyd." Her eyes light with amusement. "I'll make sure he turns in the *right* bottles."

"You think you can convince him?"

"I have to, don't I?" she says with a confident shrug. "And Gerard, we're going to need to sanitize the bottles we still have here at the center. In case the cops come to check."

"I'll dump the ones containing the secret sauce."

Adèle reaches out and massages his shoulder. "We'll work it out, *chéri*. We always do."

"Maybe," he sighs. "But I'm beginning to regret ever going down this road."

Adèle's perfect lips break into a loving smile. "What choice did we have?"

She's right, as usual. Even with the Hunters' support, Mind Over Body was hemorrhaging cash after they opened their first center in Vancouver. Despite their quality product and polished pitch, clients weren't willing to pay what the center needed to charge to make their holistic approach profitable.

That all changed when, one day in line at a coffee shop in West Hollywood, Gerard bumped into a personal trainer he used to work with at a forgettable gym that had since gone out of business. After greetings, Gerard flicked a finger, indicating Aiden Cowell's taut form under his Lycra outfit. "Look at you, Aiden. You've gone full Adonis."

Aiden tilted his head. "You switch teams, Gerard?"

"Nah." Gerard chuckled, remembering what a dimwit his former colleague was. "I thought you were ripped back then. But now . . ."

"Yeah, well." Aiden shrugged. "I might have a picked up a trick or two."

Gerard had no real interest in chatting with him, but the line was hardly moving, so he asked, "Anything you can share?"

Aiden glanced around to ensure no one was listening. "Remember Katie?"

"Your girl, right?" Gerard pretended to have to scour his memory, when in fact he had been casually bedding Katie even after Aiden started dating her. Gerard found her as uninteresting as her boyfriend, but he enjoyed playing with her natural breasts and full butt.

"Yeah. Katie's been doing the supplement thing forever. Always fighting her mom's 'thick' genes, as she calls them. Anyway, she found this one that works. Like *works*, dude. Transformed her in a month or two into nothing but muscle and sinew."

"Transformed her, huh?"

"Me, too. As you noticed."

"What is this miracle supplement?"

"DNP."

The name meant nothing to Gerard, but he didn't want to sound igno-rant. "Some bodybuilders use that stuff, right?" he guessed.

Aiden laughed. "Those crazy fucks will take anything. But yeah. They do. For good reason."

"Where do you get it?"

Aiden looked over his shoulder and then lowered his voice. "Dr. Beef-cake Pharmaceutical. Ships right to your door. You should check it out."

Gerard had no intention of ordering anything from the ridiculously named website—let alone becoming one of their most loyal customers—but the conversation piqued his curiosity enough to do some online dig-ging. Aiden wasn't exaggerating. DNP was for real. Users raved about it online, posting photos to back up the claims of whole body transforma-tion. Gerard also saw the many reports about DNP's deadliness, which Aiden had failed to mention. But Gerard eventually saw a way around that risk by diluting the amount of DNP in their supplement to the point where it would still work but wouldn't be poisonous. He also recognized that he wouldn't have to add their "secret sauce" to all the bottles. They only had to succeed with a few key clients to create enough of the word of mouth—the *tipping point*—that Mind Over Body desperately needed. And his instincts proved right. Within weeks of giving out the first laced supplements to a few select customers, business began to boom.

Gerard was shaken when he later heard about Katie's death. But, by that point, he had already perfected their system. And months in and multiple bottles later, they had not had any scares with their own cli-entele. Katie's death only cemented his resolve to be even more careful while preparing the supplement.

Damn you, Cecilia, for making me deviate from the formula!

CHAPTER 31

"Theo had to go to Children's Hospital?" Cari frowns at Anson from the passenger seat. "Is his kid OK?"

"Are you kidding me?" Anson grunts. "Would be cheaper for Theo to get monthly parking there. Between sports injuries and sketchy boyhood decisions, seems like he's at that hospital all the time with one of his five sons."

Cari grins. "What's the occasion today?"

"I think it's the youngest, Alex. Or maybe the second youngest, Stefan. One of them needs a cast changed on a broken wrist." He smiles. "Possibly both."

"Wrists or sons?" Cari asks.

He chuckles. "Again, possibly both."

The skies have opened again, and Anson speeds up the wipers in a race to beat back the reaccumulating moisture. A thought occurs to him. "Maleeka said they weren't going to leave until later today, right?"

"Yup."

"OK." Anson flicks on his dashboard police light and then abruptly crosses over to the left lane.

"We're not going back to the station?" she asks as he completes the U-turn and shuts off the light.

"Let's go see if Maleeka knows whether Rain had any connection to Mind Over Body."

"Gerard said she didn't."

"And you trust Gerard?"

"Fair enough." Cari goes quiet for a few moments. "I can't stop thinking about that TikTok ad Theo showed us."

"Disgusting, wasn't it?"

"Could you imagine how effective it might've been on someone with body image issues? The promise of a cheap, effective, and painless panacea like that?"

Something about the way Cari says it makes her outrage sound personal to Anson. He's reminded of her intense reaction to the topic over dinner last night. Not wanting to pry, he only nods.

Cari stares dead ahead for a few seconds. "My sister died of an eating disorder. She was the same age as Rain. Twenty-three."

"Oh, Cari." Anson clears his throat, caught off guard by the intimate revelation. "I . . . that must've been tough."

"Very. On the whole family. Before and after she died."

"I mean, like, how could it not be, right?" he stammers.

She turns to him. "I keep imagining how susceptible Luci would've been to the kind of devious marketing we saw in that online ad."

"Very. No doubt."

"Sorry, Anson. Maybe that's TMI."

"I get it, Cari." He offers her a heartfelt smile. "I do."

"Thank you."

They go quiet for a while, until he motions to the precipitation pooling on the window beyond the arc of the wipers and says, "You must be looking forward to getting back to sunny and dry California."

"Not necessarily. The rain—even the cold—is a nice change. Our weather can be kind of monotonous from one season to the next."

"Trust me, seasonal variation is highly overrated."

She laughs. "Well, trust me. This rain is nothing. The storm I'm facing back home is more of the shit variety."

"Departmental politics?"

"Not only. The mother of one of the victims is a powerful state senator. Maybe a future governor. She is—understandably—out for blood. But it doesn't help me do my job."

"It never does when others get involved." He thinks of Julie momentarily. "No matter how well-meaning they are."

Anson pulls into the driveway of the Sutton Place Hotel again. They leave the car by the bell desk and head up to Maleeka's room. Anson knocks on her door, but no one answers. He knocks again, harder. After a few moments, he looks to Cari with a shrug. Just as he is about to turn away, the door opens.

Shawna is standing on the other side in another baggy sweatshirt, her bespectacled face creased with concern. "Yes?"

"We'd like to speak to your sister," Anson says.

"She's . . . resting."

"I thought you two were flying home today?" Cari says.

Shawna shifts from foot to foot. "Our flight doesn't leave till six or so."

"We need to speak to Maleeka before she leaves," Anson says.

Shawna hesitates and then says, "Maybe it's good you dropped by." She turns away from the door.

They follow her inside. "Why's that, Shawna?" Cari asks.

She motions to the closed bedroom door. "Before Mal lay down, she was acting weird."

"Can you be more specific?" Cari presses.

"I dunno. Irritable. Just kind of out of it. As if she'd taken something trippy. Like mushrooms or acid or whatever. But she bit my head off when I asked her. And then she insisted on lying down."

Cari rushes past Shawna and throws open the bedroom door. Anson and Shawna follow her inside.

Maleeka is lying under the covers. Her eyes are open but glazed over, and her cheeks are almost cherry red. At first, Anson assumes she is mumbling to herself, but then he realizes that she's humming. Maleeka doesn't even look at them. Instead, she stares up at her hands, her fingers weaving above her face.

Cari steps over to the bed and gently shakes Maleeka's shoulder. "Can you hear me, Maleeka?"

Maleeka turns her head abruptly. "Looky-who! The *poh-lease*! Back again. Ray-Ray is still gone. Long, long gone."

"What did you take, Maleeka?" Cari asks her.

Maleeka rotates her head away, focusing her attention back to her fidgeting fingers.

Cari rests her palm against Maleeka's forehead. "She's burning up, Anson!" she says as she reaches for her phone. "I'll call 911!"

Anson instinctively turns for the bathroom. Inside, he yanks open the drawer below the sink. It's filled with multiple cosmetic products, but his gaze is drawn to the pill bottles at the back of it. They all have the same white-and-blue packaging with a slick logo that reads "UltraHealth." He grabs them out of the drawer and begins popping off their lids. The first two bottles, labeled "Biotin" and "GABA," are full of the usual colored and shaped pills that he would expect to find inside a vitamin bottle. But the third one—labeled "Alpha Lipoic Acid"—contains only red-and-black capsules.

Are these the same DNP capsules Rain was also taking?

Anson pulls out his phone and taps Julie's number. She doesn't pick up until the fifth ring. "Hey, can I call you back later?" she says, sounding rushed. "I'm on shift and it's very—"

"I'm in a hotel room with a friend of Rain's," Anson says. "She's delirious and burning up. It has to be DNP, Julie. I found the capsules!"

"Call an ambulance!"

"It's on the way."

"Get her here as soon as you can, Anson!"

CHAPTER 32

Gowned, masked, and gloved, the team gathers in the resuscitation room. No one speaks, but most are busy tending to their own equipment. The whir of fans and the beeps and buzz of monitors fills the void. Julie doesn't even realize her foot is tapping the polished concrete until the charge nurse, Gayle, points it out with a raised eyebrow and a nod.

"Sorry." Julie stills her foot. "It's the anticipation. Never get used to it."

"Uh-huh," Gayle says.

Then Julie hears the distant pounding of feet and the distinct creak of wheels. "They're here!" she says, moving toward the doorway moments before the ambulance gurney flies through it.

"What have we got?" Gayle asks the two male paramedics—one redheaded and stocky, the other lean and bearded—who gently roll the young woman off their stretcher and onto the one in the room.

"Maleeka Khan," the bearded paramedic says. "Twenty-four years old. Presumed drug toxicity. Blood sugar normal. Vital signs—pulse, blood pressure, and oxygen saturation—all stable. But sensorium confused."

"Restless as anything, to boot," the redhead pipes up. "She practically flipped the stretcher rolling around so much. We almost had to restrain her."

"And the temperature?" Julie asks, stepping closer to the stretcher.

"We were too focused on starting IVs and keeping her in the stretcher to get a reading," the redhead says. "But it's gonna be high."

"Forty-one degrees," Sarah, the petite bedside nurse, calls out as she pulls the probe away from Maleeka's forehead.

"OK, team, let's get an IV dantrolene drip running," Julie says. "Give her two liters of cold saline as a bolus. Spray her down with ice water and start the fan."

"Any midazolam, Dr. Rees?" Sarah asks.

"Start with two point five milligrams IV. Repeat every five to ten as needed."

Maleeka keeps trying to raise her arms in the air and bring her hands to her face. Megan, the second nurse, a broad-shouldered Welsh woman who towers over Sarah, has to pin down Maleeka's arm so that her colleague can access the IV port.

Julie leans closer to the patient's face. "Maleeka, I'm Dr. Rees. Do you know where you are?"

"YVR," Maleeka mutters, using the initials for Vancouver's airport.

"That's right, Maleeka, Vancouver." Julie indicates their surroundings with a sweep of her finger. "But what kind of place is this?"

"Hospital?" She writhes on the stretcher, as if trying to slow-dance while horizontal.

"You're in the Emergency Department," Julie says, feeling the gust from the fan against her ear. "You took too many pills. DNP."

"Ray-Ray . . ."

"Exactly. The same ones Rain took. How many capsules did you swallow today, Maleeka?"

"Red-and-black, red-and-black. So lit. The way Shawn adores them." Maleeka giggles.

"Right. Red-and-black. Those are the DNP capsules, Maleeka. But how many did you take?"

Her eyes dart off to the far side, as if someone else is talking to her. Just as Julie is about to ask the question a third time, Maleeka says, "Two."

"You're sure, Maleeka? You only took two of them?"

Maleeka tries to raise her arm again, but the nurse keeps it pinned down. Instead, she extends two fingers with the hand that's held against the stretcher. "Only two. Never more. That's what I'd tell Ray-Ray. We can never take more."

"You were taking DNP with Rain? At the same time?"

Maleeka nods, then her gaze drifts off again. "Oh, Ray-Ray, I miss you . . ."

Julie exhales. If Maleeka did only take two hundred milligrams of DNP, she stands a better chance of surviving. She turns to Gayle. "Can you page ICU?"

Gayle flashes her a thumbs-up.

Out of the corner of her eye, Julie notices Maleeka's legs begin to twitch. "And another dose of midazolam. She could seize at any—"

Before Julie can even finish, Maleeka's eyes roll back. Then she begins to blink rapidly as her arms and legs thrash noisily against the stretcher. Megan lunges forward to pin her to the bed with her chest draped across Maleeka's midsection.

"Five milligrams of midazolam STAT!" Julie cries.

Sarah struggles to attach the syringe to the IV port in Maleeka's still flailing arm but manages to administer the medication. "Given."

"Prep for intubation, Tia," Julie says to the young respiratory tech at the head of the stretcher, thankful she remembers her name this time.

"Now?" Tia asks.

"Yes. We need to paralyze her and get her on the ventilator! We can't wait." Julie's heart sinks, remembering the CT scan images of Cecilia Hunter's fatally swollen brain after she had seized for too long.

Just as Tia wheels over the cart bearing all the intubation equipment, Maleeka's limbs stop moving, and she goes limp on the stretcher.

"Are you still going to intubate?" Tia asks.

"Absolutely," Julie says. "She could seize again any second."

With the patient unconscious and motionless, the intubation proceeds seamlessly. Julie easily passes the tube between her vocal cords. And in under two minutes, Maleeka is hooked up to the ventilator.

"Her temperature is down to thirty-eight point five," Sarah announces after a second check with the forehead probe.

"That's hopeful," Julie says. "Let's lower it even more. Can we place some ice packs in her armpits and groin?"

Five minutes later, the porter arrives to wheel Maleeka off for a CT scan, accompanied by Megan.

While her patient is in the CT scanner, Julie steps out of the resuscitation room to catch up with Anson and Cari, who wait inside the family room across the way.

"How's Maleeka?" Cari asks as soon as Julie steps inside.

"She's on the ventilator now," Julie says. "We've stopped her seizures. At least for the time being."

"Is she going to make it?"

"I can't say for sure, but I think so. Her temperature is coming down, which is a positive sign. And according to Maleeka herself, she only took two DNP capsules today."

Cari squints. "Two capsules can do all that damage?"

"And then some. DNP has an unpredictable metabolism. For example, someone might be OK if she were to swallow two pills after eating, but it could be a whole different story on an empty stomach . . ."

"Jesus! Could this crap be any more toxic?" Anson mutters. "Maleeka didn't happen to mention where she got them from, Julie?"

"Maleeka kept muttering about Rain. She admitted she was taking DNP along with her. But she wasn't clear about who gave the capsules to whom." Julie frowns. "And she also said something about a Shawn. Who's he?"

"Her sister, Shawna," Cari says.

"Oh," Julie says. "I couldn't really follow, but she was muttering something about Shawna liking the color scheme."

"The color scheme?"

"Yeah, she said something like 'red-and-black, the way Shawn adores them.'"

Anson rubs his chin. "Why would Shawna care?"

Cari turns to Anson. "You think the sister is taking them, too?"

"Who isn't these days?" he grumbles. "We better find out what Shawna really knows."

"Agreed. And the moment I touch down in LA, I'm going to track down this Dr. Markstrom character."

"Yeah. Him, too. For sure."

Beyond their words, Julie picks up on the fluid rapport between the two of them. As if they're on the exact same wavelength. Unlike her and Anson. But Julie dismisses the thought, feeling sheepish for thinking of herself while her patient is in critical condition. "I better get back to Maleeka."

"When will we know if she's going to be OK?" Cari asks.

"The next twelve hours are crucial. If she makes it through them, then she should be all right."

"Makes sense. Thanks."

Julie takes a couple steps toward the door but then turns back to them. "Two DNP capsules just about killed that girl. And if Maleeka didn't know any better—after seeing what happened to her best friend— then who the hell will?"

CHAPTER 33

As Cari walks out of the ER beside Anson, her phone buzzes in her hand. She recognizes the number on the call display and picks up immediately. "Hi, Zach. What's up?

"Rain, if you believe my Twitter feed, Detective."

"Rain? The singer?"

"One and the same," Zach says. "Fully resurrected, apparently. She's been spotted alive and well all over the place. Dancing in a park in Anaheim one moment, and hiking in Kauai the next. The Elvis Presley of our time."

"I'm guessing that's not why you called."

"I've also got some non-Twitter intel that might interest you."

Cari slows to a stop. She glances over to Anson, points to her phone, and mouths the words, "Have to take this."

"I'll track Shawna down," Anson says as he walks away. "See if she's already here."

"What intel?" Cari asks Zach.

"I haven't found a name behind the Dr. X Pharmaceuticals seller. *Yet.* But the Bitcoin exchange where the funds were deposited is, reluctantly, cooperating. They're working through the blockchain, and we should have more info on the seller soon."

"That's encouraging," she says, but her words come out sounding more half-hearted than she intended.

"Also, I'm now convinced the seller is based here in LA."

"Why's that?"

"I found a chink in their online armor."

"Which is?"

"They had to leave the dark web to email out order receipts."

"And that allowed you to track them?"

"Up to a point. I was able to dig up an old IP address used in one of the email receipts from Dr. Slim Pharmaceuticals."

A flicker of excitement runs through her. "Did it give you a physical location for Dr. X Pharmaceuticals?"

"Sort of."

"What does that mean?"

"I traced the IP back to a coffee shop in Inglewood. I think someone from Dr. X was tapping into the café's Wi-Fi to email those receipts."

"Brilliant, Zach!" Cari says, her chest fluttering. "And the name of the coffee shop?"

"Sip and Ponder Coffee Roasters. Just off Manchester and Cedar."

"This could be big, Zach. Really big."

"We'll see about that," he says, but he sounds pleased. "On another note, I did some digging into those prescription records for you."

"And?"

"Rain was taking those two antidepressants, but she'd never been prescribed Ozempic."

"I'm not surprised. Did you have a chance to—"

"Anders Markstrom, on the other hand, has been getting repeat prescriptions of it since 2019."

"That son of a bitch," Cari murmurs.

"Is this bad news?"

"No, Zach. It's good. All of it. You're a star! Thank you so much. I'll call you tomorrow as soon as I get back to LA."

After she disconnects, she sees a text from Anson on the screen that reads: "Shawna already here. In the family room."

Cari hurries back through the ER and into the family room. Anson is standing across from Shawna, who paces the small room like a trapped animal. As soon as she sees Cari, she spins to face her. "How's my sister?"

"I wasn't with her just now."

Shawna turns to Anson. "I'm family. I should be able to see her!"

"Like we discussed," Anson says. "As soon as the doctor gives us the clearance."

"She's on a ventilator!" Shawna cries. "We all know how that goes!"

"Your sister's poisoning is milder than previous cases," Cari says. "Maleeka took less of it. That's important, Shawna. The doctor is optimistic."

"And yet she's still on an effin' ventilator!"

"Did you know Maleeka was taking DNP?"

"If I had, I would've beaten her with a baseball bat. She's my little sister." Shawna swallows. "When Dad hears about this . . . it'll destroy him." Her voice falls to almost a whisper, and she begins to pace again. "He'll blame me. As usual. His little princess can do no wrong. Me? I can't do anything right. But of course, he always expects me to take care of her."

Cari can relate. She was in a similar predicament after the maid had found her sister's lifeless body on a bed in a random motel. Cari was the one who had to break it to her parents that Lucia was dead. The autopsy would later reveal that her heart stopped from a lethally low blood potassium level that was caused by starvation and diuretic abuse. Cari can still hear her dad's sobs over the phone, his accusing voice demanding to know why his baby daughter was staying in a one-star motel and not with her big sister.

Cari refuses to allow the empathy she feels for Shawna to get in the way of her job. "Forgive us for being skeptical, Shawna," she says. "But do you remember how adamantly Maleeka denied knowing where Rain got the DNP? Now we find out she was taking it with her all along."

Shawna sighs. "I love my little sister. I do. But we're night and day." She motions to her loose hoodie. "I hate attention. And I have trouble keeping weight on, as is. Last thing I need is DNP."

"Maleeka mentioned something to the ER doctor about you loving the colors of the DNP capsules," Anson says.

Shawna stops pacing and gapes at him. "You saw her! She was out of her head."

"Not that confused," he says. "She knew where she was. And how many pills she had swallowed."

Cari locks eyes with Shawna. "Were you taking DNP with your sister?"

Shawna shakes her head so hard that her glasses shake. "You're not going to throw me under the bus, too!"

Cari holds up a hand. "We're just trying to figure out what happened, Shawna."

"Fuck if I know!"

Anson frowns at Shawna. "Then why did your sister tell the doctor you 'adored' the capsules because they were red-and-black?"

"*Adored?* I never even saw them." Shawna's cringe gives way to a calmer expression. "Ah! I bet I know what she was talking about. I used to have this red-and-black checkered Mack jacket in school. I wore it all the time. Everyone thought I was queer, but whatever. I loved that jacket. That must've been what Mal meant."

Anson views her for a skeptical moment. "Did Maleeka or Rain ever mention anything about Mind Over Body Wellness Center?"

Shawna shakes her head again. "Never heard of it."

"And Maleeka never talked to you about DNP?" he presses. "Not even Rain's use?"

"Not until after Rain died," Shawna says. "And she told me exactly what she told you in her hotel room. That Rain admitted to using DNP, and Mal tried to talk her out of it."

"But it's possible—likely even—that Maleeka was the one who gave Rain those capsules."

Shawna shakes her head. "I can't see it."

"How else do you explain it?" Cari asks.

"Why aren't you talking to that creepy therapist? He was the one who gave Rain that diabetic medicine to lose weight. What makes you think he wouldn't have given her DNP, too?"

"Is that what you think?" Cari asks. "That Dr. Markstrom gave Rain DNP, and then your sister stole it from her after she died?"

"Maybe? Who knows?" Shawna's lip curls. "DNP was just part of that incredibly fake world of theirs. For Rain *and* my sister. All that in-crowd scene bullshit. They both needed the attention so badly. To be accepted. To be loved. They would've done anything to get that."

Cari circles a finger in the air. "Even if it meant ending up in the hospital?"

"Hundred percent. Those two would've crawled over broken glass. Or swallowed poison." Shawna chuckles bitterly. "Clearly."

CHAPTER 34

Gerard climbs off the spin bike, his quick-dry shirt soaked in sweat. He feels hot and breathless, but he is no more settled than when he began the intense ride an hour ago. "Where are you?" he asks the empty room.

Colby pops his head into the spin studio. "You looking for me, boss?"

"No, Colby. Go home. I'll lock up."

Colby taps his fingers to his brow in a mock salute. "Won't say no to that. Not on a date night," he says and then disappears again.

Gerard has no idea if Colby's date will be male or female. For a moment, he wonders if it might even be with Adèle. After all, it's almost six p.m. and there's still no sign of her. She promised to be back with their bottles long before dinner. Gerard has already texted twice, but she hasn't responded. *Where the hell are you?*

He heads into the men's room and has a long, eucalyptus-scented steam shower. But even that does nothing to quell his growing anxiety. As he's changing into clean clothes, he hears the ding of the entryway motion detector. With his shirt half-buttoned, he rushes toward the reception area.

From the hallway, Gerard spots Adèle leaning against the reception desk. His immediate relief is tempered by the pained look on her face and turns into confusion when he rounds the corner and sees Lloyd standing by the doorway, cradling one of their trademark two-liter green bottles in his arm.

"*Bonjour, chéri.*" Adèle steps over to brush her cheek against Gerard's. With their faces touching, she whispers, "He insisted. I think he knows."

Gerard kisses her cheeks and then eases out of the embrace. "Hey, Lloyd. How are you holding up?"

Lloyd's shoulders rise and fall. "You know."

I wish I did. Gerard musters a smile. "Did you try Adèle's lasagna?"

He shakes his head. "No appetite."

"No appetite required. It's that good. Trust me."

Lloyd stares back at him without comment for an awkward moment. Then he raises the bottle in his arm. "Adèle tells me you're looking for this."

She flashes Gerard a helpless look but says nothing.

"Matter of fact, um . . . yes," Gerard stutters. "Sure. We . . . er . . . thought that the detectives might want to . . ."

Lloyd straightens. "You do realize I work in mining, don't you?"

Gerard has no idea what the comment means, but he senses trouble. "Of course I do." He forces a laugh. "I've seen the splashy CoreGold logo on the side of your jet."

Lloyd takes a few steps over to the reception desk and slowly lowers the bottle onto the counter. "In the mining business, we're forever sampling new sites. Looking for specific mineral veins."

Gerard glances over to Adèle, but she looks as lost as he feels. "I . . . I guess you'd have to," he says.

"And the thing about sampling is that you need sophisticated analytics to know exactly what you're dealing with."

Gerard twigs to Lloyd's point. "Analytics, huh?"

"Liquid, multistage chromatography," Lloyd says blankly. "You should see our testing site. It resembles the bridge of some starship. And costly?" He whistles. "You have nō idea!"

Gerard squares his shoulders, willing himself to stop playing the mouse to Lloyd's cat. "What are you telling me?"

Lloyd raises the bottle again. "I had it analyzed, Gerard."

"Did you?"

Lloyd chuckles bitterly. "Cecilia, she was always more cynical than me." He points from Adèle to Gerard. "She used to say that there's no way you two could get the results you did from just yoga, spin, and positive thinking. She was convinced there had to be more to your supplement. Something a bit more . . . to use her word . . . nefarious."

Adèle holds up her hands. "Lloyd, listen—"

"But I used to tell her: look at me!" Lloyd pats his belly. "I am guzzling their supplement, and I'm no slimmer for it. So, imagine my surprise to find out that your supplement contains . . ." He reaches into his jacket pocket, pulls his out his phone, and then puts on his reading glasses. "Magnesium, Vitamins B and D, green tea extract, iron . . ." He lowers the phone. "Oh, and 2,4-Dinitrophenol. Better known as DNP."

Adèle steps closer to him. "Lloyd, we had no idea!"

But Gerard waves her back. "What do you want me to say?"

Lloyd views him with a look that borders on triumphant. "How about, for starters, 'I'm sorry I poisoned your wife'?"

Gerard shakes his head. "Just how naïve are you?"

Lloyd's eyes narrow. "I wouldn't go there if I were you," he says quietly.

Gerard folds his arms across his chest. "How do you think you get noticed in the hypercompetitive, desperately overcrowded world of fitness and health? By playing by the rules? Maybe by adding another yoga class? Or changing the mantra in your meditation sessions?"

"Gerard . . ." Adèle says in a low warning voice.

But he dismisses her with a flick of his hand. "You break the rules, Lloyd. You find something to give your pampered, entitled clients an extra edge that none of your competitors can offer them. Another way for those filthy rich assholes to cheat the system like they do in almost every other aspect of their lives."

Lloyd shakes a finger at him. "You poison them, is that it?"

"Of course not!" Gerard snaps. "That would be the worst marketing campaign ever. No. You carefully dilute the DNP to a level that wouldn't be dangerous to anyone. To a level where you would die of water poisoning before you ever reached DNP toxicity. You make it as safe as the fluoride in the drinking water. That's why we've never had a problem with any of our clients."

Lloyd huffs. "Until you killed Cecilia."

"We didn't kill her," Gerard says calmly. "As you said, Cecilia knew for months what we were up to."

Lloyd scoops the bottle off the counter. "Even if that were true—which I highly doubt—how does that change anything?"

Gerard pats his chest. "She came to me."

The bottle shakes in Lloyd's hand. "No. No way."

"She did." Gerard points down the hallway. "She stormed into my office. Days before her death. She demanded a more potent form of the supplement."

"She just waltzed in and demanded your poison, did she?"

"Yes, Lloyd, demanded. Threatened even, in her subtle way."

"What could she threaten you with?"

"Exposure."

"Oh, I get it." Lloyd snorts. "Cecilia was blackmailing you. And the easiest way to deal with that was by poisoning her."

"Poison her? How could I? She didn't even want the supplement for herself!"

Lloyd frowns. "What does that mean?"

"It was for *you*, Lloyd!" Gerard runs a finger up and down, indicating the other man's body. "She was tired of all your flabbiness. She insisted I give you something more potent. To make you more presentable!"

"No . . ."

"Yes! And what I gave her was hardly any more potent than our regular supplement. Barely double the concentration of DNP."

"She's dead, Gerard. Dead!"

"And that's a tragedy. Truly. But I've got no fucking idea why. What I gave her shouldn't have been strong enough to make her sick, let alone kill her."

Lloyd eyes him for a long, bitter moment. "Intentional or not, you did kill Cecilia."

Gerard shrugs. "If that's the case, then we all killed her."

"*We?*" Lloyd lets out what almost sounds like a cackle. "Are you out of your goddamned mind?"

"Take that analysis of yours to the cops." Gerard dares him. "Hell, give

them the bottle! And then explain to them how you were an equal partner from the ground up in a business that upended the wellness industry
in under two years. That returned ten or twenty times—maybe a hundred
times—on your original investment. And how, the whole time, you were
oblivious to the secret sauce we were adding to our supplement."

Lloyd points an accusing finger at Gerard. "That's exactly what I will
tell them."

Gerard looks over to Adèle. A familiar, almost tranquil, calm has
returned to her face. "And we will tell them otherwise, Lloyd." He smiles
for the first time in hours. "We'll say that our money guy, our business
adviser—a mining exec with access to complex analyzers and world-
class equipment—was the one who gave us the idea. To get a leg up
over the competition. He was the one who insisted we add DNP to our
supplement."

CHAPTER 35

"Thanks for choosing a place that's only two minutes from my hotel," Cari says, as she sits across the table from Anson, nursing her glass of Bia Saigon lager.

"Wish I could tell you that's why I chose it," Anson says.

"No?"

"I had a mad craving for pho tonight, and this is my favorite Vietnamese spot in town." He grins. "But I'm glad the commute worked out for you."

"Happy coincidence then." Cari tips her glass to him. "Too bad Theo couldn't make it."

"Getting Theo out on a weekend evening is no easy feat, but a weeknight . . ." He waves the idea away as if it were laughable.

"And I'm sorry Julie has to work."

"She was going to try to join us after her shift, but after what happened with Maleeka . . . she got swamped."

Anson isn't convinced that work is the only reason Julie didn't join them. "I'm pretty tied up here," she told him coolly when he called her on the way to the restaurant. "Besides, if it's just you and Cari, I'm sure you'll be able to share a lot more without me there."

Cari takes a small sip of her beer, and then says, "I don't know how Julie does it. I could never be an ER doc. All that chaos . . ."

"She says that behind all the drama we see from the outside, the ER is usually a pretty mundane place to work."

"Yeah, sure. Mundane. Maybe if you happen to be, say, a bomb squad technician with a tic."

Anson chuckles and raises his glass to toast her. "I'm going to miss you, Detective Garcia."

"Likewise."

"To be honest, having you here has been a lot more useful than I expected."

She clinks her glass to his. "Maybe that's the secret to a happy partnership?"

"What is?"

"Having it last for only a few days."

He studies her for a moment. "Hmmm."

Cari cocks an eyebrow. "Yes?"

"That's the second time you've mentioned partnerships that way . . ."

"What way?"

"In a problematic sense."

"I won't do it again. Promise." She takes a longer sip of beer. "About Maleeka . . . did Julie give you an update on her condition?"

"She's in the ICU, still on the ventilator. But it sounds like she's going to make it."

"I'd love to talk to her when she gets off the ventilator."

"Julie figures it will be a couple of days, minimum. You'll be long gone."

"Wheels up tomorrow at eight a.m.," she says. "What does your gut tell you, Anson?"

"About?"

"Do you think Maleeka gave Rain the DNP? Or vice versa? Or did Maleeka just swipe the bottle after her friend died?"

"Any of the above." Anson shrugs. "Or maybe Markstrom gave it to both of them?"

"Can't wait to chat with that guy."

Anson sighs. "This case . . . it has so many loose threads. Then again, maybe that's because it's a bunch of different cases."

"How do you figure?"

"Are the DNP deaths in Vancouver and LA even related?"

"We've tracked orders in both cities back to the same Dr. X Pharmaceuticals."

"But not to Rain. Or to Cecilia Hunter."

"It's all related, Anson." Cari studies him intently. "We have two cities with a disproportionate number of DNP deaths. Rain came from LA, only to die in Vancouver. And one of the potential suspects in Cecilia Hunter's death happens to run a wellness center in each city. How could all of that be coincidence?"

"Probably not."

"Think how much further ahead we are than we were even two days ago." Cari raises her glass again. "We have a conduit to Rain's DNP supply, through Maleeka and/or Markstrom. And we now have an address in Inglewood that's directly linked to Dr. X Pharmaceuticals, *the* main distributor of DNP."

"I guess."

"We're getting closer, Anson, we are. I feel it."

He nods, although he doesn't share her optimism. "I hope so."

The waiter arrives with a large bowl of pho noodles for each of them and a plate of *ban khot* shrimp pancakes to share.

The food smells delicious and they both dig in, but after Anson slurps down a mouthful of the soupy noodles, he says, "Tell me to beat it if I'm being too nosy . . ."

Cari finishes a mouthful of the pancake before replying. "About?"

"Considering your family's history, Cari, isn't this case kind of . . . emotional for you?"

She puts her chopsticks down. "My favorite instructor in training used to tell us never to catch feelings. That they're 'kryptonite' to an investigation."

"Yeah, well, did he share any tricks to stop being human?"

"I wish," she groans. "Yes, this investigation has brought back memories. A bunch I'd prefer not to remember."

"I bet."

"There's guilt, for sure," she says.

"Every family goes through that, right?"

"There are things I could've done differently with my sister. That I *should* have done differently, Anson. Maybe they wouldn't have changed anything, but . . ."

"Cari, if we can get to the bottom of this—at least by shutting down Dr. X Pharmaceuticals—then it might feel like justice . . . or at least retribution for what happened to your sister?"

"Shouldn't be about my sister. Or me."

"Doesn't matter what should be. It matters what is." He lowers his spoon. "Julie and I, we fell for each other while working a case together last year that affected us, personally."

"What kind of case?"

"There was this super-potent fentanyl circulating in the city and killing people. And it became very personal for Julie."

"Because of her own history with drugs?"

"Yes." Anson reaches for his glass. "Professional lines were blurred that shouldn't have been. But when it was all said and done, the closure was good for Julie. For both of us, actually."

"She slayed her demons, did she?"

"I'm way too cynical to buy into that pop psychology BS. But I do believe in karma. And trying to even the score sometimes."

"Maybe. Yeah."

He eyes her for a moment and then breaks into a little grin. "And to do that, all we have to do is glue this priceless vase of a case together from a million broken pieces."

She smiles back. "Love me a good challenge."

Anson takes another spoonful of pho. "Time will tell."

"It's encouraging to see what you and Julie have got."

"I guess," he says, though he is not feeling particularly encouraged at the moment. "Our secret is that we're both damaged souls."

"Everyone is damaged, Anson," Cari says nonchalantly. "At least anyone who's interesting."

"Maybe, but we each lost our previous partner. Julie, her fiancé, and me, my wife. As in, they died. And talk about self-blame." Anson surprises himself with his candor. "In one sense, that binds us. But it also . . ."

"Makes you more vulnerable?"

He shrugs. "Moving in together has been more of an upheaval than I think either of us expected."

"I get the strong sense that you two will work out the kinks."

He looks down, embarrassed for having shared more than he'd intended. "Hope you're right."

CHAPTER 36

Gerard loves the feel of Adèle's breast against his arm as they lie naked and sweaty in their bed. They made love again as soon they got home, after already having frantic sex in the yoga studio after the speechless Lloyd stormed out.

"That performance, *chéri*," Adèle says, as she snuggles her head into the crook of his neck. "Like watching a ballet master at work. Brilliant! And you know how attracted I am to intelligence."

Gerard laughs. "Not sure about brilliant. But I was getting tired of that clown pulling all the strings."

Her tone turns serious. "You're not worried he'll still go to the police, are you?"

"He has no evidence other than the two bottles I gave Cecilia, and he left one of those here," Gerard says with confidence. "As I told him, it would be his word against ours."

"But *chéri* . . ."

He caresses her cheek. "At the end of the day, he's a businessman, babe. Even if he could turn us in without getting caught in the crossfire, he would end up losing everything he sank into Mind Over Body. Not to mention the lawsuits. He'd probably lose his CEO job. And his precious jet! How could he risk all that? Why would he?"

"He loved Cecilia," Adèle says. "A lot."

"When he calms down, he'll realize that she did this to herself. And he has nothing to gain by exposing us."

"But how do we stay partners with him?"

"That's the beauty of it!" Gerard laughs again. "We don't."

She sits up in the bed and twists her lithe upper body to face him. "I'm not following, *chéri*."

"You know we've been wanting to buy him out forever, babe, but he was never willing."

"Why would he be any more cooperative now?"

"It never was about the money for Lloyd. Not really. Lloyd—and especially Cecilia—they loved being part of this ride. It made them feel important."

"It's true."

"But do you think he's going to want to stay in a partnership with us now?"

"Probably not, no."

"Definitely not," Gerard says. "It won't be cheap. Lloyd will grind us for every dime. But let him. In six months, it won't matter what we have to pay."

Adèle's face creases as she does the mental calculation. "Let's assume we do buy him out. What stops him from turning us in the minute the deal closes?"

"Part of the sale will include an ironclad nondisclosure agreement. Besides, he now knows that if we're ever exposed, he will be, too."

"You think so?"

"I know so, babe." He rubs the side of her abdomen, his arousal stirring. "As annoying as Cecilia was, I'm sorry for what happened to her. I am. But in a way, things are working out even better because of it."

"Gerard!"

"What? It's true."

"But without our supplement . . ."

"We still have our supplement! It looks the same as ever."

"Yes, but it won't work the same."

He reaches over and cups her chin. "Don't you see, babe? We don't need the secret sauce anymore."

"Why not?"

"Because we've already established our brand. The word is out. Mind Over Body is the best wellness product on the market. Bar none."

CHAPTER 37

Julie steps into Leanne Melnyk's office inside the Eating Disorder Clinic to find her friend behind her desk, typing at her laptop. At the sound of Julie's approach, Leanne yanks off her glasses and looks up with a lopsided grin. "That was quick."

"I was just downstairs in the ER. Your text sounded important."

"Don't know if it is or not," Leanne says. "But after our last chat, I thought you'd want to hear this."

"Regarding DNP?"

"Possibly."

Julie taps her chin. "You're being kind of mysterious, Lee."

"No one's ever used that word to describe me before. I mostly get 'open book.'" She chuckles as she rises from her seat. "Might be best if you hear it from the horse's mouth?"

"One of your patients?"

"Yeah. Tracy McGowan. She's a forty-one-year-old real estate agent who's fought anorexia since her teens. She's been in remission—for the most part—for the past few years." Leanne motions to the door. "I asked her to hang around in the waiting room, in case you could join us."

"I'd love to hear what she has to say."

Leanne heads for the door. "Let me get her."

While Julie waits, she studies the only framed photo on the desk. In front of a snowy backdrop, Leanne and her husband, Phil, flank their three kids, who are bundled in winter jackets. Their oldest child, Thomas, is holding up the youngest, Jillian, whose smile is almost ear to ear, while the middle child, Angela, looks down shyly. The photo is so idyllic that, were it any other family, Julie might have rolled her eyes in disbelief, as though it were some deliberately staged portrait of family bliss that had popped up on her Instagram feed. But the slightly exasperated look behind Leanne's smile epitomizes her as a mother—happy and loving, but not afraid to let it be known when her kids are annoying her, which is not infrequently.

Leanne steps back into the office followed by a lean woman in a loose sweatshirt and jeans. "Tracy, this is my friend, Dr. Rees," Leanne announces.

"It's Julie," she says as she returns the woman's bony handshake.

Leanne gestures to the chairs in front of her desk. "Please." Once they're all seated, she says, "You're comfortable telling Julie what we discussed, right, Tracy?"

"Absolutely! I want to share, if it's relevant to what's going on," Tracy says in a rapid-fire cadence.

"I'd love to hear," Julie says.

"Obviously, I wouldn't be in this office if I didn't have an eating disorder," Tracy says. "I think I've been doing a lot better over the past year or two."

"You absolutely have," Leanne says.

"But as with any addiction, eating disorders never go away. You just try to manage them." Tracy nods to herself. "My weight has been fairly stable. But I'm never going to stop obsessing over it. All I can do is try to eat healthy. Stay off the scales. And exercise. In moderation, of course."

"Makes sense," Julie says, impatient to find out how any of this is relevant.

"At some point or other, I've joined almost every fitness place on the Westside. You name the fad—spin, Pilates, CrossFit, HIIT . . . I could go on forever. Not to mention the thousands of hours with personal trainers. But about three months ago, I found a gym that really fits me. It's more than a gym, actually."

"How so?"

"They call it a wellness center. Mind Over Body Wellness Center, to be exact. And, believe me, the membership price tag more than matches the fancy name. But a good friend of mine, Darlene, she swore by it. And I thought to myself, 'You've tried everything else, Tracy. Why not give this a whirl?'"

"OK . . ." Julie glances over to Leanne, who reassures her with a subtle nod that it's all relevant.

"I loved it from Day One!" Tracy says. "I'd never seen anything like it. Such Cadillac service. And the couple who runs it offer such a personal touch. Like you really matter to them. Like they care about your results. And trust me, in that business it's not always the case. I've had some—"

"Sounds great, Tracy, but . . ." *Get to the point, woman!*

"As I said, it's not just a gym. For example, they run the best yoga classes I've ever been to, especially when Adèle teaches. And they have these fascinating experts on health and anti-aging who come give lectures three times a week that you can watch in person or online. Also, they offer this supplement—"

"As in a dietary supplement?" Julie sits up straighter.

"More of a general health supplement. It comes premixed. The stuff costs an arm and a leg! But Darlene raved about it. She convinced me to try it, and within a couple days, I was hooked. It gave me this noticeable boost in energy. You're only supposed to drink up to a liter a day. But me being me and all, sometimes I'd drink two."

Julie can feel her neck tingle. "Does this bottle list its ingredients?"

"No. The label only says that it's nut-free and hypoallergenic. They claim it's a proprietary formula or something."

Leanne shifts forward. "Tell her, Tracy. What you told me."

"I've been trying this kind of stuff for most of my adult life. I've taken so many different supplements over the years. But the one from Mind Over Body was different." Tracy squeezes her bony nape between her thumb and forefinger. "It worked! I felt so energized. I was thrilled with it. Absolutely thrilled. That is, until I heard about Rain."

"What does Rain have to do with Mind Over Body?" Julie asks.

"Well, her death hit me hard. Not only was I a big fan, but I felt . . .

connected. Through our eating disorders, and all. Until Rain died, I'd never even heard of DNP. Then I began to read up on it. Look, I'm not trying to present myself as an expert or anything, but—"

Julie could shake the woman. "What about the DNP, Tracy?"

"I found this webpage that described DNP poisoning as a spectrum. It listed all the symptoms, from practically nothing to death. And when I read about the mild symptoms—like dizziness, heart pounding, sweating, and especially the heat sensitivity—it reminded me exactly of how I'd been feeling since I started taking the supplement. In fact, my mom has thyroid problems. She convinced me to get my thyroid tested. It was normal, of course, but you can never be too safe with these things . . ."

Tracy keeps chattering, but Julie tunes out the rest of her words. She reaches out and grabs Tracy's skinny forearm. "Are you still taking it?" she asks.

"The supplement? No! That article freaked me out. I haven't taken any in days."

"And the bottles?" Julie asks, as she frees the other woman's arm. "Do you still have any of them?"

"No. I panicked and drained the last two bottles down the sink."

Leanne stares hard at Julie. "You're the toxicologist. Could this wellness center have been dissolving DNP into their supplement? Would anyone take that kind of risk?"

Julie considers it. "If they truly control the dilution, they could ensure—at least, theoretically—that the DNP level is subtoxic." She turns to the other woman. "You said you were drinking twice the daily recommended amount, Tracy?"

"Most days." She looks down, sheepishly. "Some days I would drink three times."

"Which is probably why you began experiencing symptoms. And also, you're on the lighter side. You'd be more susceptible."

Leanne's face scrunches. "Who would play that kind of Russian roulette with people?"

"In a twisted way, it does kind of make sense," Julie says, thinking out loud. "They dilute the DNP to a level where there's still a degree of weight loss, but low enough to where you'd have to guzzle gallons of the stuff to make it poisonous."

"That's insanity!" Leanne cries. "Not to mention a crime."

"It's not as crazy as you think," Tracy says. "People are so desperate for results, Dr. Melnyk. And with the prices this outfit charges . . ."

Julie hops to her feet. "Thank you so much for taking the time to talk to me, Tracy," she says. "I happen to know the detectives who are investigating these DNP deaths. I hope you don't mind if I pass along—"

"I'd be happy to speak to them!"

"I'll get your contact information from Dr. Melnyk, and I'll put them in touch with you." Julie adds as she hurries to the door. She blows a quick kiss to Leanne on the way out, without slowing.

The moment Julie reaches the hallway, she calls Anson.

"Hi, you," he answers cheerfully. "How's work?"

"Mind Over Body Wellness Center," she says.

He pauses a long moment. When he speaks again, his voice is subdued. "What about it?"

"You know it?"

"Yes."

"I'm just leaving the Eating Disorder Clinic. I spoke to one of Leanne's patients. Who also happens to be a client of Mind Over Body's. She thinks that this wellness center is lacing their supplement."

"*Lacing?*"

"With DNP." Anson goes quiet again. And Julie senses the distance growing between them once more. At least, that's how it feels to her. "What is it, Anson? What aren't you telling me?"

"Your patient," he finally says. "Cecilia Hunter."

"What about her?"

"She was a co-owner of Mind Over Body."

CHAPTER 38

Stepping outside the terminal at LAX, Cari appreciates the warmth of the California sun on her face. But she can't stop thinking about the texts that popped up on her screen as soon as the plane touched down and her phone reconnected to cellular service.

The first shock came from Anson. He'd texted her about a client of Mind Over Body's who suspects the wellness center of lacing their supplement with DNP. But the other text, from Mattias, was even more unsettling. "Coming to LA tomorrow," he wrote. "Can't wait to see you!"

For a moment, the prospect of seeing him gave her butterflies. But anger soon edged out the nostalgia. More than his manipulativeness, Cari is annoyed with herself for being so needy and susceptible. As she waits for her driver at the rideshare pickup zone, she sends an intentionally terse reply: "Don't bother. I won't see you."

Her driver pulls up to the curb in a green Toyota RAV4 with a prominent dent in the front fender. After Cari climbs in and greets the driver with a small wave, her phone rings and "Benny" appears on the call display. "Hi," she answers.

"How was Canada?" Benny asks. "Cold, I bet."

"Rainy, for the most part," she says as the car pulls away. "Still, Vancouver is such a gorgeous city."

"Don't I know it! I've played there with the Philharmonic. And the scenery doesn't end with the mountains or the ocean." He whistles. "How about the men in that town?"

She thinks of how stylish Anson always looked in his form-fitting suits, but all she says is, "I was a bit busy for that kind of sightseeing. But it was a productive trip."

"Better have been. Your task force is all over the news these days."

Cari sighs. "Wonderful."

"Mainly because everyone is dying to know who killed Rain. Including yours truly."

"Rain took the pills herself, Benny."

"I mean who her Dr. Conrad Murray was."

"Who's that?"

"Remember? The cardiologist who went to jail for killing Michael Jackson with that elephant tranquilizer. Propofol, wasn't it? He took it as a sleeping pill."

Another doctor—of the PhD variety—comes to mind. "We're not there yet, Benny."

"Hurry up! The suspense is killing me."

"Mattias texted," she says, deliberately changing the subject. "Said he was coming to LA tomorrow."

"*No!* To see you?"

"Sounds like."

"Don't you dare, Caridad!"

"I told him I wouldn't see him."

"Thank God! Now block his number."

Why haven't I yet? she asks herself. Her phone dings with another incoming call, which reads "Captain" on the call display. "I gotta run, Benny. Dinner tomorrow?"

"A given. But you better not show up with a plus one."

Cari taps the button on the screen to switch calls. "Hi, Captain. I just landed."

"Welcome back," he says. "Are you coming in now?"

"Soon. I've got a couple stops to make on the way."

"All right, but I expect a full debrief by this afternoon. The media is restless. And hungry."

Which explains your interest.

Twenty minutes later, the driver drops Cari off at her condo in the Echo Park neighborhood. She considers leaving her bag and grabbing a quick shower but decides instead to head straight down to her car in the garage. She realizes Dr. Markstrom might not be at his Santa Monica office, but since she doesn't want to give him any warning of her visit, she decides to take the chance.

With a drab gray waiting room which only has space for a handful of chairs, Markstrom's fifth-floor office is more modest than what Cari was expecting. A woman with stringy gray hair and thick glasses looks up, uninterested, from behind the reception desk. "Do you have an appointment with Dr. Markstrom?"

"I'm Detective Garcia with the LAPD." Cari flashes her identification. "I need to speak to him now."

"He's in a meeting."

"This can't wait, ma'am," Cari says as she strides past the desk and down the short hallway toward the closed door at the far end.

Cari knocks at the door. "Dr. Markstrom?"

"Yes? Who's there?"

"Detective Garcia, LAPD." She turns the knob and opens the door without waiting for a reply.

Inside, a diminutive, balding man with a polka-dotted bow tie pops up from behind his desk. Across from him sits a man in a tight gray suit with one leg crossed over the other, his Gucci loafers on full display.

"What's this concerning, Detective?" Dr. Markstrom demands.

The other man rises to his feet. "I probably should give you two some privacy."

"And you are?" Cari asks, although she already has a strong suspicion.

"Braden Hollands," he says, offering her a Hollywood smile.

"Why don't you stay as well, Mr. Hollands?" she says. "I was planning to interview you later anyway."

Shrugging, Braden eases himself back onto the chair.

"If this is concerning Rain Flynn, I already gave a statement to the police in Vancouver," Dr. Markstrom says pointedly, as he lowers himself down, too.

Ignoring the remark, Cari looks from one man to the other. "Were either of you aware that Rain was using DNP?"

"Definitely not," Braden says.

"I'd never even heard of it until after she died," Markstrom says. "As her therapist, I would have intervened."

"Ah," Cari says. "You mean if you knew she was abusing substances for weight loss?"

"Yes. Certainly, one as dangerous as DNP."

"But not if she were abusing say . . . something like Ozempic?"

Markstrom eyes her impassively, but Braden grimaces. "What's that?"

"A diabetic drug that's also popular for weight loss," Cari says.

"As I told the Vancouver detectives," Markstrom says evenly, "I do not have a license to prescribe medication."

"Maybe, but what you *failed* to mention to them is that you've been prescribed Ozempic yourself for the past two years."

Braden's eyes dart to the therapist. "What's she talking about, Anders?" he asks.

But Markstrom only glares at Cari.

"Were you giving Rain your own prescription medication?" she asks.

Markstrom stares at her for another few seconds before he says, "To be accurate, Rain was taking it from me."

"But you didn't stop her?"

He shakes his head.

"Why not?" Cari asks.

"Because I was afraid if I did, she would only abuse something much more dangerous in its place."

"I thought you said you'd never heard of DNP?"

"That is not what I'm referring to, Detective."

"No? What then?"

Markstrom leans back in his seat. "When Rain first came to me as a client, she was abusing cocaine and other stimulants, such as Adderall."

Cari tilts her head. "Are you saying she was addicted?"

Braden holds up a hand. "You sure you don't want your attorney present for this, Anders?"

"Oh, I wouldn't describe it as an addiction," Markstrom says to Cari. "She wasn't looking for a high, per se. Rain took those drugs purely to suppress her appetite."

"I see," Cari says. "And as a responsible therapist, you substituted a diabetic medicine instead?"

"No. I looked the other way when she took my Ozempic, in exchange for her promise that she wouldn't use street drugs."

"That's a convenient explanation."

"It's also the truth." Markstrom folds his hands together on the desk. "You must understand, Detective, that when I first met Rain as a client, she was in an extremely fragile state. Her heart had been shattered." He glances over to Braden. "Her weight was out of control, yo-yoing up and down. Sometimes by the week. She had a clinical depression and, much of the time, she was actively suicidal. But after a few years working with me—obviously there were multiple factors, and I do not mean to take the sole credit—much of her volatility had settled. Certainly, her most toxic impulses."

"Settled?" Cari bites her lip, trying to focus on the information rather than her disdain for the self-righteous man sharing it. "But she still died at twenty-three from a very toxic impulse?"

Markstrom views her defiantly. "Without my intervention, she probably would have died at nineteen by her own hand."

"Her best friend wasn't as glowing in her description of your influence on Rain."

Markstrom lets loose a bitter laugh. "Maleeka Khan?"

"And her sister, Shawna. Both implied we should be looking into your involvement in her death."

"Talk about toxic influences," Markstrom scoffs. "Those two are as toxic as they come. Why don't you suspect Maleeka of providing Rain DNP?"

"We haven't ruled anything out."

"Well, you can rule me out. The night of Rain's party, I did everything

I could to intervene. I had no idea what she had taken, but she looked ghastly. I begged her to let me take her to a doctor. But I could not get her to listen."

Braden nods emphatically. "It's true. We both tried!"

"And half an hour later," Markstrom says, "when she didn't respond to my knock, I was the one who insisted they break down the door."

"None of that proves you weren't involved." Cari looks at each of them for a moment. "If you know anything about how Rain got the DNP, now is the time to tell me."

"I do not," Markstrom says unequivocally.

Braden waves both hands in front of his face.

After leaving Markstrom's office, Cari intends to drive straight to LAPD Headquarters, but, on a whim, she heads over to Inglewood and parks out front of Sip and Ponder Coffee Roasters. She steps inside and is greeted by a rich, nutty waft of brewed espresso. Three people are spaced out at individual tables, but no one is lined up at the counter. Behind it, a young man, his blond hair tied back in a bun and a sleeve of tattoos on each arm, leans back against the espresso machine and types on his phone.

Cari introduces herself to the barista, whose nametag reads "Dallas."

"A detective? That's wicked!" he says in a valley drawl.

"We're investigating a criminal enterprise," Cari says, being deliberately vague. "We believe that at some point, someone used your Wi-Fi for illicit transactions."

"No way! A criminal enterprise?" Dallas's whole face scrunches. "Here?"

"We believe so, yes. Do you offer free access to Wi-Fi for your customers?"

"Sure do." He points to the sign above him where the Wi-Fi password, *cappuccino*, is scrawled in pink chalk.

"Have you worked here long, Dallas?"

"Eighteen months or so. I DJ a lot of nights, but I'm here most days. When was this big data breach?"

"Early last month."

"I was probably here then when it happened," he says, appearing awed by the realization.

"No one out of the ordinary comes to mind?"

"Aw, man, we get all types here. Some pretty sketchy ones, too. Even apart from the usual suspects—actors, writers, models, students, et cetera. At least half the customers come here for the free Wi-Fi."

Cari pulls out her phone. While waiting for her flight, she cobbled together photos from online searches and the social media pages of the more prominent names in the investigation, including Maleeka, Braden, Markstrom, Owen, and most of the LA victims.

Dallas studies the photos intently as he scrolls back and forth through them. "Nope. Nope." He pauses momentarily at Owen's photo and then shakes his head. The same with Maleeka. When he gets to the photo of Aiden Cowell, the trainer whose fiancée died from DNP, he stops and studies it from different angles. "This dude looks kinda familiar? But can't say for sure."

"Thanks, Dallas," Cari says, though she assumes it must be a dead end. Why would Aiden be selling DNP from the same website where his fiancée ordered it?

CHAPTER 39

"The good news is that the judge signed it," Theo says, waving the search warrant document in his hand, as he gets into the passenger seat.

"And the bad?" Anson asks as he pulls away from the curb.

"The judge excluded the client records we asked for in our affidavit."

Anson sighs. "Meaning we can't touch their computers or phones."

"That'll change in a hurry if we can show that their energy drink contains DNP instead of green tea extract or whatever."

"They could've done a lot of housecleaning since my last visit," Anson mutters.

"Is what it is." His ever-unflappable partner shrugs. "Team is already assembling down the block from the shop. I said we'd meet them there in ten."

"How big a team?"

"Four uniforms. Two crime techs." And then Theo adds wryly, "I didn't request an emergency response team or any snipers."

"What if we walk right into an ambush of rose water and scented towels?"

Theo chuckles. "That's why we get danger pay, partner."

The phone rings, and Anson picks up on speakerphone.

"Good afternoon, this is Klaus Gruber calling."

"Hi, Doc," Theo says. "You're on with me and Anson."

"Of course. I thought you would like to hear the preliminary autopsy results on your latest victim, Ms. Cecilia Hunter."

"Very much so," Theo says.

"Ideally, even before Desmond announces the findings to the press," Anson adds.

"*Ja*, that was most unfortunate," Gruber says. "I am informing you before I have a chance to speak to the coroner. Possibly, long before."

"Thank you."

"Ms. Hunter died, as I'm sure you expected, from multi-organ failure secondary to acute DNP toxicity," Gruber says. "This is also why, ultimately, she did not qualify as an organ donor. However, there were some anomalies in the specific autopsy findings."

"Anomalies?" Anson echoes. "As in different from the previous victims?"

"Exactly so," Gruber says. "For example, unlike the young singer, Ms. Hunter had a normal body habitus. Lean and muscular, yes, but no evidence of the starvation state we find in typical eating disorder victims like Ms. Flynn. Moreover, I could find no skin discoloration or other changes on Ms. Hunter to suggest chronic DNP poisoning."

"Are you saying Cecilia did not use DNP prior to her fatal overdose?" Theo asks.

"Not necessarily. It could be true that it was her first time ingesting DNP. But it also could indicate that she was not taking it regularly or, at least, in high enough concentration to cause any end-organ damage earlier." He pauses. "Of course, that would be less consistent with the other anomaly."

"Which is what, Doc?" Anson asks.

"The DNP level in Ms. Hunter's blood was fifty-two milligrams per liter at the time of her death."

"That's high, right?"

"To put it in perspective," Gruber says. "Ms. Flynn's blood level was eleven milligrams per liter when she died."

Anson glances at Theo. "Does that mean Cecilia Hunter took roughly five times as much DNP as Rain did?" he asks.

"It is not such an exact science, Detective," Gruber says. "There is timing of ingestion and metabolism to consider. In a way, it is comparing apples to oranges. But I am confident to say that Ms. Hunter consumed a significantly larger ingestion, *ja*."

Anson thanks Dr. Gruber. and as soon as he disconnects, Theo says, "That doesn't exactly fit with someone drinking an extra bottle or two of supplement that happens to be laced with small doses of DNP."

Anson considers his point. "Not unless someone really screwed up. And spiked a batch of supplement with way too much DNP."

"But if it were a whole batch, wouldn't we be expecting to see their rich and famous clients dropping like flies across the city?"

"Maybe Cecilia got tired of microdosing and decided to make her own DNP supplement?"

"Or maybe she just swallowed a bottle of DNP pills instead of the supplement?"

"We're getting ahead of ourselves," Anson says, as he turns onto Mainland Street and rolls slowly past the entrance to the wellness center. "First step is proving whether or not they are lacing their supplement."

"Agreed."

Anson turns another corner and spots a group of uniformed officers already assembled beside a VPD van. After parking the car nearby, he and Theo do a quick round of introductions with the team. Theo flashes them the search warrant and explains, "We're entitled to take any bottles, containers, capsules, pills, or other materials that we deem potentially suspicious. But we cannot touch their computers or mobile devices."

"In other words, if it doesn't have a plug, grab it," Anson says to a few chuckles.

"Ready?" Theo asks, and after everyone nods, he turns for the street.

They walk down the block and Theo leads them through the entrance of Mind Over Body. Sitting behind the desk again, Colby appears flustered by the large police presence. "I'm sorry. Can I . . . help you, officers?"

Theo lays the signed form on the desk. "We have a legal warrant to search the premises for suspicious substances. You are ordered by the court to cooperate and to not impede our search in any way."

Colby jumps up. "I . . . I better get Gerard," he says, more to himself than the others.

"You do that." Anson turns back to the rest of the team and rotates his finger in a helicopter blade motion. "Let's spread out and cover it room by room."

The team wordlessly separates in different directions. Anson heads over to the closet behind the reception area. He opens it and sees that the top two shelves are lined by matching green containers, the size and shape of two-liter soda bottles but made of glass, not plastic. Lifting one down from the shelf, he is surprised by its weight—it's as heavy as a magnum of champagne. He studies the label, which has the Mind Over Body logo printed prominently across it in raised lettering. The only other words on the front read: "hypoallergenic" and "nut-free." On the back the directions read: "We recommend two cups, or five hundred milliliters, twice per day, to a maximum of one bottle per day." A heart symbol is embossed beside the directions.

"What's going on?" Gerard asks as he appears in front of the reception desk, followed by a stunning, dark-haired woman in yoga wear. Gerard doesn't introduce her, but Anson assumes she must be the girlfriend he mentioned on their previous visit. While Gerard stands still, she practically bounces on her toes.

"We're executing a search warrant," Theo says.

The woman stabs a finger at him. "On what grounds?"

"And you are?" Anson asks.

"Adèle," she growls. "Why are you storming our center?"

"No one is storming. We are executing a legal search warrant."

She waves away the distinction.

"We have reason to believe that Mind Over Body has been providing a health supplement that contains illicit substances," Theo says.

"What reason could you have to believe that?" Adèle's voice cracks.

"I'm afraid that's between the VPD and the issuing judge," Anson says.

Gerard sweeps a protective arm over Adèle's shoulders. "They're just doing their job, babe."

"Their job?" Her head swivels toward him. "By raiding our business? Disrupting our clients in the middle of the day?"

"There is that." Gerard squeezes her shoulder. "Not to mention making us look guilty by association."

"Association with what exactly, Mr. Martin?" Anson asks.

"Really? After Rain and Cecilia? You don't think people will try to put it all together?" Adèle glares at Anson. "How long do you think it will take before the rumors spread? Before our business is decimated?"

"Mr. Martin is right, ma'am," Theo says. "We're just doing our job."

"Cops," she huffs as she pivots away. "You're all the same!"

Theo catches Anson's eye. His expression tells Anson that he's thinking the same thing: her words were spoken like someone who's had run-ins with the law before.

CHAPTER 40

The captain stands up from behind his desk and greets Cari with a warm smile. "Welcome home, Detective," he says, as if she has been gone for months, not days.

"Thank you, Captain."

"Detective," the senator says, looking over her shoulder from the seat in front of the desk. Despite her impassive gray eyes, she seems to have aged years in the past two weeks. She wears the naked toll of her son's death in her sunken cheeks and the deep bags under her eyes, which appear to be makeup-proof.

Cari realizes that behind the senator's polished political exterior is a deeply grieving mother, and she feels sorrier for her than she has before. "Good afternoon, Senator."

After Cari sits down, she recaps what she has learned since leaving for Vancouver.

Once she finishes, the captain says, "We'll need a search warrant for the Beverly Hills location of this Mind Over Body, too."

"Absolutely," Cari says. "But we've yet to establish any connection between that wellness center and Dr. X Pharmaceuticals."

"Isn't the DNP connection enough?" the captain asks.

"Even if Mind Over Body is lacing their health supplement with DNP, they might not have any link to Dr. X."

"Other than using the same poison?"

"Unfortunately, Dr. X Pharmaceuticals is by no means the only supplier," Cari says.

The senator raises an eyebrow. "They're both active in the same two cities. How do you explain that?"

"I can't. At least, not yet."

"Maybe one will lead you to the other?"

"That would be ideal, Senator."

"What about that coffee shop you checked out in Inglewood?" the captain asks. "If Dr. X Pharmaceuticals is using their Wi-Fi to fill online orders, then we should stake it out and see who comes and goes."

The idea has already occurred to Cari. "We certainly can try. The problem is that after Rain's death and since we publicized the aliases of the various Dr. X Pharmaceuticals sites"— she forces herself not to make eye contact with the senator—"their website has gone dark. They don't appear to be active right now. Which makes sense considering all the public scrutiny."

"Unless they've just reopened shop with some equally tacky new theme for a business name?" the senator suggests.

"We've been monitoring for that," Cari says. "So far, we haven't picked up on any such activity."

"I want that stakeout set up, Cari," the captain commands, almost puffing out his chest out.

"Will do."

"Meantime, you ought to familiarize yourself with the rest of the task force's work." He motions to the glass wall. "We've converted the second conference room into an operations center. And I've seconded Detectives Ronning and Yoshida to help with the investigation."

"Oh, Sheila and Phil will be a great fit," Cari says, genuinely pleased.

"Glad you approve," he says, but his tone doesn't match the words. "They've been digging into the other DNP deaths that happened before . . . the senator's son."

The senator turns to Cari with uncharacteristically plaintive eyes. "Are we any closer to finding the people who killed Owen, Detective?"

"I believe we are, Senator."

"Thank you," she says softly.

Shortly after Cari has left the captain's office, her phone rings with a call from Zach. "Hi. What have you got?"

"I found her," Zach says nonchalantly.

Cari's heart pounds. *Her?*

"Your actress in those Dr. Pharmaceuticals viral ads."

"You did?"

"I got a facial recognition match back to her TikTok feed. Turns out, she's an aspiring model-slash-actor." He snorts a laugh. "What are the chances in this town?"

"Who is she, Zach?"

"Brittany Mair. Lives out in the valley. Granada Hills. But if you believe her Insta feed, she's working today in Lincoln Heights."

"Working? As in a film or photo shoot?"

"As in a boutique clothing store. She's a salesclerk. Some place called Stepping Out. For what it's worth, it gets a four-point-nine-star aggregate review on Google."

"I could always use another dress," she says. "Thanks, Zach."

Cari heads straight down to her car. The traffic is light for midafternoon in the downtown core, and she reaches Lincoln Heights in under fifteen minutes. She finds parking in front of the store, which has a colorful array of casual dresses hanging in its windows. She could see herself in a couple of the looser-fit ones.

The bell jangles as Cari steps inside. She doesn't spot any customers, but a young woman steps out from behind the counter, and Cari recognizes her from the online ad Theo showed her.

"Hi!" Brittany says with a huge smile as she approaches. "Oh, my God, your complexion is gorgeous! We have a new line of earth tones that would be *perfect* for you."

"I'm Detective Garcia," Cari says, extending her identification. "With the LAPD."

"Oh?" Brittany's smile doesn't falter. "The break-in was weeks ago. I didn't think anyone was still following up on it."

"I'm not here about the break-in."

"You're not?"

"No, Brittany. I wanted to ask you about a promotional social media clip that you acted in."

"Um, OK . . . I've done a bunch of those. Which one?"

"Dr. Slim Pharmaceuticals."

"I only did a few of those. And not for ages."

"Do you know what DNP is, Brittany?"

The grin slips off her lips. "The stuff that killed Rain?"

"It's also what Dr. Slim Pharmaceuticals was selling in their diet pills."

"Oh, my God!" Brittany slaps a hand to her mouth. "I had no idea! It was just a gig. I didn't even . . ."

"I get it, Brittany," Cari says. "We're looking for the people behind the video."

Brittany shakes her head wildly. "I don't know who they are."

"Did they hire you through an agency?"

"No, they reached out directly through my acting and modeling page. On Insta."

"How did you get paid?"

"E-transfer," Brittany croaks.

"Did you ever meet anyone from the company?" Cari asks. "For example, did someone set up the shoot?"

"Never! It was all via direct messaging. They'd send me a script. Then they'd tell me what to wear, where to shoot it, and all that kind of stuff. They always wanted me to use my own phone. And . . ."

"And what, Brittany?"

"They told me to make it look as 'homemade' as possible," Brittany says in a small voice.

"They didn't want it to look like an ad at all, did they?"

"I guess not." Her lip quivers.

"And you never once met or even spoke to anyone from the company?"

Brittany shakes her head again. "Not except for that one call."

"Which call?"

"The first job I did. Can't even remember for what website. Dr. Beefcake Pharmaceuticals, maybe? They didn't like the camera angle on the takes I sent. They thought it looked too . . . professional."

"And someone phoned you?"

"Called me via Insta." She holds up her hand. "Just audio. It's not like she had her camera on or anything."

"*She?*"

"Yeah, a woman. She didn't sound very old. And she was so snippy." Brittany pauses. "Downright cold."

CHAPTER 41

Anson sits on the couch beside Julie, the gas fireplace lit and their favorite "dinner chill" music mix playing softly over the wireless speakers. He sweeps a hand over the takeout remnants littering the coffee table, including all the individual sauce containers. "Why do they waste so much plastic?"

"Mmm," Julie only mumbles.

"And why do I always forget to tell them not to send extra sauces?"

She only takes a sip of her red wine.

"What is it, Julie?"

"What is what?"

"You hardly said two words over dinner. Even less since."

She turns to him with a quizzical look. "Oh? I'm not sharing enough with you? Is that it?"

"Ah, I get it." he says. "I'm dying to talk to you about the case. But after last year . . . we agreed, Julie."

"Forget the case, Anson. You don't even tell me what's going on in our bedroom anymore."

"Our bedroom?" He sits up straighter. "What's that supposed to mean?"

She is quiet for a few seconds. "You moaned Nicole's name in your sleep again last night."

He lays a hand on top of hers and squeezes. "I don't always remember having those dreams." But that's not entirely true. The nightmares have stayed with him for weeks.

"I guess not," she says, as she eases her hand free of his.

"They're *dreams*, Julie. What am I supposed to do? Just stop having them?"

"How about talking to me? Your partner."

"I told you about them."

"Once. And only barely then."

"They don't change."

"I'm not jealous of Nicole, Anson. I love that you two had something special. And it's only natural you'd dream about her now, right after you've moved in with me. What I hate is that you exclude me from it all." A pained expression flits across her face. "You make me feel left out of your life."

Anson looks down at the empty noodle box. A blush warms his face. "It's really hard for me to talk about."

"Even more reason to. We're supposed to be there for each other for the tough conversations. The most personal stuff. That's how this works." Her voice thickens. "The only way it works."

Anson looks back up to Julie. Spotting the hurt in her eyes, he feels guilty. And protective of her. "It's been a few weeks now. The basic dream is always the same, but the setting changes every time. Usually, I don't even recognize where we are. It's never in Hawaii, where the accident happened. But Nicole is always begging for help. And I can't do anything for her. I get this overwhelming feeling of helplessness. Uselessness." His face heats more, and he assumes he must have already turned beet red. "Then I wake up."

"That must be awful."

"It's not only the damn dream."

"What else?"

"This is gonna sound kind of unhinged, but I get this worry . . . this dread . . ."

She doesn't move a muscle, waiting for him to expand.

"That something bad could happen to you, too. And there's not a thing I could do to prevent that, either."

"That's very sweet." She smiles for the first time. "And weirdly chauvinistic."

He chuckles self-consciously. "Yeah, well, that's me in a nutshell."

Julie shifts closer to him. "Have you gone to see Nicole?"

"At the cemetery?" He shakes his head.

"Maybe you should. I do that with Michael when I'm really out of sorts. When the memories get too much."

"You think it would help?"

"Definitely," she says, to encourage him. "Take Nicole flowers, Anson. Tell her you're sorry."

"Yeah, maybe," he says slowly. But he already knows she's right. He leans over and kisses her cheek. "I love you."

"I love you, too." She rubs her face to his. "But don't leave me out of your life."

They remain like that, silently, cheeks touching for a while. "We raided Mind Over Body Wellness Center today," he finally says.

She pulls her head away from his, and her face lights with an appreciative smile. "What did you find?"

"We're still waiting on the tox screen on the bottles we confiscated. The deputy chief pulled strings, and the lab's running an urgent analysis. We're supposed to hear this evening."

"And if there is DNP in the supplement?"

"Then we round up the owners. And figure out where they got the stuff."

"Do you think it's related to Rain's death?"

"It's too early to say," he says. "But we haven't found any connection between Rain and Mind Over Body yet."

Julie links her elbow in his. "Thank you for sharing."

"Now that I've spilled my guts all over the place, tell me about your work."

"Well, I had this drunk guy who decided it would be a good idea to dive off a countertop."

Anson chuckles. "It wasn't?"

"Probably not," she says. "Seeing as how he shattered his wrist and dislocated his other shoulder."

Julie goes on to describe how she had to reset both joints. And then she tells him about the latest gossip ripping through the ER, after one of the nurses spotted a fifty-year-old female vascular surgeon making out with her twenty-seven-year-old male resident in her car in the parking garage in the middle of the night.

Anson's phone rings, and as soon as he spots "DC" on the call display, he grabs for it. "Did you get the results?"

"We did," the deputy chief says. He can tell from her subdued tone that he's not going to like the news. "They didn't find any DNP, Anson."

"How could they have tested all the bottles already?" he says, feeling his optimism seep away.

"Apparently, they pooled a sample from every bottle," she says. "Nothing. Nada. Not a trace of DNP. Just a bunch of useless vitamins. Basically, glorified tap water."

"Damn it," he mutters.

"But you and Theo were right about the woman. Adèle Gagnon. She has a record in Montreal."

"For what?"

"A couple of arrests for shoplifting and other petty crimes. And one conviction for identity theft. She didn't serve any time, but she's clearly no stranger to the system."

"Those two . . ." Anson grumbles. "And Gerard was so calm when we were executing the warrant. As if he was expecting us."

"Maybe he was?"

"Yeah, maybe. Thanks for letting me know, DC," he says glumly as he hangs up.

Julie eyes him expectantly. "Don't leave me hanging now."

Anson summarizes what the deputy chief said, and as soon as he finishes, Julie asks, "Do you think they switched out the bottles?"

"Probably. Would explain why they were clean." He sighs. "But who knows? And that patient of yours, Cecilia. Her DNP blood level was through the roof. Not consistent with just swallowing too much of some laced supplement."

"Why don't you check the other bottles?"

"Which other bottles?"

"The ones their clients still have."

It's a good idea. One that Anson has already considered. "We don't have access to their client list. Our search warrant didn't include that."

Julie nods knowingly. "Maybe you don't need their list?"

CHAPTER 42

Gerard gears down, revving the engine loudly, more out of frustration than need. "This fucking traffic!" he says as his Porsche 911 slows to a crawl. "Can't they learn to fucking drive before they flock to Canada?"

"Nice," Adèle says, no doubt more put off by his swearing than the racist connotation.

"Pardon me for my gaucheness," he growls. "But I'm not having the best fucking day."

"You're not the only one, *chéri*."

He punches the steering wheel. "Lloyd threw us under the bus."

"How do you know it was Lloyd?"

"Who else could've tipped off the cops?"

She only shrugs. "The cops aren't going to find anything in the bottles they confiscated from us."

"That won't matter if Lloyd gave them Cecilia's bottles. That complete fucker."

"Calme-toi le pompon!"

"Don't start!" he snaps. "Not the time for your grandpa's little bullshit idioms. Wasn't he an abusive drunk who beat your grandma, anyway?"

"Take a chill pill. *Jesus!*" Adèle turns to look out the window.

Gerard is too unnerved to make peace with her, and so they lapse into a sullen silence for the remainder of the drive.

The tires squeal as he pulls into Lloyd's driveway. He hops out of the car and stomps up to the front door and pounds on it before Adèle has even caught up with him.

The door swings open. Unshaven and reeking of whiskey, Lloyd fills the doorway. "What do you want?"

"I was going to ask you the same," Gerard says.

"I want my wife back." Lloyd glares at him. "But that's not possible, thanks to you. And now I'd like you to get the hell off my property."

"Not until you tell us what you told the VPD."

Lloyd's face scrunches. "The VPD?"

"The detectives, Lloyd. What did you tell them about our supplement?"

"I haven't spoken to the detectives."

Gerard can't hide his surprise. "You haven't?"

"Not since the first time they came to see me. Why would I? After you threatened to ruin me with your vile lies."

"I . . . I just assumed you did."

Lloyd squints at him. "Why? What happened?"

Adèle elbows her way past Gerard. "We got a message from one of the detectives," she says.

"That's right," Gerard says, appreciating her quick thinking. "From Detective Chen."

"He said he had some more questions for us," Adèle says. "We assumed—"

"Assumed you put him onto us," Gerard finishes her sentence. *What would I do without you?*

"I wish I had," Lloyd growls. "But what's the point? Cecilia's gone. And you've made it pretty damn clear that you'd take me down with you."

"Well, now that we've sorted that out . . ." Gerard takes hold of Adèle's upper arm and gently pulls her back from the door.

"Since you're already here," Lloyd says. "I might as well tell you."

"Tell us what?" Gerard asks, although his mind is already focusing on who or what else might have directed the cops toward Mind Over Body and their supplement.

"I'm done with you. And your filthy, fraudulent wellness center. I want out!"

Gerard suppresses a smile. "Suit yourself."

"And you're going to pay me fair market value for my share."

"Mind Over Body isn't exactly peaking in value right now, Lloyd."

"That's a load of crap. Revenue has never been better. And that's before the Bay Area location opens."

"Revenue could dry up tomorrow." Gerard snaps his fingers. "What with the police sniffing around, and our product under such scrutiny. We've never been more exposed."

Lloyd jabs a shaky finger at him. "It's nonnegotiable, Gerard. My lawyer will forward the paperwork tomorrow."

Gerard glances over to Adèle. "We'll definitely consider it."

"I don't need you to consider it, asshole! I need you to sign it. Oh, and I'll need you to sign an affidavit, too."

Gerard tilts his head. "What kind of affidavit?"

"One attesting to the fact that I was only ever a financial partner. And that I knew nothing of your means or methods."

"Why would I do that?" Gerard scoffs. "So you can turn us in the moment we buy you out?"

"How many times do we have to go over this?" Lloyd's voice cracks. "I'd love nothing more than to turn you in. But you've guaranteed mutual assured destruction if I do."

Gerard snickers. "Mutual assured destructions requires . . . well . . . assurances."

"And you'll have them."

"How?"

"You sign the contract and the affidavit, and I'll sign a nondisclosure agreement." Lloyd takes a step back inside the house. "Now get the hell out of my life!" he cries as he slams the door in their faces.

CHAPTER 43

In the weak haze of dawn, Cari sits in her car out front of Sip and Ponder Coffee Roasters, listening to her favorite classic hip-hop station while impatiently tapping the steering wheel along to the beat. She glances at the dashboard clock again: 6:53. She's been parked there for over fifteen minutes, and there is still no sign of life inside the café. *Where are you, Dallas?*

Wired with anticipation, Cari hardly slept overnight. It wasn't only Brittany's description of the anonymous woman's brusque voice that had twigged Cari's suspicions. It was the TikTok ad itself. She appreciated how its message would have played perfectly to her sister's vulnerabilities, especially Lucia's desperation to find any quick fix, as well as her idolization of others she perceived as having the perfect body. It was as if whoever staged the ad intimately understood how to appeal to those with body image disorders. Maybe even someone who had a little sister like Cari's? One who would crawl over glass or swallow poison to be accepted?

As soon as Cari left Brittany's boutique late yesterday afternoon, she called into the task force and asked one of the junior officers to look up Shawna Khan's address and do a criminal background check on her. Less than fifteen minutes later, the officer called back, noting that Shawna had no criminal record and providing her most recent address as it was listed on the California electoral roll. Cari's suspicions only solidified when she mapped the location online and saw that it was only an eighteen-minute walk from Shawna's home to Sip and Ponder Coffee Roasters.

Cari wanted to head straight to the café to interview Dallas, but she struggled to dig up an image of Shawna to show him. The internet was littered with photos of Maleeka Khan—her life seemingly documented by the minute on Instagram and other social media feeds—but her older sister didn't exist online. It was only after Cari scrolled through thousands of Maleeka's posts that she found a two-year-old photo of the whole Khan family posing for a holiday shot. In it, the father stood beside his wife and behind Maleeka, with his hands resting protectively on his younger daughter's shoulders, while Shawna hovered off to the side. Cari had to zoom in on and crop the image of Shawna. The resulting picture of her sullen face was blurry, but at least she was recognizable in her usual hoodie. By the time Cari had downloaded the photo, it was well after six p.m. and the coffee shop was long closed.

Now Cari's pulse picks up as she spots Dallas rolling up to the front door on a skateboard. He hops off his board, flicks it up into his hand with his foot, and then unlocks the front door. She hurries inside after him.

"I'll be another five getting set up," Dallas calls out from where he crouches below the countertop.

"It's Detective Garcia," she says. "I only need a minute or two of your time."

"Detective!" Dallas pops up to face her with a big grin. "Back so soon. Whoa! You must be onto something big, huh?"

"Maybe, Dallas."

"Awesome!"

"Do you mind looking at a few more photos for me?"

"Mind?" He races around the counter to meet her. "This is a total trip. Makes me feel like I'm an extra in one of those gritty detective shows. Y'know?" He waves his hand in an arc. "The ones set in those miserable towns where it's always dark and raining? And I'm like that one witness who cracks the case wide open without knowing I've been holding the key to the whole shebang all along."

Cari can't help but smile. "You've got quite the imagination, Dallas."

He rests two fingers on his temple. "The mind's got to go somewhere when you're brewing your ten thousandth latte."

Cari pulls up the photo of Shawna on her phone and turns the screen outward to show him.

Dallas doesn't hesitate. "Oh, yeah." He taps the screen with his index finger. "This one. With the hoodie."

Cari's chest buzzes. "You're sure?"

"Hundred percent!"

"Is she a regular?"

"She's here often enough. A couple times a week. She's kinda chilly, if I'm being honest. Don't mind that she never tips, but would it kill her to smile like once?" He points to the counter facing the window with a few stools beneath it. "She likes that spot. At the end."

"What does she do there?"

"She'll come in and work away on her laptop. A gold MacBook. Maybe for an hour or so. Half the time, she just leaves a full cup of tea behind." He juts out his lip. "What is she? Like a terrorist or something?"

"I can't get into the details, Dallas. But this isn't a domestic terrorism investigation."

"A drug dealer, right? That'd make sense, too."

"Why do you say that?"

"She always wears the same backpack. One time, I walked past her, and it was open and full of these bubble pack envelopes. It just happened to catch my eye." He holds up his hands. "She scowled at me like I was trying to look down her shirt or something. As if!"

"When was she last here?"

Dallas strokes his stubbly chin. "Come to think of it, she hasn't been around for a while. At least a week, I'd say."

The timing fits. The Dr. X Pharmaceuticals site went dark last week right after the captain's disastrous press conference. Shawna probably hasn't filled any orders since.

Dallas shakes his head in wonder. "Wild! Like I said, not the friendliest gal. But I had her pegged more for an IT nerd. Organized crime? Didn't see that one coming."

"Never assume, Dallas," Cari says, her chest pounding as she tucks the phone into her pocket. She hands him a card. "If she does show up, please don't approach her. Just call me."

He looks disappointed. "No citizen's arrest then?"

"Absolutely not." Cari turns for the door, calling back, "Thanks for your help, Dallas. It's huge."

As soon as she reaches her car, she phones Captain Taylor. Cari doesn't trust him to keep the disclosure to himself, but she has no choice. She needs his help.

After listening to her news, he says, "Let's put out a BOLO on this Shawna Khan."

"I think she's still in Vancouver. Her little sister, Maleeka, is in the ICU there."

"Wasn't she the one who went public about Rain's DNP use?"

"Yes."

"Are you suggesting it was Maleeka who gave Rain the DNP?" The captain's voice rises in disbelief.

"Shawna probably supplied her little sister, who then shared it—maybe even sold it—to her friend, Rain."

"What a pair! Let's get the VPD to pick up this Shawna."

"I'm on it," Cari says. "But in the meantime, we need an urgent search warrant for her home."

"Get me a statement from that barista, and I'll get you your warrant."

"Will do," she says. "Thanks."

As soon as she gets off the line, she calls Anson's cell. He answers on the third ring.

"Hey, Cari," he says warmly. "Too much UV light down there for you? Are you missing our cold drizzle?"

"I know who's behind Dr. X Pharmaceuticals!" she blurts.

"Tell me!" Anson says, his tone suddenly dead serious.

"Shawna Khan."

"Shawna Khan . . ." he echoes, not sounding the least surprised.

She tells him about Dallas's positive identification.

Anson goes quiet a moment. "Guess that explains Maleeka's delirious comment about her sister adoring red-and-black."

"Absolutely." Cari pauses. "It also explains where Maleeka got the supply for her and Rain."

"True. But why was Shawna peddling this DNP crap in the first place?"

"Why else? The cash."

"Yeah, maybe. But why would she take that kind of risk with her own sister?"

"Why don't you ask Shawna?" Cari says. "She's still in Vancouver, right?"

"As far as I know, yes. We'll track her down ASAP."

"Can you wait an hour to two for our search warrant to come through before picking her up?" she asks. "It will be easier for you to hold her if we find evidence in her home linking her directly to Dr. X or DNP."

"Sure."

"How's it going on your end?"

"Ups and downs," he says. "We confiscated the supplement from Mind Over Body, but it didn't test positive for DNP. We suspect the couple who runs the place was spooked by the publicity around Cecelia Hunter's death. We think they must've sanitized their supply before we got to it."

"Those two are slippery," she says. "But even if they were lacing their supplement with DNP, they might not be connected to Shawna or Dr. X Pharmaceuticals."

"True."

"And even if they are, Anson, other DNP distributors are bound to pop up. Especially now that Rain has almost glamorized this poison."

"Probably," he says. "But this is still massive, Cari. You, unmasking the source of Dr. X Pharmaceuticals. Think how many deaths we know they—Shawna, I guess—is responsible for. Trust me. Just by stopping her and anyone associated with Dr. X, we're going to make a huge difference."

"I hope so," Cari says, filling with a warm sense of satisfaction. She thinks of her little sister again. And for the first time in a while, the memory isn't such a painful one.

CHAPTER 44

Julie sits on the couch, working on an upcoming toxicology lecture on her laptop, while waiting for a more respectable time to make the call.

She awoke early this morning, forty-five minutes before her six thirty alarm was set to go off, feeling more refreshed than she had in a week. Either Anson had tossed and turned less, or she had just slept through it. Regardless, she was relieved to have cleared the air between them. After their deep post-dinner conversation, they'd gone to bed early, watched an episode and a half of their new favorite series, and then made languid love before falling asleep in each other's arms. Anson was still sleeping peacefully when she eased out of bed.

Leanne's patient, Tracy, hadn't responded to Julie's message until almost eleven p.m., and Julie didn't see the text until she woke up this morning. "Sorry, Dr. Rees!" Tracy wrote. "Condo closing went sideways. Back on my phone. Call anytime."

At eight o'clock, minutes after Anson left for work, Julie calls Tracy, who answers immediately. "Good morning, Dr. Rees," she chirps.

"I was hoping to get the contact info for your friend," Julie explains.

"Which friend?" Tracy asks.

"The one who originally put you onto Mind Over Body."

"Oh, Darlene! Darlene Hoffman. She's my partner."

"Oh, great. Is she home with you now?"

"Home with me?" Tracy pauses and then breaks into laughter. "Not life partners! Business partners. We're real estate brokers. Although, honestly, we get along so well. We would definitely do better as life partners than we've done with the male duds we've both been picking. I mean if you'd spent five minutes with Darlene's ex-husband, you would wonder what the—"

"Do you have Darlene's number handy, Tracy?"

"Of course. Are you planning to interview her yourself?"

"No," Julie says, thinking how much she would love to, but aware that that would cross the line Anson had drawn for them. "I'm going to pass it on to the detectives who are looking into your claim."

"Oh, wonderful. But they might not be able to reach her this morning. Darlene will be at the showroom all day, overseeing the sales staff. She's going to be swamped. Today is the first presale day on this new development we're representing. The Spires. Have you heard of it? It's absolutely darling. State-of-the-art amenities and spectacular sightlines from the higher floors. But our new agents are so green. Honestly, it's like teaching kindergarten sometimes with these—"

"That's on Seymour just off Drake, right?"

"That's the one! You've seen it then?"

"I've walked past a few times. It's not too far from my place. I'll let the detectives know. But if you can still forward me Darlene's contact info, I'd appreciate it."

"You'll have it in moments."

"Thanks, Tracy." Julie disconnects before the woman can go off on another tangent.

But ten minutes pass without Tracy sending the number. Julie is considering phoning back when her phone rings with Tracy's name on the call display. "Hi. You could just text me the number," Julie says, feeling too impatient to sit through another rambling conversation.

"It's not that." Tracy's voice is subdued.

"What is it?"

"I called Darlene myself, to give her the heads-up."

Julie rubs her forehead. "You didn't have to do that."

"Darlene doesn't want to speak to the detectives." Tracy swallows. "She's upset with me for mentioning her name to you at all."

"I'm not following."

"Darlene is still drinking the Kool-Aid, if you'll pardon the pun, when it comes to Mind Over Body."

Julie isn't sure it is a pun. "It's a police matter now. Darlene has no choice but to speak to them."

Tracy goes uncharacteristically quiet. "Can you do me a favor?" she eventually asks in a small voice.

"What kind of favor?"

"Will you talk to her?"

"I don't think that's a good idea, Tracy."

"Please. It's not only for me. I'm worried Darlene could do something rash."

"Like what?"

"Get rid of the bottles, maybe?"

"She wouldn't, would she?"

"She might."

Julie ignores the voice in her head, telling her this is a bad idea. "You said she's at the showroom now?"

"Yes! She's there all morning."

Julie takes the elevator to the ground floor and heads out on foot. Outside, the sun is shining. But without the usual layer of November clouds, the temperature has dropped to near freezing. And as she bundles the light down jacket tighter and picks up her pace to keep warm, she wishes she'd worn a thicker coat.

Aware she's treading on thin ice, Julie phones Anson to alert him of the situation. But his line rings straight through to voicemail. "I think I found you another source of bottles to test," she texts him instead. "Call me, please."

Julie reaches the showroom within ten minutes of leaving her place. The bright, open space boasts a life-sized mockup of a two-bedroom unit. She doesn't see any buyers, but several attractive, young female agents mill around, all sporting matching green blazers. Julie spots an older, blond woman in a blue suit across the floor, who breezes from one agent to another with an authoritative air.

Julie makes a beeline for her. "Darlene?" she asks as she nears.

The fortyish woman flashes her a toothy smile, but the skin over her forehead and around her eyes doesn't budge. "I am, indeed. How can I help you?"

"I'm Julie Rees. A physician at St. Michael's."

Darlene's smile somehow broadens. "Then you've come to the right place! The Spires is a ten-minute walk to your hospital. Not much farther than your hospital's parking garage."

"I'm not here to buy a condo," Julie says politely.

"You're not?"

"Your partner, Tracy, gave me your contact info."

The smile vanishes. "*You're* the doctor she called me about."

"Yes."

Darlene heads over to a quiet corner of the room, and Julie follows her. "I told Tracy to leave me out of this," Darlene says.

"I understand. I do. But this is important," Julie urges. "Tracy told me you were the one who sold her on Mind Over Body."

"Why wouldn't I?" Darlene says. "I swear by their method. Never seen anything close to as good before. Not only that, but the owners really care. As a matter of fact, I consider Adèle to be a friend of mine."

"Are you still using their supplement?"

Darlene eyes her suspiciously. "The supplement is only a small part of their method."

"No doubt," Julie says. "But do you still have any bottles left?"

"I'll have to check."

"It's important, Darlene. The VPD needs to run an analysis."

Darlene slides a hand onto her hip. "What could the police possibly want with my supplement?"

"There's an . . . um . . . ongoing investigation."

"Into the wellness center? Because of Tracy?"

"I really can't speak for the police," Julie says, beginning to regret coming here. "I'm just trying to help out."

"I love Tracy. I do. Like a sister," Darlene says in a condescending tone. "But she's struggled with—how best to put it—health and weight issues as long as I've known her. She's so susceptible to everything and anything. Give that girl a Tylenol, and she'll probably faint dead away. You understand?"

"I do. But it's more than just Tracy."

"What else could there be?"

"Darlene, I am involved because I'm a toxicologist—"

"That's an expert on poisons, isn't it?"

"Yes, but—"

Darlene's eyes scrunch. "You think the supplement is poisoned?"

"No . . . well, we don't know. There were irregularities. Someone got sick."

"Who did?" Darlene crosses her arms. "What's going on, Dr. Reed?"

"It's Rees. Again, I can't say. I probably shouldn't have come to see you at all. But after I spoke to Tracy—"

"All of this because Tracy thinks the results with Mind Over Body are too good to believe?"

"Did she also happen to mention the side effects she was experiencing?"

"Yes, but again . . . Tracy." Darlene rolls her eyes. "And personally, I feel absolutely fantastic. Never better."

"Then why not put all of this to rest by giving the VPD a sample of your supplement?"

"If it's that important, why don't the police just get it directly from Gerard?"

"It's a bit more complicated." Julie stifles a sigh. "Look, if you're right—and you may well be—then Mind Over Body has nothing to hide. And the quickest way to clear up any mix-up is for you to provide the VPD a sample of your supplement."

"I don't know." Darlene hesitates. "It almost feels like I'd be betraying Adèle."

Julie leans in closer to the other woman. "This is something you're putting into your body every day, Darlene."

"True . . ."

"What if Tracy happens to be right? Don't you want to ensure that whatever you're taking is safe in the long run?"

Darlene stares at Julie for several seconds. "All right," she finally says. "You can have a bottle."

"Terrific. But not me. It's got to go directly to the police officers. Chain of evidence and all that fancy legal stuff."

"Chain of evidence? This is craziness. They're good people, Adèle and Gerard. They care. They do."

Julie cocks her head. "Darlene, you haven't spoken to anyone else about this, have you?"

She waves a hand around the room. "When have I had time?"

"You can't tell anyone else. Not yet, anyway. Understand?"

"I won't. But this doesn't sit right with me."

"I get it," Julie says, feigning a lot more sympathy than she feels.

"OK. The cops can pick up the bottle. *Provided* I get it back as soon as they've cleared the sample. The stuff costs a fortune."

CHAPTER 45

The wait for the team to arrive is agony. But in less than thirty minutes, Cari is standing at the door to Shawna's tenth-floor condo in an LAPD windbreaker alongside the rest of the five-member search team. She has worked with most of them before and knows that the senior crime tech on the team—whose name is Doug, but whom everyone calls "Willy" because of his long, braided ponytail and graying beard—is one of the best in the business.

The lead uniformed officer pounds on the door. "Shawna Khan, this is the LAPD," he calls out in a loud voice. "We have a warrant to search these premises."

No one answers.

He pounds again. "This is your last opportunity to comply. If there's no response, we will break down the door."

Cari's breathing deepens as she sees the lead officer unclip his gun and remove it from his holster. The one beside him does the same, while a third officer steps up to the door, holding a compact battering ram in both hands.

The lead officer waits a few more seconds, and then nods to his colleague, who swings the battering ram. The door splinters around the knob, and it flies open.

"LAPD!" the lead officer shouts, as he and the others storm inside with firearms extended.

Tense seconds pass until the lead officer calls from inside. "All clear. There's no one here."

Another few minutes pass while the photographer snaps evidence of the scene prior to the search commencing. Then finally, Cari files inside with the rest of the team.

The condo is bright and modern—all white except for the stainless steel appliances. But its barrenness makes the strongest impression. There's not a single piece of art on the walls or a rug on the hardwood floor, and every visible countertop and surface is clear. For a moment, Cari wonders if Shawna has already moved out and simply abandoned her furniture. But as the team spreads out and starts to open the kitchen cupboards and drawers, Cari sees that it's stocked with food and supplies. And looking up, she notices the motion detector and video camera perched discreetly in the corner above one of the cabinets.

Cari heads past the living room and down the hallway to the master bedroom and ducks her head inside. The bed is made with four pillows and there's a digital alarm clock on the nightstand, but otherwise, it's as soulless as the kitchen and the living room. She heads into the bathroom, which is equally sterile. She opens the mirrored cabinet above the vanity. A few generic products line the shelves, including toothpaste, a hairbrush, a nail file, and an unopened bar of soap, but she doesn't see any pill bottles.

Cari moves on to the second bedroom, which has been converted into a home office. There, she sees the first signs that suggest Shawna might live here. Two large monitors stand on the desk beside a microphone and a pair of headphones, along with a scattering of computer accessories that Cari doesn't recognize. There are even a few knickknacks, including a Rubik's cube and a fidget spinner. With a gloved hand, Cari opens the desk drawers and leafs through the flash drives, pens, and assorted papers inside. But she doesn't spot anything that might tie Shawna to Dr. X Pharmaceuticals.

"Hey, Cari!" Willy calls from the walk-in closet in the same room. "You might want to check this puppy out."

Cari hurries over to the closet, where Willy is standing in front of a gunmetal-gray safe that is as tall and wide as a standard fridge. Its front bears the same sort of heavy metal dial that she has only seen on a bank safe.

Her neck tingles. "That's a good size for locking up the family jewels."

"Definitely a TL-30," Willy says with an appreciative whistle.

"TL-30?"

"Highest grading for a commercial safe. Means it would take a professional a minimum of thirty minutes to break into it."

"How long will it take you, Willy?"

"Not me," he says, pulling out his cell phone. "We'll need the department's safe engineer to crack this bad boy. Guessing Marty will have to use his angle grinder."

While they wait for the safe engineer to arrive, the team combs the rest of the condo. They find a few more personal items and clothes in the master bedroom, including hoodies, T-shirts, and a couple pairs of black sneakers that are very similar to what Shawna was wearing when Cari and the other detectives interviewed her in Vancouver.

"If Shawna really does live here," Cari says. "Then she keeps a pretty monastic existence."

Willy only shrugs. "I've seen all types."

She waves around the bare living room. "What's the point of the black-market DNP sales? What's she doing with all the money?"

"Saving up for a getaway pad in Tahiti?" Willy hypothesizes. "Squirreling it away in cryptocurrency for the day after Armageddon? Stuffing that big safe of hers full of greenbacks? Who knows? Not everyone who craves money actually spends it."

"I suppose," Cari says, unconvinced. Based on her interactions with Shawna and what she now sees—or doesn't see—in her home, Cari wonders if Shawna is driven more out of spite or even by the thrill of it rather than profit.

The expert locksmith, whose name tag reads "Marty," arrives within thirty minutes, carrying a tool bag over his shoulder. Diminutive and silent, he stands motionless in front of the safe's door for a good minute, before he kneels and pulls a large device out of his bag that looks to Cari like a sander.

"Told you," Willy says with a satisfied nod. "Angle grinder."

Cari watches with anticipation as Marty begins to cut at the door with the grinder. His progress is slow but steady. Halfway through, he has to stop and replace the blade on his device. Finally, Marty puts the grinder away and then snakes his fingers into the edges of the square gap he has just cut within the actual door to pry free a makeshift opening. The entire search team watches in dead silence as he inches it free.

"Good," Marty mutters to himself. "No booby trap."

The thought hadn't even occurred to Cari, but she holds her breath as the heavy piece of metal that is almost the size of the door itself falls away, exposing the safe's contents. Her eyes graze over the two large, round canisters, one with a skull-and-crossbones on it and the other with a triangular yellow hazard symbol. Her gaze rests on the clear jar on the top shelf that is filled with red-and-black capsules.

"Gotcha!" Willy hoots.

We do, Cari thinks as she glances up to the corner of the closet, where another video lens stares back down at her. *But you already know that, don't you?*

CHAPTER 46

"This still all sounds like a witch hunt to me," Darlene says as she stands in the doorway to her house, cradling the bottle in both hands as if it were a family heirloom.

"You could be right, Mrs. Hoffman," Anson says. "But we still have to check."

He remembers the knee-jerk defensiveness he felt after Julie told him that she had gone to see Darlene before he'd had a chance to return her call. But sensing Julie's genuine contrition, coupled with the fact that Darlene had agreed to hand over her bottles with potentially pivotal evidence, he held his tongue. And now Anson feels only appreciation for Julie's resourcefulness.

"Just because the Mind Over Body system is so effective, it's no reason to punish them," Darlene says.

"We're not trying to punish them," Anson says, mustering his patience.

"Kind of feels like you are," she snorts. "You promise you'll give it back to me as soon as you've run your little tests?"

"Right after," Theo says as he extends his hands toward her.

She hesitates another moment and then, with obvious reluctance, passes him the bottle.

Anson manages to maintain his polite smile until it's safely in Theo's grip. "Thank you, Ms. Hoffman," he says, spinning away from the door. "We'll be in touch."

As they walk back to the car, Theo says, "Wow, those two really have her under their spell."

"Like any decent con artists, huh?" Anson says.

"Yeah, I suppose. But Darlene sounds like she would take a bullet for Gerard and Adèle. You sure she hasn't spoken to them yet?"

"Almost doesn't matter at this point."

"Unless she gave them the opportunity to swap out this bottle, too?" Theo says, raising it up.

"I don't see it, Theo. Darlene's just not that good an actor. Not after the fuss she just made."

"Probably not, no."

They load into Anson's car and head for the forensic lab. On the way, Theo asks, "How are things back at the ranch?"

"Better," Anson says without hesitation.

Theo raises an eyebrow. "You took my advice and talked to Julie?"

"When have I ever taken your advice?"

Theo grins. "You're welcome."

Anson takes a deep breath. "We did talk, yeah."

"How did it go?"

"OK, I guess." He pauses. "I'm not normally a heart-on-my-sleeve kind of guy."

Theo chuckles. "You don't say."

"But at least the nightmare didn't recur last night."

"See. As they say, partner, one day at a time."

Anson motions to the bottle in Theo's arm, eager to get back to business. "DC told me the lab would make this their top priority," he says. "We should have an answer within a couple hours."

"I'll write up another warrant for Mind Over Body and Gerard's home that will give us access to everything once the test results come back."

"If it's positive."

"Are you expecting otherwise?"

Anson pulls up in front of the forensics lab. He leaves the car running, while Theo hurries inside to drop the bottle off with the accessioning clerk. As soon as he climbs back into the passenger seat, the phone rings with a call from Cari.

"The search of Shawna's condo paid off!" Cari blurts over the speaker phone. "We found kilos of raw DNP and thousands of capsules in an industrial-strength safe."

"Good work!" Anson says. "We'll pick her up now."

"Do you even know where she is?"

"The hospital. With her sister, who's still in the ICU."

"Shawna spends most of her time there," Theo adds.

"Out of guilt, no doubt," Anson grunts. "If she's even capable of it."

"I'm not sure she'll be that easy to find," Cari says. "Her place was wired with an advanced security monitoring system. Cameras every-where."

Anson grimaces. "You figure she knows you were there, huh?"

"I'm assuming."

"She could well be on the run," Anson says, as he flicks on his lights and sirens. "We'll go to the hospital now. And we'll send someone to check out her hotel."

"If we don't find her right away, we'll put out a BOLF," Theo adds.

"A *bolf*?" Cari asks. "Is that like what we call a BOLO?"

"Yup. Canadian style. A be-out-on-the-lookout-for."

"You'll call me the second you find her, right?" Cari asks.

"Absolutely," Anson says. He hangs up and uses the voice command to dial the deputy chief's number.

"What's up, Anson?" she answers.

"We dropped the bottle off at the lab," he says. "But Cari just called to confirm she found proof Shawna Khan is *the* DNP distributor behind Dr. X Pharmaceuticals. We're on our way to the hospital. We also need to send units to check out her hotel."

"On it."

"And DC," Anson says, "can you track her phone?"

"Without a warrant?" the deputy chief asks.

"Exigent circumstances. She's a huge flight risk."

"You know that's not enough."

"And at extremely high risk to re-offend. There are multiple deaths directly attributable to her product. If Shawna gets away, more will follow."

"I guess that'll have to do," she sighs. "Send me the number, and we'll trace it."

Anson switches off the siren as he pulls into the loading bay in front of St. Michael's. They bolt up the stairs to the ICU on the third floor. Anson flashes his identification to a frazzled young clerk. "We're looking for Maleeka Khan's sister, Shawna," he says.

"Don't know if she's still here." The shocked young woman waves a frantic hand over her shoulder toward the rooms behind her. "The patient's in room twelve. You can check with her nurse."

Inside room twelve, they find Maleeka lying motionless on the bed, still connected to a ventilator. A nurse in a gown, gloves, and a mask tends to one of her IV lines. But the chair pulled up beside the bed is empty.

After they've introduced themselves to the nurse, whose ID tag reads "Gwen, RN," Theo asks, "Have you seen Maleeka's sister?"

"Shawna left about fifteen or twenty minutes ago," Gwen says as she connects the IV tubing to a new bag. "Said she was just going to grab a bite."

"And then come back here?"

"That's what she told me."

Anson picks up on her skepticism. "You didn't believe her?"

"Well, the way she said goodbye to Maleeka. Hugging her like that. Felt to me like she might be leaving for longer than just lunch."

Anson shoots Theo a look and then asks, "Do you have Shawna's cell number?"

"I do, yes." Gwen steps away from the IV line and over to the bedside laptop computer. She dictates the number to Anson, who immediately texts it to the deputy chief. "I was kind of surprised that she left when she did."

"Why is that?" Anson asks.

"Dr. Jansson is supposed to come by anytime now. The plan is to extubate Maleeka—to take her off the ventilator."

"And then she'll wake up?"

"Soon after, yes," Gwen says. "Since Shawna has been here pretty much day and night, I expected her to want to be here for that, too."

Theo nods. "We'll be sending officers here. For observation. But if Shawna comes back before then, please do not mention we were here."

Gwen puts a hand on her hip. "What's this about, detectives?"

"Shawna's a suspect in a major crime," Theo says.

"Shawna?" Her eyes go wide. "Is she . . . dangerous?"

"Not to you or her sister, no," Anson says. "But she's a fugitive now."

They leave the shaken nurse and head back downstairs. Just as they reach the car, Anson gets a text from the deputy chief. "Damn it!" he mutters.

"What?"

Anson turns the screen out to show Theo the message that reads: "Shawna's cell phone offline. Last reported location was St. Mike's."

"She's gone to ground," Theo says. "We need to get that BOLF out."

"And check the airports and other transport hubs."

Theo eyes Anson with concern. "Shawna is gonna to try to flee the country, isn't she?"

CHAPTER 47

Adèle looks up from her laptop where she sits across the desk from Gerard. "Trust me, *chéri*. If the cops had found anything, they would've come back by now."

"We knew they weren't going to find anything in the bottles they confiscated." Gerard sucks his teeth. "Doesn't mean they won't look elsewhere."

"Even if they do, we won't let them find anything," she says with a reassuring smile. "Have you read through the offer?"

Gerard pulls off his glasses and rubs his eyes. "Yes. And I just heard back from our lawyer."

"What does he think?"

"Like me, he thinks what Lloyd is asking—demanding, actually—is expensive but not outrageous," Gerard says. "If we refinance, we'll be able to cover it."

"But we'll be carrying too much debt, no?"

"A lot, yes. Too much? I don't think so. In a year, we'll probably look back and think we got a great deal." He exhales. "Besides, we've got no choice, babe."

Adèle reaches across the desk to caress the back of his hand. "I guess not."

Her touch is welcome. He craves her physical reassurance. "How's it going on your end?"

"Not bad," she says. "Of the fifteen outstanding bottles, I've reached nine of the clients holding them so far."

"Thank God we've been so selective." Their policy has always been to only give the DNP-laced bottles to clients they deem most influential for growing their business. The majority of their members have bottles that are as free of DNP as the ones the VPD already confiscated.

"What's the reaction been so far among the ones you've reached?" Gerard asks.

"No one's questioned it. I just say that the B vitamins are outdated and prone to crystalize in the bottles." Adèle laughs. "As soon as I tell them we will replace their bottles and throw in a one-month free supply, all they want to know is how soon it will happen."

"Brilliant. Devious. Sexy." He lays his other hand over the back of hers and squeezes it. "I really would be lost without you, babe."

"*Moi aussi, chéri.*"

"Who's left to reach?"

Adèle glances over to her screen. "The Coopers, Wongs, Howards, Tracy McGowan, Raj Sandhu . . . Oh, and my little girl crush—at least on her part—Darlene Hoffman."

CHAPTER 48

Had he not known better, Anson would've assumed the hotel room had been ransacked. Every drawer is open with random clothes poking out. The bedding is twisted in a heap. One shoe lies on its side outside the closet, its mate nowhere in sight.

"Someone forgot to do a final room scan before checking out," Theo says, deadpan.

"Shawna must've been frantic." Anson motions to the open suitcase in the corner. "Wonder why she came back at all?"

Theo points to the room safe inside the closet, its door wide open. "To pick up her passport?"

"Yeah, probably. That and a few essentials."

"We should head to the airport," Theo says. "A flight is her best escape route."

"DC has already sent officers there and alerted the on-site RCMP officers," Anson says. "And Border Services is checking all flight manifests."

"Shouldn't we have our own eyes on the departure lounges, too?"

"Wouldn't hurt."

Anson's phone rings, and seeing Cari's name on the call display, he answers it on speakerphone. "You were right, Cari," he says. "Your search must've tipped off Shawna. She fled about fifteen minutes before we got to the hospital. We're in her hotel room now. Looks like she left most of her stuff behind."

"No luck on tracing her phone?" Cari asks.

"She dumped it at St. Mike's," Anson says. "Anything on your end?"

"Her driver's license expired last year, and she never renewed it. So at least she won't be able to rent a car."

"There are still taxis, buses, trains, ferries . . .'"

"Air is her best bet," Theo says.

"My captain wants me to be there when you bring her in," Cari says. "I'm catching a flight back to Vancouver in just over an hour."

"We'll try to have her in custody by the time you touch down," Anson says.

"I'll text you when I land," she says and then disconnects.

"OK," Anson says to Theo as he turns for the door. "Let's go to the airport."

As they're driving through downtown, Anson's phone rings with a call from the deputy chief, and he answers over the car's Bluetooth speaker. "Any luck with the manifests?" he asks her.

"No," she says. "According to Border Services, there are no flights leaving in the next forty-eight hours booked under the name of Shawna Khan."

"What about other Khans? Maybe she travels under a different first name?"

"Good luck with that," the deputy chief says. "'Khan is like the Smith of surnames in the Middle East and parts of Africa."

"Don't we have her passport info?" Theo asks.

"No," she says. "We don't know which flight or airline she came in on."

"Do you have any good news at all for us, DC?"

"Not related to Shawna. But I thought you might like to hear that the toxicology screen on the bottle you dropped off at the lab is back."

Anson grips the steering wheel tighter. "And?"

"It looks like your fitness club was adding a little pick-me-up to their energy drink after all," she says. "It's positive for DNP."

Theo punches the dashboard triumphantly. "Of course it is!"

"Thanks, DC," Anson says with a satisfied nod to his partner.

"Oh, and DC," Theo adds. "Can you get a judge to sign off on a new search warrant for Mind Over Body? This one with access to all their electronic records, too? And also a search warrant for Gerard and Adèle's home?"

"Send me the paperwork," the deputy chief says. "I'll get the warrants."

After Anson hangs up, he turns to his partner and says, "We should make one quick stop before the airport."

"Where?"

"Her nurse made it sound as if Maleeka would be off the ventilator by now."

Theo nods. "The hospital is on the way to the airport, anyway."

Anson does a quick shoulder check and then veers into the right lane, before turning down Burrard Street. He pulls into St. Michael's, parks in the same loading zone again, and then heads up to the ICU with Theo. Through the window of her room, Anson notices that Maleeka is moving on her bed and the ventilator tubing is no longer in her mouth.

Gwen meets them outside the room. "Shawna didn't come back," she says.

"We've come to speak to Maleeka," Theo says. "Is she awake enough?"

"It's only been a few minutes since we took her off the ventilator. The sedation hasn't fully worn off. She's still pretty groggy."

"Please, Gwen," Theo says. "It's important."

She steps out of the way, and the three of them enter the room together.

Maleeka looks up with glazed eyes. Without makeup or fake eyelashes, she looks much younger to Anson. Just a kid.

"Hi, Maleeka," Theo says. "Remember us?"

"The *poh-lease*," she says with a croak in her voice.

"That's right." Theo smiles. "How are you feeling?"

"Kinda ripped."

"You almost died, Maleeka. You took the same type of pills as Rain did."

She waves a hand in front of her face. "Not the same type."

"Your toxicology tests confirmed it was DNP."

"Not the same type," she repeats with a dreamy smile. "The same pills."

"You and Rain shared those pills, didn't you?" Anson asks.

Maleeka nods. "Then that night at her pad, I snapped them back up."

"The night she died?"

"The night we lost Ray-Ray."

"Why did you grab them?"

"I would've been in deep shit if I'd left them behind," Maleeka says. "Besides, why waste quality product?"

Anson rests a hand on the bedrail and kneels closer to the level of her face. "Maleeka, we know your sister supplied you with the DNP."

"No. Not Shawn. She's a techie geek. She doesn't dabble."

"We know about her online sales business," Anson says. "Dr. Slim Pharmaceuticals and all the other offshoots."

Maleeka's eyes seem to focus and, for the first time, she looks concerned. "No. You're off base."

"You know we're not, Maleeka," Theo says gently.

"Leave Oshana out of this!"

"Your sister's on the run, Maleeka," Theo says. "We need to find her. Before she does something rash. Can you help us?"

Maleeka rolls away from them. "Nurse, I'm not feeling so good."

Gwen looks from Theo to Anson with a helpless shrug. "She does need to rest. Maybe come back later?"

"We will," Theo says.

As soon as they step out of the room, Anson turns to Theo. "You hear that?"

"Yeah. She called her Oshana. That doesn't sound like one of Maleeka's little pet names."

"Hopefully it's the one on Shawna's passport."

"Worth a shot."

As they head down the hallway, Anson texts the deputy chief: "Please ask Border Services to check the manifests for an 'Oshana Khan.'"

By the time they reach the car, his phone vibrates with a response from their boss. He reads it aloud to Theo: "Oshana Khan booked on Air India to New Delhi. Departs 21:35. Has connection through to the Maldives."

Theo chuckles. "What do you want to bet that the Maldives has no extradition treaty with Canada or the US?"

CHAPTER 49

The Customs agent waves Cari through, and she steps into the arrival area where Anson and Theo are waiting for her. "No sign of Shawna?" she asks.

"Not yet," Theo says. "But her flight doesn't leave for two hours. And she's already checked in online."

"There's no visible police presence in the departure terminal, is there?"

"Nothing but plainclothes." Anson folds his arms in mock outrage. "You thought we'd march in in full parade dress?"

Cari smiles, glad to be back with her two Canadian colleagues. "Can't promise you the LAPD wouldn't have stormed in in SWAT gear."

Theo wiggles a finger between Anson and Cari. "We're going to have to hang back a couple of departure lounges away from her gate so Shawna doesn't spot us."

"Where do you plan to make the arrest?" Cari asks.

"Hopefully before the gate," Anson says. "We have an officer in an airline uniform at the check-in desk and another who's undercover as a baggage loader waiting in the walkway in case she gets past. The rest of the team will be scattered around the lounge, all dressed as passengers."

"Sounds right."

Theo taps his ear, indicating a discreet headphone. "We'll hear once anyone confirms a sighting."

Cari's heart thrums as they stride in to the international departure gates. Outside the security checkpoint, Anson flashes his ID to the RCMP officer, who pauses the rest of the line to expedite their passage.

Since Shawna's flight is scheduled to depart from Gate 79, they stop to wait at Gate 76. The lounge is already filled with passengers waiting for a British Airways flight, which is supposed to leave for London ten minutes after Shawna's flight. Anson sits two rows over from Cari and pretends to read a paper he picked up from a seat next to him, while Theo is seated at the end of the aisle, working on his phone.

Cari holds her phone in her hand, too. Out of the corner of her eye, she studies each female passenger who heads by, focusing on the ones traveling alone. The gates are crowded with an eclectic mix of travelers. A young, heavily tattooed couple doze on each other's shoulder, a few seats over. Behind Cari, an exasperated mother tries to contain her two sons, who act as if they're wired on too much sugar and too little sleep. Many of the people heading for Shawna's gate are dressed in Punjabi attire—the men in turbans and the women wearing saris along with headscarves.

Minutes pass without a sighting. *Has she changed plans?*

Cari's worry intensifies when the gate agent welcomes passengers seated in first and then business class to board Shawna's flight. She studies the passengers lined up to board, but none of them look familiar.

A pit forms in her stomach as the agent opens the boarding to the lower zones, and more passengers flood into the line. Then Cari notices an elderly couple in traditional garb who emerge from the restaurant just beyond the gate accompanied by a younger woman with a backpack slung over her shoulder. Dressed in a similar sari and headscarf as the older woman, she appears to be the couple's daughter or granddaughter.

But despite how close the young woman is standing, the couple ignores her and chats only to each other. Cari glances over to Anson, who has lowered his paper and is watching them, too.

Cari's chest hammers as the three passengers inch closer to the gate agent who's scanning tickets and passports. The young woman reaches the desk and holds up her passport. The agent glances over her shoulder to the officer posing as an airline employee.

Time freezes. Everything stills.

Then everyone erupts into motion at once. Anson hops up from his seat, Theo just behind him. Cari fires out of her chair after them.

The young woman at the gate pivots and shoves the turbaned man backwards. Someone screams as he falls over, knocking down the man closest to him. The woman sprints back toward the main terminal.

"Police! Freeze!" an undercover officer shouts as she rushes past him.

Anson reaches her first. He lunges and catches her with an arm around her midsection, tackling her onto the carpet. And the scarf falls away from Shawna's flushed face.

Struggling like a roped calf, Shawna rolls onto her belly. She shoots her hand to her mouth and then grinds her face into the carpet.

As Anson scrambles to his feet, Theo grabs Shawna by the shoulder and Cari grips her thigh. Together, they forcibly roll her onto her back.

"Get the fuck away from me!" she cries, sounding as if her mouth is full of marbles.

Two more plainclothes officers, one in jeans and the other dressed as a cleaner, yank her up to her feet.

"What's in your mouth, Shawna?" Cari asks.

Without replying, Shawna wipes her damp face on her shoulder.

"Was it DNP?" Anson demands.

Shawna glares back, her eyes filled with hate. "Is my sister off the ventilator?"

"Maleeka is doing OK," Theo says.

Shawna's eyes narrow to slits. "Did she tell you how to find me?" she spits, her voice clear now after another noisy gulp.

"Call an ambulance!" Theo says to one of the other officers.

"What's the point?" Shawna laughs bitterly. "Didn't you see what happened to those stupid vain bitches?"

"How many pills did you take?" Anson demands.

Ignoring the question, Shawna says, "I just gave them what they wanted. What most of them deserved."

Cari looks over to Anson. "We gotta get her stomach pumped."

"Too late!" Shawna cries. "You think I'd let Dad watch me go down for this? Or blame me—*again*—for what happened to his little princess? Fuck that!"

CHAPTER 50

Julie can't believe anyone would need a screen as huge as the ones lining the wall of the electronics showroom in front of her. But Anson has been teasing her lately about her ten-year-old TV that he describes as "too small for a laptop." So she has decided that, with his birthday coming up in a week, she will surprise him with a new TV to watch his beloved football and hockey games.

Her phone rings and Julie holds up a hand to interrupt the young salesman's stream of meaningless technical jargon. "Excuse me, I have to take this," she says as she answers it.

"Are you at the hospital, Julie?" Anson asks urgently.

"No, I'm running a couple of . . . late errands," she says.

"We need your help!"

Julie hears multiple sirens wailing in the background of the call. She steps away from the salesman. "What's going on, Anson? Where are you?"

"The airport. Maleeka's sister just OD'd on DNP!"

"The sister, too?" Her voice cracks. "What the hell?"

"Turns out Shawna is one of the main online suppliers for DNP. It's how Rain and Maleeka got theirs. We tracked her down at the airport. And she swallowed a handful of pills in front of us."

"How many?"

"Don't know. She wouldn't say. The paramedics are packaging her up now."

Julie turns away from the bewildered salesman and rushes for the exit. "Are they taking her to St. Mike's?" she asks Anson.

"No," he says. "Richmond Hospital is the closest ER. They've got to pump her stomach ASAP, right?"

"Depends," Julie says. "It's not safe to do if she's not alert enough. She could aspirate—inhale—everything into her lungs."

"I'm guessing it was a lot of pills, Julie."

Julie leaves the store and runs to her car. "I'm in south Vancouver now," she says, panting. "I could meet you at Richmond Hospital in fifteen minutes."

"Perfect."

In the light evening traffic, Julie flies over the Oak Street Bridge and reaches Richmond Hospital in twelve minutes. She races through the ER entrance and flashes her ID to the triage nurse, a stocky, balding man who is leaning over to measure the blood pressure on the elderly woman seated in front of him.

"Julie Rees," she says. "ER doc at St. Mike's and a toxicologist with Poison Control. Has the overdose from the airport arrived?"

"They're less than five minutes out," the nurse says calmly as he pulls the blood pressure cuff off the patient.

"Who's the ER physician on right now?"

"Dr. Ho."

"Vincent?" Julie says, hoping it's her old classmate from their ER residency.

"Yup." The nurse points to the sliding door behind him. "He should be with the rest of the team in the resus room, getting prepped."

Julie hurries into the main ER and heads straight for the resuscitation room. It's smaller than the one at St. Michael's, which houses three mirrored bays. But the controlled chaos feels the same. Everyone is active, preparing IV bags, donning protective equipment, or manning computer stations.

"Julie? Julie Rees?" A shorter man in a mask and gown asks from across the room. "What brings you out to the burbs?"

"Hi, Vince," Julie says. "I got the heads-up about the DNP poisoning coming from the airport. I've dealt with a handful of cases in the past few months."

"Glad to have you here then," he says, without a trace of territoriality. "Don't know much about DNP except what I've seen and read regarding Rain."

"It's brutal, Vince. Just brutal."

"Seizures and hyperthermia, right?"

"Exactly," Julie says. "Also, volatile blood pressures and malignant arrythmias. It's like you're chasing one crisis after another. Sometimes, simultaneously. The key is to get the temperature down. Active cooling with cold saline, fans, and sprays. And do you have dantrolene available?"

He motions to an IV pole where a bag is hanging. "It's waiting."

She flashes him a thumbs-up. "I was told the patient took the pills only minutes ago."

He nods. "We got a large-bore NG tube and suction ready, if she's awake enough for us to pump her stomach."

"Excellent." She is about to ask about other drugs when she hears the banging noises and raised voices coming from beyond the room.

"They're here!" one of the nurses calls out.

"Mind if I stay?" Julie asks Vincent.

"I insist!" he says. "And feel free to offer any tips."

A pair of paramedics slam their gurney into a corner of the glass door, trying to navigate it into the room. One of them leans over the patient and pins her to the stretcher as she thrashes away on it. Two police officers follow them. It takes both paramedics with the help of the cops to transfer the flailing patient onto the hospital stretcher.

"Twenty-six-year-old picked up from YVR," the second paramedic reports as they finish moving Shawna. "Apparently consumed a handful of DNP pills. She was alert but noncooperative when we loaded her. Then she spiked a temperature of forty-one degrees and became delirious. Blood sugar normal, but her blood pressure plummeted as we were approaching. And she started seizing just as were pulling in."

"Have you given her any meds?" Vincent asks as he leans forward and tries to flash a light in her twitching eyes.

"Nope. Only barely got an IV in her right elbow."

"Terry, load her up with five milligrams of midazolam," Vincent calls.

Another bedside nurse says, "Her temp is forty-one-point-six, Dr. Ho. I've never seen one that high."

Vincent looks uncertainly over to Julie, who nods to the IV pole.

"Let's infuse the dantrolene," he says. "Run in cold IV Ringer's lactate. Four degrees. And get the fans going with cold sprays of water."

Shawna keeps jerking on the bed. It's hard for Julie to watch, keenly aware of the brain damage the electrical storm might already be causing.

"We're going to have to paralyze her, aren't we?" Vincent asks.

"You don't have a choice," Julie murmurs.

"OK," he announces to the rest of the team. "Let's get set up for intubation."

Just as Vincent says it, Shawna flops back on the bed and goes utterly still. For a fleeting moment, there is serene peacefulness. But then the bedside nurse cries, "We've lost the pulse!"

On the monitor above the bed, the heart tracing squiggles up and down with the chaotic pattern that signals ventricular fibrillation. The same nurse shoots out her locked hands, leans onto Shawna's chest, and begins compressing it with CPR.

"Let's shock her!" Vincent calls.

It's the right the decision, the only one, but Julie's heart still sinks.

She watches as one of the nurses applies the pads on Shawna's chest, while skillfully working around her colleague who's pumping away at Shawna's chest like a piston engine. "All clear?" the nurse calls, applying paddles to the pads as the other nurse yanks her hands away from the chest.

The jolt of electricity stiffens Shawna's body. But the squiggles don't budge on the monitor. And the bedside nurse immediately resumes CPR.

"Epinephrine every three minutes, guys," Vincent instructs. "And let's give her three hundred of amiodarone."

The nurses push in IV medication after medication. They pause CPR to shock Shawna every two minutes. Nothing changes.

For Julie, it's like watching the ending of the same tragic play she has seen several times before. She admires the effort and resourcefulness of the staff, but she knows it will make no difference.

After eight rounds of shocks, the line on the monitor dwindles down from its frantic squiggles to a lazily drifting single line across the screen.

"She's flatlining," Vincent says. "Asystole. Let's give her some atropine and more epi." He looks to Julie with helpless eyes. "Maybe we should try an external pacemaker?"

Julie shakes her head.

"Thrombolyze her with clot busters? In case it's a pulmonary embolus."

"It won't help, Vince."

"There's got to be something," he argues. "She's so damn young."

Julie rests a hand on his shoulder. "There's nothing, Vince. When it gets to this point . . . she's already gone."

CHAPTER 51

Anson yawns again, having slept less than four hours the previous night. He glances at Theo, who looks as exhausted as he feels. By the time they left Richmond Hospital and filled out their preliminary report, it was well after two a.m. And they had to be up in time to meet the search team at seven o'clock to coincide with Mind Over Body's opening.

Cari, on the other hand, seems alert and energetic as she sips her coffee while she paces beside the parked cars. "At least one of us had a decent sleep," Anson says to her.

Cari shrugs. "It could've been longer, but it was satisfying."

Theo frowns. "Even after what happened at the airport?"

"Obviously, I'd rather we took Shawna alive," she says. "But either way, Dr. X Pharmaceuticals has been shut down. Permanently."

"I'd feel better if we had the chance to interrogate her," Theo says. "And made sure she didn't have any partners."

"She behaved more like a lone wolf," Anson says, draining the last of his coffee.

"Let's hope," Theo says.

"We still have her laptop and her home computers, Theo," Cari says. "If she had any partners, we'll find out."

"Hopefully, they'll also lead us to her supplier and her clients."

"And to a bunch more arrests," Anson adds.

"Not to mention stopping the supply of this poison to those most vulnerable," Cari says.

"That, too," Anson says. He suspects she must be thinking of her sister again. "With any luck, we're about to make another dent in that supply chain this morning."

"No time like the present." Theo lifts up the search warrant to show the assembled team, which, aside from Cari, consists of the same six members who conducted the last search of the premises. "OK, gang. This time, we're entitled to access anything we find on-site."

He leads the team around the corner, down the street, and through the entrance of the Mind Over Body Wellness Center.

"You're back again?" a wide-eyed Colby murmurs from behind the reception desk as the officers spread out through the lobby and beyond.

"We are, indeed." Theo lays the new search warrant on the desk. "But this time, we have a judicial order for all of your electronic and paper records."

"I . . . I better . . ."

"Yeah," Anson says. "You better get Gerard."

But before Colby has even left his chair, Gerard bursts into the reception area. "You didn't make a big enough mess the last time you were here?"

"We didn't have a court order for your computer and other records last time we were here," Anson says.

Gerard squints at them. "Are you saying you found something suspicious on your last search?"

Anson shakes his head. "We're not saying anything, Mr. Martin."

"Then what's going on?"

"Those bottles we confiscated last time weren't the only ones in circulation, were they?"

Gerard scowls. "Haven't you ever reused a bottle, Detective?"

"Not those kinds of bottles," Anson snorts.

"We can't be responsible for what happens to our supplement after we give it out, can we?"

"You are facing multiple charges, Mr. Martin." Theo raises his index finger. "One, administration of a noxious substance." He lifts a new finger for each subsequent allegation. "Two, trafficking in a controlled substance. Three, consumption by fraudulent means."

"And don't forget manslaughter and possible homicide," Anson adds.

Gerard grimaces. "Manslaughter?"

"In the death of your business partner, Cecilia Hunter."

"Are you arresting me?"

"Not quite yet," Theo says.

"Help yourself to the computers and the files." Gerard spins away and stomps off down the hallway.

Two officers immediately follow him to ensure that he doesn't tamper with potential evidence.

The entire search takes a little over an hour. They find no obviously incriminating evidence, but Anson isn't discouraged. He's confident the electronic records will provide more answers.

A VPD van pulls up onto the curb at the front entrance for the officers to load the confiscated boxes of files, computer components, and bottles into the back.

As the three detectives stand back and watch, Cari says, "He's not going to make this easy for us, is he?"

"Doesn't matter," Anson says. "He's guilty as sin."

"Gerard might have a point," Theo says. "One tainted bottle might not be enough to convince a jury beyond a reasonable doubt."

"Once we go through his client list, we'll find more bottles."

"Plus," Cari says. "They have a whole separate client list in their Beverly Hills office that the LAPD is about to raid."

CHAPTER 52

Cari sits beside Anson and Theo across the desk from Deputy Chief Brower. Cari didn't meet her on the previous visit to Vancouver, but she likes the other woman instantly. Despite her gruff exterior, there's a sincerity to the deputy chief that Cari finds missing in her captain.

"That was solid police work connecting Shawna Khan to the DNP distribution, Detective Garcia. Are you sure you don't want a job with the VPD?" The deputy chief wags her finger playfully between Anson and Theo. "I could make an opening."

Anson rolls his eyes. "Thanks for the unwavering support, DC."

Cari grins. "It was very much a team effort."

"So where are we now?" the deputy chief asks them.

"Babar is pulling Mind Over Body's client lists from their hard drives," Theo says. "According to him, he'll get them to us by the afternoon. And also, according to him, I better not ask again until at least after lunch."

The deputy chief chuckles. "He puts the *cur* in curmudgeon."

"With their client list, we should be able to track the outstanding bottles to test," Theo says. "And find more of the laced supplement."

"I don't like the wait," Anson says. "They could be cleaning house with their clients right now—swapping out bottles—the same way they did with their own supply before our first search."

The deputy chief frowns. "But surely the clients will tell us if they do."

"Better to ask forgiveness than permission. We won't be able to prove a thing after the fact."

"What do you suggest, Anson?"

"Why don't we pick up Gerard and Adèle now?" he says. "Hold them for a few hours while we're waiting for their client list. Divide them up and question them separately. One of them might crack."

"Do you have enough to hold them on?"

The two VPD detectives share a look. "Not sure we do yet," Theo admits.

"If we don't, they might make a run for it like Shawna did," Cari points out.

The deputy chief leans back in her chair, considering it. "Couldn't you pick them up on a lesser charge? Like criminal negligence causing bodily harm?"

"Works for me," Anson says, rising from his chair.

"By the way, we got the final toxicology result on the bottle you left with the lab." The deputy chief reads from her computer screen. "The concentration of DNP in the bottle was roughly point oh-two-five milligrams per milliliter."

Cari does the mental calculation. "That's about fifty milligrams per two-liter bottle."

The deputy chief chuckles. "If you say so. I'd be a rich accountant like my brother if I was any good at math."

"That's a half of a capsule for every bottle," Anson says. "With that concentration, you'd probably have to drink five or six bottles—ten liters, minimum—to get yourself into the toxic range."

"That must have been what they were counting on to avoid killing their clients," Theo says.

"It didn't help their partner Cecilia, though," Cari says.

Theo shakes his head. "The pathologist told us that Cecilia Hunter had super-high levels of DNP in her system. Way higher than Rain's."

Anson gestures to the deputy chief's screen. "With those concentrations, Cecilia would've had to drink a bathtub full of the supplement to end up with the blood level she did."

"Like you suggested, Anson," Cari says. "Either someone screwed up on a colossal scale preparing the batch of supplement that killed Cecilia. Or she took the capsules straight out of the bottle."

The skin around Anson's eyes creases. "There's one more possibility."

The deputy chief raises an eyebrow. "Which is?"

"What if Cecilia didn't even know she was taking DNP?" Cari answers for Anson.

"Yeah, maybe Gerard and Adèle wanted to permanently silence their silent partner," Theo suggests.

The deputy chief studies them for a moment. "All good hypotheses, detectives," she says. "Why don't you go ask them?"

The three of them leave the VPD building and step out into a sudden deluge. Cari's hair is soaked by the time she crosses the street to Anson's car. As they drive, the rain pelts the windshield so hard that even with the wipers on maximum, there's a constant film of moisture across it.

Cari feels her phone buzzing in her pocket, and she pulls it out to see an incoming call from Zach.

"Man, what a nightmare that was!" Zach gripes.

"Shawna's computer?" Cari asks.

"Yeah," he says. "That one taxed my hacking skills to the max."

"But you were able to get into her system?"

"Course."

Cari taps the speaker button on her phone. "Zach, I'm putting you on speaker. I'm in the car here with two Canadian colleagues, Anson and Theo."

"Sure," he says. "But what's with the noise in the background?"

"Hey, Zach. Theo here. What you're hearing is the soundtrack of Vancouver in November. Sheer rainfall."

"Zach, it's Anson. Thanks for all the good leads you've dug up for us."

"Couldn't agree more," Cari says. "Speaking of, what did you find on Shawna's system?"

"In terms of her supplier," Zach says, "Shawna was ordering the DNP in bulk from a chemical factory outside Mumbai. But don't blame them."

"Why not?"

"The company is aboveboard. They screen their clients. Well, sort of. Shawna had these bogus certificates claiming to be some kind of dye manufacturer who needed DNP to make her product."

"Could you tell if Shawna was working with anyone else?" Cari asks.

"From everything I've seen, it looks like Shawna was a one-person outfit. She handled it all, from marketing to shipping."

"How about her clientele?"

"Now, that was a challenge. Holy! But I was able to crack the app that sent out the email purchase receipts."

"You genius, you," Cari says.

"You figure? Three-quarters of my Cal Tech classmates are running multimillion-dollar IT startups, and I got a union job with the LAPD. You do the math." He snorts. "Anyway, I exported the list of her clients' emails and shipping addresses to a database."

"No names?" Cari asks.

"Oh, there are names, too, but I wouldn't trust them as far as I could throw them."

"Can you search the database by their shipping address?" Anson pipes up.

"Sure. Easy."

"Can you see if there's a match for Mind Over Body Wellness Center?" Theo glances down at his phone. "Eleven seventy-three Mainland Street, Vancouver, BC."

"Hang on a sec," Zach says.

The pounding of the rain against the car's roof fills the silence as they wait in tense anticipation.

After a minute, Zach says, "Looks like they're not just any client."

"What does that mean?" Cari asks.

"Judging by the number of orders I see here, Mind Over Body was one of her oldest and most consistent clients."

CHAPTER 53

His mahogany desk has never looked so oversized to Gerard as it does now that the cops have confiscated his iMac and everything else he kept on it. He sits behind it, staring helplessly at his phone while wondering how to plug the gaping holes in their operation.

Where the fuck are you, Adèle?

Gerard slept overnight at the office and hasn't seen Adèle since yesterday. She hasn't answered any of his calls or texts this morning.

Slut! Of all mornings to sleep over at some random's place.

Gerard squints at the tiny font on his phone as he scrolls through the list of names, trying to jog his memory. He is going to have to figure out for himself which of the last few clients Adèle hasn't reached who still might have incriminating bottles in their possession. He recites the names in his head that he recognizes: the Wongs, the Coopers, Raj Sandhu, Darlene Hoffman, and Tracy McGowan.

That's only five. He's sure there is a sixth. Just as he starts to go through the list again, the door to his office flies open and the detectives march in. The slob, the second-rate Asian Armani model, and the cute, full-figured Latina.

"Again?" Gerard groans, as he pockets his phone.

None of them say a word until they reach his desk. Then Detective

Kostas looks him dead in the eye and says, "Gerard Martin, we are arresting you for the offense of administration of a noxious substance and for trafficking in controlled substances. You have the right to retain and instruct counsel without delay."

"You are not obliged to say anything, but anything you do say may be given in evidence," Detective Chen adds. "Do you understand?"

"Yes," Gerard mutters, resisting the urge to tell them to go fuck themselves.

"Where is Ms. Gagnon?" Detective Garcia asks.

Exactly! "I haven't seen Adèle this morning."

Detective Chen extracts a pair of handcuffs and motions for Gerard to get up.

"Is that necessary?" Gerard asks as he rises to his feet.

"You tell us."

Gerard holds up his hands. "Happy to cooperate."

The two male detectives flank Gerard as they walk him out of the building and through the rain puddles to where a black police wagon is parked at the curb with lights flashing.

Gerard sits alone in the back of the wagon as two uniformed cops drive him back to the VPD Headquarters. Inside, they leave him with a bored-looking officer who processes his information. After the officer completes the form, he pushes a phone across the desk. "Would you like to make your call now?"

Gerard doesn't know any criminal lawyers, so he dials the office of his corporate attorney, Stephan Kohler.

The receptionist puts him on hold, and almost a minute passes before Stephan finally comes on the line. "Gerard, hi. I thought we already have a meeting in the books for later today?"

"I've been arrested, Stephan."

The line goes silent.

Gerard briefly explains his predicament.

Stephan doesn't speak for several more seconds after Gerard finishes. "Do they have proof the supplement from Mind Over Body was tainted?" he finally asks in a tone so strained that it sounds as if he's being strangled.

"They have a bottle that tested positive for DNP. But there's no proof—to the best of my knowledge—linking it directly to me."

"All right," Stephan says. "I'm not a criminal lawyer, but my colleague, Laura Mazur, is one of the best in town. I'll send her down there."

"When?"

"As soon as she gets out of court."

"Shit. OK. Ask her to hurry."

"I will. Meantime, Gerard, do *not* speak to anyone else."

Another officer escorts Gerard to a room down the hallway. Inside, there is only a desk and a few chairs that are bolted to the floor. The door has a window that looks shatterproof. A camera is mounted prominently in the corner.

After half an hour or so, Detective Kostas ducks his head in the room. "Can we talk now, or would you rather wait for your lawyer to be present?"

Gerard understands that he should wait, but he's desperate to find out what the cops discovered in the hour between searching his premises and coming back to arrest him. "I've got nothing else to do."

Five minutes later, the two male detectives return without Detective Garcia and sit down across from him.

Detective Chen eyes him impassively. "Are you familiar with a website called Dr. Slim Pharmaceuticals?"

How could they know? I don't keep those records on our computers. Gerard rubs his face. "Sounds vaguely familiar."

"It should. Considering it's the biggest supplier of DNP in both Vancouver and LA."

"And Mind Over Body is one of Dr. Slim's top clients," Detective Kostas adds.

Gerard snorts. "As if."

"We have their records, Mr. Martin," Detective Chen says. "And we can prove you have been ordering from them, regularly and for a long time."

Gerard tries to swallow away the tightness that is forming again at the base of his throat. "Maybe it would be better if I do wait for my lawyer, after all?"

"Not a problem. And by the time he or she gets here, we might have added manslaughter or homicide to your list of charges."

"That's bullshit. And you know it!"

"Look it at from our point of view, Gerard," Detective Kostas says. "We know beyond a shadow of a doubt that you were ordering DNP and using it to lace your supplement. And that one of your partners died from a DNP overdose. Pretty hard to believe they're not connected."

Detective Chen nods. "The only question left is: Was her death accidental or deliberate? In other words, manslaughter or murder?"

"That's craziness!" Gerard scours his brain, trying to figure out what they already know with certainty. He holds up a hand. "OK. OK. Let's say *hypothetically* that someone was adding small but very safe amounts of DNP to our supplement. The only reason to do so would be to get the most positive results for the clients. To encourage membership. To grow a business. Killing someone—accidentally or otherwise—would blow the whole thing apart in a flash."

"Someone made a mistake, then?" Detective Chen suggests.

"No, no, no." Gerard waves his hand. "*If* I were to have done what you're accusing me of, I would've staked my life on not making that kind of mistake."

"Then how did Cecilia Hunter wind up poisoned from an overwhelming amount of DNP?"

Confused, Gerard lets his arm drop to the table. "Overwhelming amount?"

"A way higher concentration than what was in your regular supplement."

Gerard shakes his head, his mind filling with possibilities. "I have no idea."

Detective Chen leans forward. "Were the Hunters aware you were adding DNP to your supplement?"

A thought begins to take hold. "I'm admitting to absolutely nothing." Gerard pauses to rehearse his next line in his head. "But let me ask you this: What kind of business operates without all of its principals knowing what's in their product?"

CHAPTER 54

"What did you think?" Anson asks Cari, as he and Theo join her in the conference room where she had watched the interview on the monitor.

"He seemed flustered," Cari says. "Kind of all over the map."

Theo nods. "He panicked once he found out we tracked his DNP order from Shawna's website."

Anson looks from Theo to Cari. "I've got zero doubt he was the one lacing those bottles of supplement. But when it comes to Cecilia . . ."

"Not as clear-cut, is it?" Cari says.

"His outrage did seem more believable."

"And that surprised look when you told him that Cecilia had such high levels of DNP in her system . . ."

"It was about the only time he seemed genuine."

"Do you buy his inference about his partners?" Theo asks. "That they were all in on it?"

Cari shrugs. "We should definitely ask his girlfriend."

"She hasn't surfaced this morning," Theo says. "I've left messages."

"Another BOLF?"

"Probably," Anson grunts. "Meantime, why don't we go talk to the only other living partner?"

"Good idea," Theo says.

Anson turns to Cari. "Can you get Zach to check on another address for us?"

"The Hunters?" she asks.

"Yeah. Maybe they had their own supply of DNP, independent of the supplement?"

"Sure." Cari calls Zach, but his line rings through to voicemail. "No answer. If you give me the address, I'll text him instead."

Theo sends the address to Cari, who forwards it on to Zach.

They head down to the car and, twenty minutes later, pull into the Hunters' driveway. Theo has to ring the doorbell twice before Lloyd answers. He wears the same tracksuit as on their previous visit, but his five-o'clock shadow has grown into a patchy beard. "Hello, detectives," he says.

"Sorry to bother you, Mr. Hunter," Theo explains. "We just had a few things we wanted to follow up on from our previous conversation."

"Of course." He opens the door wider and beckons them inside.

"We arrested Gerard Martin this morning," Theo says.

"*Arrested?*" Lloyd's eyes widen. "On what grounds?"

"Administration of a noxious substance," Theo says.

"In other words," Cari says. "For lacing Mind Over Body's supplement with DNP."

"Wow." Lloyd goes quiet for a few moments. "You obviously have proof?"

"We do."

Lloyd shakes his head. "Do you think that's how Cecilia got poisoned? Through the laced supplement?"

"We don't know, Mr. Hunter," Cari says.

Lloyd's chin drops. "It would make sense, though, wouldn't it?"

"Except," Anson says and deliberately draws out his pause, "it doesn't quite fit."

"Why not?"

"The blood levels of DNP they found in your wife's system were too high. She would've had to drink gallons and gallons of the supplement to reach them. More than a person could consume at any one time."

"What else could it have been?"

Anson stares hard at him. "Did you know about the DNP in the supplement?"

"Absolutely not." Lloyd hesitates and then adds, "Well . . . not before Cecilia's death, anyway."

"What does that mean?"

"I . . . I really can't discuss it."

"Why not?"

"Because I signed a nondisclosure agreement."

"When?"

"When I sold my share of the business to Gerard."

"That wouldn't be enforceable if a criminal offense had been committed," Theo says. "Especially manslaughter."

Lloyd shakes his head adamantly. "I better consult my lawyer before I say anything else."

"When did you sell your share of the company?" Theo asks.

Lloyd clears his throat. "The deal closed yesterday."

"That's some coincidence, Mr. Hunter," Cari says.

"I suppose," Lloyd says. "After Cecilia passed, I didn't want anything to do with the business anymore."

Anson nods. "Are you aware that Mr. Martin implicated you in the tainting of the supplement?"

Lloyd gapes at him. "He wouldn't!"

"He did. Gerard implied that all of the company's principals knew about the scheme to lace the supplement."

"That son of a bitch. It's not true!"

"Do you now want to tell us how you found out about the DNP in the supplement?" Cari asks.

"I would love to. I really would. But I'm still going to have to speak to my lawyer first."

"All right, Mr. Hunter," Anson says. "But if you can't provide us an answer very soon, we'll have to charge you, as well."

"Soon. I get it." Lloyd looks lost in thought.

"Last time we were here," Theo says, "we asked you if your wife could've ordered the DNP for herself."

"I still can't see it," Lloyd says. "Like I told you, Cecilia was averse to anything that wasn't natural. Or organic."

"Mind Over Body must have had their own supply of DNP," Cari says. "Maybe Cecilia got into that?"

"Doesn't sound like Cecilia," Lloyd says hoarsely.

After they leave, on their way back to the car, Theo says, "At least one of these guys is lying."

"My bet is on both of them," Anson says.

"Mine, too," Cari says.

They get into the car and head back for the station. As they're driving over the Granville Street Bridge, Cari punches Anson's headrest. "Oh, my God!" she cries. "Why am I not surprised?"

Anson views her in the rearview mirror. "About?"

She holds up her phone. "Zach just texted. He doesn't have a name, only a spam email address. But he confirmed that someone at the Hunters' residence ordered DNP from Dr. X Pharmaceuticals. Though, unlike with Mind Over Body, it was a onetime order. Four months ago."

CHAPTER 55

"As I see it," Anson says, after they're all seated in the deputy chief's office, "there are three possible explanations for the DNP order to the Hunters' home."

The deputy chief laces her hands behind her head. "I'm all ears."

"One, the Hunters were in on the conspiracy to spike the bottles of supplement from the get-go. And for whatever reason, they had to order the DNP for Mind Over Body that one time last summer."

"What kind of reason?" Cari asks skeptically.

"Who knows?" Anson says. "Maybe Gerard and Adèle were indisposed? Or away? Or they were having issues with financing that month? We can check his bank accounts, check their whereabouts . . ."

"Nah, don't buy it," the deputy chief says. "They could've ordered it from anywhere. And if it was a cash shortfall, the Hunters could have just lent Gerard and Adèle the money directly."

"OK," Anson says. "Two, Cecilia was so impressed with the effect of DNP, she wanted her own supply. And then later, she ended up poisoning herself. Intentionally or not."

The deputy chief grimaces. "Four months after ordering it?"

"Exactly," Cari says. "Her supply would've run out before then if she'd been using it all along."

"OK." Anson shrugs. "So Lloyd ordered the DNP. And used it to poison his wife."

"But why would he wait four months?" Theo asks.

"Besides, how could we prove it?" the deputy chief asks. "All we know is that someone ordered DNP to the Hunters' home. Could've been the wife."

"I'll check with Zach," Cari says. "See if he can track down which credit card the order was placed on."

"Even if he can," Theo says, "it won't prove Lloyd was the one who ordered the DNP. Couples share their credit cards all the time. I borrow Eleni's, sometimes. And vice versa."

"True," Cari says, feeling a bit deflated.

The deputy chief looks around the room. "Any other ideas?"

None of them speak, and Cari can feel the energy being sucked out of the room. But then Anson breaks into a small grin.

Theo turns to him. "You've got that look on your face . . ."

"We've already got Gerard—maybe all three of them—for distributing the DNP," Anson says.

"The evidence against Gerard is the strongest," the deputy chief says.

"And the guy is desperate not to take the fall for Cecilia's death."

"What are you suggesting, Anson?"

He shrugs. "Maybe it's time to chum the waters?"

CHAPTER 56

"I thought you were in jail," Lloyd says as soon as he opens his front door.

"My lawyer got me out on bail," Gerard says.

"Too bad."

Lloyd starts to close the door, but Gerard wedges a foot in it. "We need to talk."

"I'm done with you," Lloyd snaps.

"You mean now that you have taken all my money?"

"I kept my end of the bargain. You're the one who broke it."

"What the fuck are you talking about?"

"You implicated me. In your dirty scheme to poison your 'wellness' drink. The detectives told me as much."

"That's going to be the least of your worries," Gerard growls. "Unless we settle some things. Right now."

Lloyd hesitates a moment and then opens the door wider. He turns around, and Gerard follows him into the living room.

They stand with arms folded on opposite sides of the granite coffee table, glaring at each other. "Cecilia didn't die from drinking the supplement," Gerard finally says.

"*This* again?"

"You never thought she did," Gerard says. "Not for a millisecond."

"What makes you say that?"

"Because the cops told me her blood level of DNP was through the roof. Way higher than what she could have reached from the supplement."

Lloyd only shrugs.

"The cops told me something else, too," Gerard says.

"Are we playing Twenty Questions? Get on with it. Or get the hell out."

"They told me I wasn't the only one who has been ordering DNP," Gerard says. "They've traced another order. To this house."

Lloyd considers that a moment. "Guess I was wrong then. Cecilia must have been ordering it for herself after all."

"Bullshit!"

"What would you know?"

"I'm not an idiot, Lloyd." Gerard taps his temple. "What's more, all the cops have on me is that someone ordered DNP from Mind Over Body. Unlike you, *I* never ordered it to my home."

"This your latest angle? Setting me up again?" Lloyd scoffs. "You're a one-trick pony."

"Doesn't it stand to reason that the same business partner who was ordering it to his home would've also been buying it for the company?"

"Oh?" Lloyd laughs bitterly. "I'm the one who was spiking your pathetic supplement all along?"

"Maybe you were."

Lloyd shakes his head. "Still more of your empty threats."

"Not empty, Lloyd. Adèle will back me up. Who's gonna back you?"

Lloyd flashes an ugly smile. "We're back to the two-against-one thing, are we? Like the last time you tried to blackmail me?"

"Looks like."

Lloyd's smile grows. "It's probably better to be on the side with the two then."

"Much better."

"I agree." Lloyd looks over his shoulder and calls upstairs, "Sweetheart? Can you come down here?"

Gerard is bewildered for a moment. Then a pit forms in his stomach as he watches the woman glide down the circular staircase, recognizing her by her fluid stride before he can even see her face.

"I'm sorry, *chéri*," Adèle says when she reaches the last step. "There wasn't much choice."

Gerard's head spins as the love of his life ambles over to Lloyd and wraps an arm around his midsection. "What the fuck . . . ?" Gerard gasps.

"The walls were closing in on us, *chéri*," Adèle says. "Cecilia figured out about the DNP. On her own. Others were going to, too. It was only a matter of time until it all caved in on our heads."

"You . . . and *Lloyd*?" Gerard croaks.

"I thought you understood me, Gerard. I'm sapiosexual. Intelligence is what turns me on. And the way this one's mind works . . ." She snuggles in closer to Lloyd. "Always steps ahead. It's very, very sexy."

"You're too sweet." Lloyd kisses the top of her head. "But I think your share of the buyout might have played into the attraction."

"*Un peu. Peut-être.*" A little. Perhaps. She smiles as she squeezes her thumb and her forefinger close together.

The sense of betrayal is so overwhelming that Gerard can hardly speak. "How . . . ?"

"Ten years, Gerard!" Lloyd says. "I put up with that pretentious, promiscuous, cruel cunt of a wife of mine for ten years!"

Gerard can only gawk at them.

"You think I didn't know about Ibiza and the other affairs?" Lloyd asks calmly. "It wasn't enough that Cecilia was hopping from one bed to another with lowlifes like you. She also had to belittle me all the time. Constantly putting me down. Embarrassing me."

"Cecilia could be harsh," Adèle agrees. "Especially with Lloyd."

"She had me cornered. For starters, we didn't have a prenup! Don't get me wrong. To be free of her, I would have forfeited fifty percent of my net worth in a heartbeat." Lloyd shakes his head. "But that wouldn't have been enough for her. Cecilia knew where my skeletons were buried."

"What skeletons?" Gerard asks.

"Let's just say it's not possible to mine in Central America without some off-the-books work." Lloyd chuckles. "Cecilia reminded me of it all the time. She could have ruined me. She *would* have, too."

"You killed her, didn't you?" Gerard mutters, still astounded at the idea of it, as he remembers how browbeaten and submissive Lloyd always seemed to be around her.

"Cecilia was right about one thing, at least," Lloyd says. "She knew your formula was too good to be true. That you had to be manipulating it. It was her idea to use my company's lab to get it analyzed."

"You've known all this time?"

"About the deadly pick-me-up in your sludge? For at least a year." He strokes Adèle's hair. "Even before this gorgeous lady came into my life. What I couldn't quite figure out was how to take advantage of it. I kept thinking there had to be a way to kill two birds with one stone. That was why I placed my own order of DNP. I was planning on an accident. But the timing never seemed to be right."

Adèle looks up at Lloyd and smiles. "Until Rain."

"Exactly! Rain's DNP overdose was like a gift from the gods. Everything fell into place. Especially, with the help of this angel." Lloyd pulls Adèle in tighter.

She beams. "I was the one who convinced Cecilia that Lloyd needed stronger medicine. A higher dose. And that she should persuade you into making it for her, *chéri.*"

"Cecilia always used to complain about my gut." Lloyd pats his belly. "It was almost too good to be true. You literally handed me my alibi with those special bottles you prepared for her. She had the gall to tell me I needed to double my dose of your stronger concoction if I wanted meaningful results. Oh, how I thanked her that morning! I even brought her a gift."

Adèle winks at Gerard. "Me."

"And while Adèle was entertaining that nympho bitch, I dissolved ten capsules into her kale smoothie. It already tasted so godawful I could've mixed horse manure in without her noticing. Then later, when she started seizing, I might have waited a bit too long to call 911."

"You set me up!" Gerard isn't talking to Lloyd, though. He's staring at Adèle, simultaneously heartbroken and enraged.

Adèle gazes back at him with an expression that could pass for pity. "Couldn't be helped, *chéri*."

After all I've done for you? For us. The outrage steals his voice. *How could you?*

"She's right, Gerard," Lloyd says. "And thanks to the contract we just signed, I got my money—and then some—out of your business fiasco." He shakes his head. "Honestly. From spin coach to CEO? Come on." Even his laugh is ugly.

"You bastard!" Gerard hisses.

"What can you do, Gerard? I mean, really? You signed an affidavit swearing to my ignorance of your criminal scheme. And your own girlfriend—ex-girlfriend, I guess, all things considered—will back me up. She'll say we both only learned about your plot after Cecilia's death."

Gerard takes a step toward Lloyd, but he shoots out a hand. "Think, Gerard!"

"About what?" he snarls.

"I still have one of the bottles you gave Cecilia. The one you made more potent."

"Who the fuck cares?" Gerard croaks.

"I also have the texts between you and Cecilia. From her phone. Where you promise to drop the 'special bottles' off with her. They're from the evening before she died."

Gerard hesitates.

"And when the cops test this last bottle," Lloyd says. "They're going to find it's even more potent than the double-strength one you made for her."

"You added more DNP to it, didn't you?"

Lloyd shrugs. "I'm no scientist, but I'd guess the concentration is now high enough to kill an elephant or two."

Gerard's hand begins to tremble involuntarily.

"Walk away now," Lloyd says, "and we'll make it look like Cecilia accidentally overdosed on her own DNP order. Maybe you'll do a year or two in prison for administering a noxious substance or whatever. Your life will go on." His eyes narrow. "But make a big deal of this, and you'll go down for Cecilia's murder."

Gerard's temples pulsate. "You figure?"

"You lost, Gerard. Accept it."

Adèle nods. "You did, *chèri*. You really did."

Gerard lunges.

Adèle screams as she falls backwards and hits the coffee table.

Lloyd's fists strike Gerard in the face, but, sick with rage, Gerard overpowers him in seconds. He straddles Lloyd's chest, wraps his fingers around the other man's neck, and squeezes with all his might.

"You're killing him!" Adèle cries from where she sits on the floor, pressing a hand to her forehead, blood leaking through her fingers.

But Gerard only tightens his grip. Even as Lloyd gurgles. Even as his eyes bulge out of their sockets. Even as the door explodes open and someone shouts, "Police!"

Gerard keeps squeezing until someone slams into his chest with a thud that winds him, as they topple over together.

CHAPTER 57

Cari stands between Anson and Theo in front of the Hunters' house. The overcast skies and steady drizzle soften the harsh lights of the emergency vehicles surrounding the place, making the scene feel slightly surreal.

"That was more than I expected," Anson says as he rubs the shoulder that he landed on after tackling Gerard.

"That wasn't exactly 'chumming.'" Theo laughs. "More like you filled the sea with blood, and the sharks went berserk."

"It didn't take much." Anson shrugs. "As soon as we told Gerard that someone ordered DNP from the Hunters' home, he put most of it together himself. You saw how eager he was to go in with a wire and take Lloyd down."

"Literally," Theo says. "Another minute and Gerard would've finished Lloyd off."

"Lloyd was just as keen to rub it in Gerard's face," Cari points out.

"Man, did he sing," Anson says.

"Lloyd thought he had all the leverage," Theo says. "He believed that tainted bottle of supplement and those texts between Gerard and Cecilia were his get-out-of-jail-free card."

"One thing Gerard didn't count on was Adèle being there," Cari points out.

Anson chuckles. "That, he did not. Then again, neither did we."

"If Gerard and Lloyd wind up in the same prison, the communal exercise block could get dicey for one of them," Theo says.

"Yeah," Anson says. "For whoever takes longer to make a shiv."

"That's a bit dark." Cari laughs, as she checks her watch. "My flight leaves in just under three hours."

"You sure you can't stay for a celebratory dinner?" Anson asks. "Theo might even come."

"I just might," Theo says. "Let the boys reign free at home. *Lord of the Flies*-style. After all, how often do you close two major cases in the same week?"

"I'd love to, but I have to get back to LA," Cari says.

"Too bad," Theo says. "I wanted you to meet Eleni."

"When I come back? Hopefully, this summer!" Cari smiles and then turns to Anson. "Do you think we could stop in at the hospital on the way back?"

"To get a statement from Maleeka?" he asks.

"I'd like to try. To close the loop."

They load into Anson's car and head for St. Michael's.

As they drive, Cari's phone dings with a text, but she doesn't recognize the number. She opens it and reads, "Detective Garcia, Congratulations on your excellent investigative work. It means a lot to know Owen's killer met justice. That my son's death was not in vain. And that it will help prevent others. With deep gratitude, Suzanne Galloway."

Theo looks over his shoulder at her. "What are you grinning about?"

"Just a nice text from home," she says, putting away her phone as the car pulls into the hospital's parking lot.

They find Maleeka in her private room, sitting up in bed, staring past the TV screen on the bedside table. She's not wearing any makeup, and there's a frailty to her that Cari hasn't detected before.

"You were there?" Maleeka asks. "When Shawn . . ."

Cari nods. "We were there, yes."

"It's my fault," Maleeka mumbles.

"No," Cari says. "Your sister made her choices."

"I asked her."

"What did you ask her?" Anson asks.

"I didn't know jack about DNP or Shawn's online biz," Maleeka says. "But Ray-Ray was cutting me out. Treating me like I was a stan, or something."

Theo frowns. "A stan?"

"A superfan. A hanger-on. I thought Ray-Ray and me were BFFs." Maleeka's chin drops. "I asked Shawn to help. Like make me relevant, again."

"And she told you about DNP?" Cari asks.

"Yeah, she said Ray-Ray would be so into it. Grateful and all." Maleeka snorts. "After Braden FedExed her, Ray-Ray would do anything and everything to get scrawnier. For fuck's sake, that skeevy Dr. Markstrom even had her on those diabetic shots!"

"And Shawna gave you DNP capsules to give Rain?" Anson asks.

"Yeah. Reluctantly."

"Why reluctantly?"

"'Cause she knew me. Fretted I'd start popping them myself. She warned me she'd beat me with a club if she found out I was. She would have, too." Maleeka's shoulders slump. "Ray-Ray loved me for getting her those caps. I warned her to go easy. I really did. But Ray-Ray, she had zero moderation."

Cari nods, thinking of her own sister. "And you started using DNP at the same time Rain did?" she asks.

"A couple weeks after, maybe. How couldn't I? I saw it was like this super-pill for Ray-Ray. And I had a pound or two to shed myself. Besides, I didn't want BFF to take it alone. Wanted to go through it with her. But I sure as shit didn't tell Shawn I was taking them. That woulda been a death sentence."

"Did Shawna tell you much about her online business?" Anson asks.

Maleeka shakes her head. "Shawn was ultra-furtive."

"Do you think she had any partners?"

"*Shawn?* Uh-uh. She was solo all the way!" Maleeka says. "Big sib never fit in growing up. Dad was hard on her, too. He's kinda traditional. He expected her to look after me, being the baby in the family and such. She tried to, in her way. But Shawn also grudged both Dad *and* me for it."

Cari gets it. At times, she too had resented her little sister's dependency on her for help cleaning up her messes. Especially when Lucia kept repeating the same self-destructive mistakes. "Shawna didn't have many friends?"

"As in none," Maleeka says. "Other kids treated her like a freak. She was bullied, too. But she just swallowed all that bitterness. Me? I always wanted to fit in among the white-teeth teens. Not Shawn. She resented the fuck out of the in-crowd. She had a special hate on for those flossy-flossy bitches."

"You're sure, Maleeka?" Cari asks again. "That Shawna had no partners."

"I'm the only person in the world Oshana trusted." Maleeka swallows. "The one person she shouldn't have."

Sympathy wells up in Cari for the helpless girl. "We would've caught up to Shawna one way or the other."

"We're not pressing charges, Maleeka," Anson adds. "You can go home now."

Maleeka's lip trembles. "Yeah . . . home."

None of the detectives speak after leaving Maleeka's room. It's not until after they load into the car that Anson says, "All families have their dynamics, but the Khans . . ." He shakes his head. "That one sounds messy."

"Ain't that the truth?" Theo says. "The little sister with all her insecurities, and the big sister with all that seething resentment."

"Agreed," Cari says, hoping that her own family dynamic wasn't too similar. "I get the feeling Shawna's business was as much about exploiting—maybe even punishing—the kids from the 'in crowd' as it was about making money."

"I do, too," Theo says. "Ironic that her little sister inadvertently became one of her targets."

Anson taps the steering wheel. "Bound to be a lot of collateral damage when you're trying to settle a score with your entire past."

"Especially if you use an explosive to do it," Cari adds, and the chillingly accurate assessment silences everyone again.

Theo asks Anson to drop him off at the body shop where his wife's SUV is waiting to be picked up. They pull into the parking lot, and Cari gets out of the car with Theo to say goodbye to him.

Theo points to Anson, who's still behind the wheel. "Can't believe you're going to leave me stuck alone with old Zoolander over there."

Cari grins. "It's been a pleasure, Theo. I learned some tricks from you."

"Likewise. You're a good cop, Cari."

After they leave Theo, Anson and Cari head for her hotel. Along the way, her phone dings again with another text, this one from Mattias. "Disappointed I didn't get to see you this visit. But I'm not giving up. I love you."

Cari stares at the screen. So many responses come to mind. But after a moment, she deletes the message, opens the contact for Mattias, and, without hesitating, clicks on "Block this Caller."

"Everything OK, Cari?" Anson asks.

She looks over to Anson with a smile. "Yes. It really is."

CHAPTER 58

Rare November snowflakes drift past the window. For Julie, it's the perfect complement to a lazy afternoon. The burning fireplace. The half-empty bottle of Syrah on the coffee table. Anson's warm breath on her ear as he lies with an arm draped over her shoulder. And Rain's *Cloudburst* playing softly in the background.

Julie fights off the fatigue that has crept over her since she finished the glass of wine. She doesn't want to sleep through a moment of it. All she wants is to read her book in Anson's warm embrace.

But he shifts on the sectional and exhales heavily as he lowers his tablet onto his chest.

"What's wrong?" she asks.

"Did you see the news out of New York?"

She rolls to face him. "I thought we weren't doing news this afternoon."

"Busted," he says. "But I didn't really mean to. I was flipping through some online posts. And there it was."

"What was?"

"Three more DNP-related deaths this week in the Northeast. Two in New York, one in Baltimore."

"It wasn't going to just disappear, Anson. We knew that."

"We didn't know it was going to get worse, either. Rain's death seems to have turned into some kind of promotional campaign for DNP."

Julie shakes her head. "That's not true. Maybe, in the short run, it's led a few impressionable people to experiment with DNP. But in the long run, it will raise awareness."

"You think?"

"There's already public pressure mounting to tighten up the restrictions on the distribution of DNP for industrial purposes."

"Not sure that'll be enough."

"Word is out now, Anson. It's only going to get harder for the Dr. X Pharmaceuticals of the world to distribute this poison."

"Maybe, but after we caught Shawna Khan and shut down Mind Over Body . . . I thought it would make an actual difference. Like immediately."

"Are you kidding me? You disrupted the biggest distributor of DNP on the West Coast. And stopped a conspiracy to spike health supplements with it. Who knows how many lives you might have saved?"

"*We* might have saved."

"Uh-uh, I was better this time." She kisses him lightly. "I didn't stick my nose in your business. At least . . . not as much."

"You launched this investigation." He chuckles. "And we wouldn't have exposed Mind Over Body without your help."

"Aww. Does that mean you want me back on your cases?"

"Not a freakin' chance!" He laughs as he squeezes her in a bear hug.

After he loosens his grip, Julie thumbs to the huge TV screen mounted above the fireplace. "You happy with your birthday present?"

"Best gift ever! I'm only sorry there's no football on this afternoon."

"That makes one of us."

He cocks his head and studies her. "I'm happy, Julie."

"With the TV?"

"With this." He spreads out his hands. "With you."

Out of nowhere, Julie begins to tear up. She feels the same. Her own regrettable history is finally receding into the past. "And the dreams?"

"They're not as frequent as they were. Not as scary, either."

Julie smiles, relieved. "Nicole was a big part of your life. She always will be."

"Maybe." He brushes his hand over her cheek. "But being here . . . living with you . . . this is my home now."

AUTHOR'S NOTE

One of the many joys I get from writing my form of fiction is the opportunity to share relevant medical, scientific, and social themes within the context of telling a suspenseful story. Never has this been truer than with this book. It focuses on the treacherous phenomenon of body image and eating disorders, which are perpetuated by a toxic weight loss industry and a social media rife with body shaming. And in this story, I shine a specific light on one very real and very deadly diet pill that is growing in popularity.

As a medical doctor and a father of two young women, I am acutely aware of the dangers posed by the body image and eating disorders. They can be insidious and sometimes fatal diseases. What I had not realized until recently is how pervasive these conditions are, and how they afflict people of *every* age and gender.

Only in the past two years did I hear about DNP, or 2,4-Dinitrophenol, an explosive agent that was synthesized to fill the howitzer shells fired on the battlefields of World War I. In the past two decades, this industrial chemical has resurfaced for sale on the net as a highly lethal weight loss pill and bodybuilding supplement. The consequences have been predictably tragic. There have been multiple unintentional deaths—both in single poisonings and clusters of overdoses—reported across North America and Europe. Most of the victims are young people who are conned on-line into believing DNP is "safe and effective" for weight loss or body-building.

Law enforcement agencies all over the world have struggled to thwart the anonymous sales of this toxin, while their respective legal systems have failed to adequately punish the sellers who distribute it remotely from the corners of the dark web without ever meeting the purchasers they sometimes kill.

In bringing any attention to this poison, I did worry that I might inad-vertently open the eyes to even one person who would then be vulnerable to such deceptive marketing. But for me, awareness is the most potent preventive measure we have in staring down such threats. I hope and believe that this story, which repeatedly illustrates the fatal consequences of experimenting with DNP (even when taken at a dose "recommended" by online dealers), might serve as a deterrent to its use. And I like to think that I am bringing a measure of attention to a threat that is already hiding in plain sight.

ACKNOWLEDGMENTS

As always, I depend on my friends and family for their unwavering support and belief in my writing—my passion. But I owe too many debts of gratitude to the village of people involved to name everyone who helped carry this story from an inkling of an idea to the completed novel. There are, however, certain individuals who go above and beyond, whom I do need to single out.

I strive to be as accurate as I can be in the technical details behind my fiction. This story involves dual police investigations in separate cities, in fact in different countries, and tackles themes around eating disorders, online body shaming, and toxic diet supplements. I am so grateful for the guidance I received from two supreme experts in their respective fields. Superintendent Howard Tran of the Vancouver Police Department walked me through the ins and outs of law enforcement and the nuances of the legal procedures involved in an investigation of this imagined scale. And Dr. Jane McKay generously shared her vast expertise and experience in managing eating disorders.

As always, I relied heavily on the insightful feedback of my freelance editor, Kit Schindell, and my dependable first reader, Mariko Miller, to mold the first draft into the best shape possible.

There was considerable transition in my literary world during the crafting of this novel. Henry Morrison, my longtime agent, retired, while Laurie Grassi, my previous editor at Simon & Schuster Canada, moved on to explore other career options. While they remain friends, professionally I will miss them both. But I was fortunate to team up recently with two accomplished agents, Carolyn Forde and Samantha Haywood, and a talented in-house editor, Brittany Lavery. Their invaluable advice helped to shape the final draft. And I'm excited to be collaborating with them on future works.

Of course, none of this would be possible without the support of the wonderful team at Simon & Schuster Canada, including Kevin Hanson, Jillian Levick, Nita Pronovost, David Millar, Mackenzie Croft, Adria Iwasutiak, and Felicia Quon.

And finally, thanks to you, the reader. I would be nowhere without your willingness to invest the time and energy into reading this latest effort. I so hope you find it worthwhile.

"Kalla is a clever master of surprise."

#1 internationally bestselling author
Samantha M. Bailey

Also by DANIEL KALLA

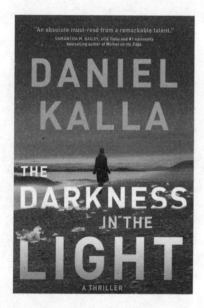

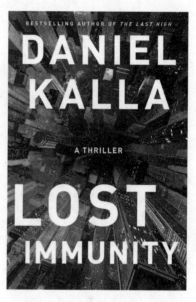

"One of Kalla's best."
The Globe and Mail

"Kalla . . . has a knack
for writing eerily
prescient thrillers."
CBC Books

SIMON &
SCHUSTER
CANADA